The Lights Out Club

THE LIGHTS OUT CLUB

Copyright 2019 E.C. Woodham

For information contact:

E.C. Woodham

emma.c.woodham@gmail.com

Emma C Woodham

https://www.authorecwoodham.com

Cover Design: Mandi Lynn, Stone Ridge Books

Editor: Emmye Collins

Formatting: Ashley Felder, The Educated Writer

Author Photo: Ryan Woodham

ISBN: 9781074857752

First Edition, 2019

✿ Created with Vellum

To the Ragsdales —

THE LIGHTS OUT CLUB

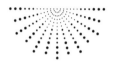

E.C. WOODHAM

EC Woodham

To the
Ragsdales

For Ryan, who pushed me to write it until I wrote it.

And for my Mama, who taught me everything I know about grammar and sentence structure.

CHAPTER ONE

SUMMER 2007

"*E*llie, this is crazy!"

"No, it's not!"

"Yes, it is! We're going to get in trouble!"

"No, we're not!"

Darkness blanketed Sullivan's Island, but that didn't stop eleven-year-old Ellie Taylor from jogging up the beach towards a brightly-lit house. Close on her heels were her two best friends, Charlie and Olivia Tanner, but they were following her reluctantly. Their voices echoed across the dunes, the only disruption to the peaceful night.

"You can't just march up to someone's house and tell them to turn their lights off," Charlie called after her. "They might call the cops or think you're a robber or something."

"That's really unlikely," Ellie said. "Besides, I'm not going to *tell* them to turn their lights off. I'm going to ask them very politely."

"C'mon, Ellie, let's just go back to the house and play a

game!" Olivia lagged behind the other two, almost distraught. Ellie thought for a moment that her friend might start crying if they didn't turn back soon.

"No!" Finally, Ellie found the path through the dunes that she had been looking for—the one that led up to the street. "If you two want to go home, just go. You don't have to come with me."

"We're not letting you go alone," Charlie muttered, "but I'm starting to wish we hadn't run into that crazy turtle lady on the beach this morning."

Earlier that day, a few minutes after daybreak, the three friends had ventured out onto the beach to see what treasures the tide left behind overnight. An older woman was bent over the dunes in front of the beach house, driving skinny wooden stakes into the sand. She had greeted them warmly and informed them that a sea turtle had laid a nest in the dunes. Ellie asked the woman half a dozen questions, and the woman had patiently answered each one of them. She gave them pamphlets about sea turtle nesting, and she instructed them on the importance of filling in deep holes on the beach and making sure lights were turned off along the beachfront at night. Lights on the beachfront during nesting season could disorient the turtles, she said.

"It's past eleven o'clock," Ellie insisted, slowing down to a brisk walk so she could catch her breath before she reached the house. "They're supposed to have all their lights off. The Turtle Lady said so!"

"So? It's not our job to tell these people to turn off their lights," Charlie said. "We're not part of the Turtle Team."

"Our parents are going to be mad if we stay out too late," Olivia added.

At the end of the path through the dunes, Ellie stopped and whirled around to face both of her friends. "So what? Those lights could confuse a sea turtle, and they need as much help as they can get. All I'm going to do is knock on the door and politely ask them to turn out their lights."

Olivia folded her arms across her chest and shook her head. "Well, I'm not going any further. This is silly!"

"I'm with Liv on this one, Ellie," Charlie agreed, shoving his hands into the pockets of his shorts uneasily. "Sorry, but I think this is kinda crazy, too."

"Fine," Ellie huffed. "You're both scaredy-cats! You might as well go back to the house. *I'm* going to do my part to help the sea turtles!" With that, she turned her back on them and squared her shoulders. She marched up the unfamiliar steps with only a slight hesitation. Olivia and Charlie were whispering loudly behind her, and Ellie could feel their stares boring into her back. When she pulled the screened door open, the hinges squeaked loudly, and her heart began to pound heavily in her chest. She hoped that whoever came to the door wouldn't yell at her or, as Charlie had suggested, call the cops.

Taking a deep breath, Ellie raised her hand and knocked on the door.

SUMMER 2018

It was still dark outside when Ellie climbed into her car and pulled onto the highway. The drive to Sullivan's Island would take her at least five hours, and she wanted to arrive in time to have lunch with her uncle. It was also the Friday before Memorial Day, and she knew traffic would be hectic.

With a travel mug of coffee tucked safely into the cupholder, Ellie set off. The sun came up slowly as she drove, and she sighed as she settled into her seat. The long drive to the South Carolina coast had never bothered her, mostly because she knew her destination was a beautiful and relaxing island. And after the busy year she'd had, Ellie was looking forward to a vacation. This year's trip to Sullivan's Island was going to be different for her, though; Ellie's uncle, who owned a beachfront home on the small barrier island, was spending his summer traveling through Europe. He'd asked his only niece if she was interested in house-sitting for him. Normally, Ellie worked during the summers—usually a typical summer job, waiting tables or folding shirts in a retail store—but after talking it over with her parents, they had all agreed that taking the last summer off before her senior year of college would be good for her. Ellie had just wrapped up a grueling semester with several tough classes and a demanding round of final exams. Her brain was utterly exhausted, and she was looking forward to three months at the beach.

BY NOON, Ellie was crossing the Ravenel Bridge over the Charleston Harbor, and she rolled her windows down and eased off the accelerator so she could inhale a deep breath of the coastal air. Growing up, she had spent lots of time in the Charleston area, and all of the surroundings were familiar. A few miles down the road, she left Mount Pleasant behind and drove over the causeway towards the Ben Sawyer Bridge, the link between the mainland and Sullivan's Island. Fortunately, the ancient swing bridge wasn't open for any boat traffic, and Ellie breezed over the Atlantic Intracoastal Waterway, slowing her speed again as she finally reached the island. She could already feel the majestic spell of the island renewing her energy and welcoming her back.

ELLIE TURNED onto Middle Street and passed half a dozen familiar island restaurants and businesses. The island's only barbeque restaurant was one of her favorite places to eat in the Charleston area, and her mouth watered when she thought about their smoked chicken wings. Just past the restaurant, she turned down Station 22 Street and slowly drove to the end. Another right turn onto Pettigrew Street brought her uncle's house into view, and she pulled into the yard, parking her car in the driveway behind his.

STRETCHING her stiff arms and legs, Ellie climbed out of her car and stared up at the large house. She had spent many summer vacations in the house that loomed before her, and dozens of memories flooded back, wrapping around her like a warm blanket. It was as if she were arriving home after a long, long absence, and a slow smile spread across her face.

"Hello, house," she whispered softly. "I've missed you so much." She clapped her hands together, giggling quietly to herself. She could hardly believe that she was spending her entire summer on Sullivan's Island.

The beach house was a beautiful three-story home, elevated on ten-foot pilings and painted a beautiful Santorini blue. All the trim on the house and even the louvered window shutters were a soft, dark brown wood. Dozens of windows lined every side of the house, giving everyone on the outside a brief glimpse into the beautifully decorated interior. In addition, the house had two porches—a wrap-around screened porch on the main floor and an open-air deck on the second floor. On the third floor, a small cupola overlooked the island, and Ellie had spent many hours in that tiny room, examining the island with a pair of binoculars. She loved every part of the house. Sometimes she thought she loved her uncle's beach house more than she loved the childhood house she'd grown up in.

. . .

THE SCREENED door on the back porch swung open with a shuddering squeak, and Ellie's uncle stepped out into the sunshine, grinning down at her. "You gonna stand there all day, or do you think you might come inside at some point?"

Ellie laughed aloud, pleasantly startled from her reminiscing. "Hi, Uncle Jim! Yes, I'm coming up. I was just stretching and getting some fresh air." She bounded up the back porch stairs two at a time and greeted her uncle with a warm hug. "I've missed you."

"It's good to see you, kid," he said, ruffling her hair playfully.

"You, too!"

"Come on in. We'll get your bags later."

"So, tell me what's going on with you!" Jim smiled at his young niece when she was seated at the kitchen bar with a cold drink.

"Not too much. I spent a week at home with Mom and Dad, and Mom cooked me all my favorite meals. We went to the movies, and she took me shopping for new summer clothes."

"And now you get to spend three months relaxing in my beach house. Sounds like you're having a pretty good summer so far."

"I am," Ellie agreed. "You have no idea how happy I am to be here."

"Good. Now, what do you say we go grab a bite to eat? I was waiting on you to get here before I ate lunch."

Ellie's face lit up, and she nodded eagerly. "Let me get my bags out of the car, and then we can go."

ELLIE HAULED her suitcases up to her bedroom. Her uncle had allowed her to redecorate it one summer, and since then, it had been considered "her" room. She had painted the walls a soft, sky blue and spray-painted the iron bedframe a navy blue. The bedspread was a soft white coverlet, trimmed in pale blue, with matching shams and a few decorative pillows.

She set her duffel bag on the end of the bed and pulled out a fresh shirt that wasn't wrinkled from hours of riding. After changing, Ellie ran a brush through her messy blonde locks and then checked her reflection in the mirror. Before leaving for Sullivan's earlier that morning, she hadn't bothered to apply any makeup, and now she frowned at her appearance. Her skin looked washed out and oily, so she took a few extra minutes to wash her face and apply a touch of blush and mascara.

UNCLE JIM DROVE them to Home Team, easily the most popular restaurant on Sullivan's Island. The quirky barbeque joint was always crowded, and with the holiday weekend already underway, Ellie and her uncle were lucky to snag one of the last tables on the porch.

"I have been craving this place for weeks," Ellie declared, tucking her napkin into her lap.

"You must have left home early to have gotten here so soon," her uncle said, glancing at his watch. "It's not even one o'clock yet."

"I left before six and only stopped a couple times. I wanted to get here as soon as I could."

A waitress arrived to take their drink orders and tell them about daily specials. When she left again, Ellie looked back at the menu, trying to decide what she wanted.

"How did you do in your classes this semester?" Uncle Jim asked, patting down some of his white hair that was ruffled by the coastal breeze.

Ellie set the menu down and squared her shoulders proudly. "Five As and one B. The B was in some stupid Operations Management class. I actually failed the first test in that class, so I'm pretty proud of how I turned that grade around."

"Good job, kid! That's great!" He smiled at her, beaming with pride. "You really have earned this vacation, haven't you?"

"I really have."

ELLIE'S UNCLE was one of her favorite people. He was her mother's older brother, and he had never married, despite the fact that he had seriously dated several women over the years. He had lived in the Charleston area since Ellie was a toddler, and he purchased his Sullivan's Island beach house when she was in the second grade. Ellie wasn't sure exactly how he'd earned his wealth, but she knew he spent his time traveling all over the world, driving expensive cars, and collecting bottles of rare bourbon and whiskey. He called it retirement.

Uncle Jim welcomed his sister and her family into his beach-front home many times a year. Ellie was the closest thing he had to a daughter, and even when she was growing up, she would stay with him for several weeks during the summer. Always his faithful sidekick, Ellie loved traipsing all over the Charleston area with him. She had even traveled to Europe with him during her senior year of high school.

The summer Ellie was ten, one of her uncle's trips had left his beach house vacant, and her parents had invited the Tanner family to join them on vacation. The Tanners had two children close to Ellie's age—Charlie and Olivia. Ellie had been friends with Olivia since they met in kindergarten, and the families forged a strong friendship over the course of many years. That trip was the beginning of an annual tradition where both families spent a week together on Sullivan's Island, and Ellie loved reminiscing about the fun times she had spent with Olivia and Charlie in the beach house. Through middle and high school, the three of them had remained close friends, and because she knew that three months of solitude on Sullivan's Island might get a little lonely, Ellie had invited Olivia to stay with her for a few weeks.

"So, are you looking forward to spending time with Olivia?" Uncle Jim asked once they had been served their drinks and had placed their orders.

"Yes! We haven't hung out much since she got married and I left for college. I feel like we've grown apart a little as we've grown up, and that sucks. She's so busy now that she's married *and* going to school. And I'm always busy and haven't gone home much over the last year."

"I'm sure y'all will pick right back up where you left off," her uncle assured her.

Ellie thought for a couple of moments, not allowing her expression to betray anything. "To be honest, I think I've done more of the pulling away from the friendship than she has. Every time I see her, I just feel so jealous."

"Jealous? Why?" Uncle Jim shook his head, confused.

The waitress returned, bearing their appetizer. Ellie helped herself to a wing, but quickly realized it was too hot and dropped it onto her plate.

"It's silly, really, but Olivia's life always seems so perfect. She always has the perfect clothes, she had the perfect boyfriend, and now she's married to what seems like the perfect husband. She lives in the cutest little house, she and Daniel are basically the perfect couple, and I don't even have a boyfriend right now!" Ellie shook her head, frustrated with herself.

"You're right—that *is* silly. You and Olivia are nothing alike, Ellie. You might think you'd want to have her life, but you wouldn't be happy if you had it. I know you, kid. You've got some big dreams and some big goals, and your time is coming. You shouldn't be jealous of your friend."

Ellie bit into the chicken wing, rolling her eyes with delight at the delicious taste. "I know, but it still sucks. I try not to feel so envious, but sometimes I can't help it. And not only that, but she's so pretty and thin, and I always feel so frumpy and over-weight next to her."

"First of all, it's not a race, Ellie. You and Olivia are at different stages in your life, which is normal," her uncle told her comfortingly. "At my age, most people have a wife and children, but I don't. Instead, I date different women from time to time, and I have a niece to spoil—not a hoard of grandchildren. But I don't spend time comparing myself to my friends. And secondly, you need to stop selling yourself so short. You're a beautiful girl, and I don't want to hear another word about it."

"Thanks, Uncle Jim." Ellie wiped her greasy fingers on a napkin. "Growing up, Olivia and I made all these plans, and I always thought we'd get married and have kids around the same time. But that's not how it's turning out."

Jim inhaled deeply and wiped his mouth neatly. His blue eyes were stern and fierce. "When you least expect it, things will start happening for you, but you're going to make lots of plans in your life. Many of those won't turn out the way that you thought, but that's okay. First of all, you need to get your head on straight. Start feeling as confident as you act all the time. Stop beating yourself up about your weight."

Ellie smiled and nodded, taking a deep breath. "I know you're right, but that's easier said than done."

AFTER LUNCH, Ellie unpacked and took a short nap. When she woke up, she walked downstairs and out onto the screened porch. She stood at the door for a moment, staring out at the beach with a smile. A boardwalk stretched across the front yard, through the dunes, and down to the beach. Ellie walked slowly, the salt air permeating her body and easing all the tension in her muscles. She paused again for a few moments at the crest of the dunes, staring out over the shoreline. The beach was dotted with a rainbow of umbrellas and tents, and beachgoers swarmed across the sand like ants. Children splashed in the surf, squealing loudly as they chased each other up and down the beach. The latest Cole Swindell song drifted along on a breeze, emanating from someone's portable speaker. On the horizon, a cargo ship was easing its way into the harbor, enormously majestic as it sliced through the waves. Ellie noticed the familiar orange tape wrapped around three stakes up in the dunes in front of the house—a loggerhead turtle nest. A sense of pride swelled from deep within her because the female loggerhead had picked her uncle's dunes to lay her nest. Ellie would certainly keep an eye on that nest throughout the summer.

Leaving her flip-flops at the end of the private boardwalk, Ellie danced her way across the scalding hot sand towards the ocean. A small wave washed over her feet, and she shivered with delight.

For the next three months, she would wake up every morning to the sound of waves crashing onto the beach, and she would fall asleep every night to the same melody. She would swim in the Atlantic Ocean daily and then let her hair dry in the hot summer sunshine. Ellie watched dolphins surface only a few hundred yards out and hugged herself tightly, sighing deeply. She felt certain that this summer was going to be a memorable one, and she was excited to see what the next three months would hold for her.

CHAPTER TWO

"*D*on't cry, don't cry," Olivia repeated to herself out loud willing the tears to stop filling her eyes. She struggled to think about something else—anything else—but it was no use. She could only think about one thing: her failing marriage. She glanced at her GPS for the hundredth time, feeling as if she had been traveling down the interstate forever. She only had an hour left, but the drive to Sullivan's Island was mind-numbingly dull —nothing but interstate for hundreds of miles. Olivia had listened to the radio for the first part of her trip, but once all the songs started to sound alike, she turned the volume down and had been driving in silence for the last half hour.

TURNING off the radio had been a mistake, though, because silence was dangerous. Silence left her alone with her thoughts, and Olivia was trying not to dwell on all the different thoughts swirling around inside her brain. She gripped the steering wheel tighter and shifted in her seat, shaking her head. Her life wasn't supposed to have turned out this way. She wasn't supposed to be miserable. She wasn't supposed to *want* to spend three weeks away from her husband. She and Daniel were supposed to be happily married—and from all outward appearances, they were —but in fourteen months of marriage, Olivia had learned that appearances could be deceiving.

The only people who knew about her marital problems were her parents and brother, Charlie. Olivia hadn't breathed a word of it to Ellie, and that made her feel even worse. Ellie was her best friend, and Olivia had never kept such a big secret from her. She wasn't even sure how to bring the subject up without dissolving into a blubbering heap of emotion, and that was the main reason she hadn't brought it up yet. Even though Ellie had seen her cry before, this was different somehow, and Olivia had decided it would be better to bring the subject up in person instead of over the phone.

UNTIL FOUR MONTHS AGO, Olivia hadn't even known what Asperger's Syndrome was, but now it was all she could think about. Asperger's had invaded her life and was threatening to destroy her marriage. How had she not seen the signs? A tear slipped down her cheek, and she wiped it away angrily. If she had known that Daniel had Asperger's, she didn't think she would have married him.

Quirky. Socially awkward. Those were the words people used to describe Daniel, but Olivia had never minded when she and Daniel were dating. They had started going out when she was a sophomore in high school and he was a senior, and he had been an amazing boyfriend. Daniel had never been one to skimp when it came to big gestures—expensive jewelry, lavish dinners, and thoughtful gifts for every holiday and special occasion. At least once a month, he sent her flowers and chocolates. Olivia had been swept off her feet, and all of the gifts made it easy to overlook his little quirks. Those idiosyncrasies were what made him who he was, and Olivia fell in love quickly. Their engagement and wedding were straight out of a Southern bridal magazine. With an engagement party, numerous bridal showers, and a bachelorette party, the months leading up to the marriage seemed like something right out of a fairy tale. Due to the many activities scheduled for the day of the wedding—hair-styling and makeup appointments, getting into her elaborate gown and veil with all its intricate buttons, and hundreds of photos—Olivia remembered only small snippets of that day. The important thing, though, was that at the end of that momentous day, she was married to the man of her dreams.

A few hours after the wedding, Olivia and Daniel boarded a flight to Grenada to spend a week in paradise. While she had been eagerly anticipating the wedding, Olivia was even more excited about their honeymoon. She and Daniel had both grown up in Christian homes, and they had chosen to wait until they were married to have sex. They made love on their wedding night, but in the days that followed, Olivia sensed something wasn't right. Daniel didn't seem interested in intimacy once the wedding night was over. In fact, during their honeymoon, they only had sex twice, and Olivia had initiated it both times. Confused, she told herself that Daniel was weary from all of the wedding chaos and that everything would be fine when they got home.

IN THE DAYS and weeks following their honeymoon, Olivia began to feel as if she was living in a horrible nightmare, unable to wake up. Daniel her husband was completely different from Daniel her fiancé. It was as though someone had flipped a switch, completely replacing the man she had loved before the vows had been said with a total stranger. Within a few weeks of sharing a home with him, Olivia realized that Daniel was a man of strict, rigid routines. The slightest interference with his schedule caused him to freak out, leading to angry outbursts and bringing out a side of him Olivia had never seen before. When they were dating, Daniel seemed to have endless hours to spend with her, but once they were married, he worked long, exhausting hours at the office, even on the weekends.

Olivia couldn't count the number of times she had cried in the first few months of their marriage. As time wore on, she learned that Daniel ironed his clothes in a specific order, loaded the dishwasher in a specific way, and never adjusted the thermostat except when the seasons changed. Gradually, she adapted to fit his needs, all while wondering how she had failed to glimpse this side of him before they married. Some days, usually when Daniel was at work, Olivia would wonder if she was just imagining it all, perhaps blowing it all out of proportion. But when he came home, the reality and the severity of the situation blindsided her all over again.

As time wore on, Olivia began to wonder if a baby would bring them closer together. She and Daniel had always planned to have a family, but she had been taking the pill since before the wedding. When she finally brought up the subject, Daniel had been more than willing. He was eager to start a family, but he soon wanted to know Olivia's ovulation cycle and began initiating sex at times she was likely to conceive so that now making love seemed like one more item he could check off his "to-do" list. Instead of bringing a new intimacy to their relationship, sex began to feel like a chore. Daniel was simply indifferent to sex; he didn't mind if they went weeks without it. And Olivia grew angrier with each passing day. She felt betrayed. Daniel had deceived her. She wasn't even twenty-two years old, but she felt as if life with him was aging her at an alarming rate.

LATE ONE SATURDAY NIGHT, when Daniel was working late again, Olivia sat down with her laptop and a mug of hot tea. She opened a search browser and typed in the first thing that came to mind: *Why doesn't my husband want to have sex with me?*

The majority of the articles that popped up were religion-related, and many of them shamed women for desiring intimacy with their husbands. A few suggested that a husband who wasn't interested in sex with his wife was having an affair, but Olivia didn't think that Daniel was seeing anyone else. Next, she decided to research some of his particular quirks—the ones that seemed most peculiar. This time, the search engine brought up dozens of hits on ADHD, but it didn't take her long to realize that those weren't going to offer any helpful answers. Just to be thorough, though, she had scrolled to the bottom of the first page of search results, and suddenly two words jumped out at her:

Asperger's Syndrome.

With some apprehension, Olivia had searched for the symptoms of AS in adults. She read faster and faster, devouring all the information she could find. It was as though someone had written all the articles about Daniel personally. She kept reading and finally searched *'I think my husband has Asperger's'* on the web.

And that's when she knew for sure.

Olivia wasn't the only one feeling utterly betrayed and miserable. To the contrary, countless other women were at a loss to understand why the men they married had changed so drastically after the wedding. Asperger's Syndrome. It explained why Daniel had changed so much. Except that he really hadn't changed. Daniel had finally allowed himself to be who he truly was around her. No more pretenses, no more imitating other boyfriends and fiancés. Daniel had swept her off her feet and married her; now, he didn't have to try so hard. Olivia was crushed.

OLIVIA CRIED QUIETLY AS she drove along the highway, but after a few minutes of self-pity, she forced herself to stop. She refused to arrive at the beach house with swollen eyes and a red nose. Keeping an eye on the road, she dug around in her purse until she found a crumpled tissue. She wiped the tears away and sniffed loudly, then shoved the tissue into the cup-holder.

"Get it together," she told herself. "You're going to relax and have a good time, and you're going to forget about all of this for a little while." Saying the words aloud seemed to help.

Even though the South Carolina Lowcountry was the most peaceful place Olivia could imagine to escape her troubles, she knew nothing could make her forget the stress and anxiety that weighed heavily on her mind. It couldn't make it any worse, though.

She smiled wistfully when she saw the sign announcing that Charleston was only forty miles away. She was almost to Sullivan's Island, and she could hardly wait to see her best friend.

CHAPTER THREE

"*B*ye, Uncle Jim! Have a safe trip!" Ellie waved goodbye to her uncle as he walked into the terminal of the Charleston International Airport to catch his flight, wheeling his luggage behind him.

"Bye, Ellie," he waved back at her. "Have a great summer! Let me know if you need anything!"

Ellie pulled away from the curb under the stern eye of a police officer who was monitoring cars dropping people off at the curb and headed back to the island. It was barely eight-thirty in the morning, and Olivia wasn't supposed to arrive until sometime mid-afternoon, so Ellie had several hours to herself.

AFTER PICKING up breakfast on the way home, she decided to spend her morning on the beach, getting a head start on her summer tan. When she pulled on one of the swimsuits she'd purchased the week before, Ellie scowled darkly at her reflection in mirror, turning from side to side to examine herself from every angle. When she left for college, Ellie had been slim—not thin, but definitely slim. Now, she was so frustrated with her body.

Her breasts had always been uncomfortably large, but only surgery could change that, and she hated the extra pounds she carried around her waistline. Some days, she felt as if all the other girls in her classes were sizes smaller than her, and Ellie thought maybe that's why she hadn't had a date in months. Those extra pounds made her feel horribly unattractive, and she hated each one of them. The swimsuits she had chosen for the summer had features to help draw attention away from her waistline, but Ellie still felt uncomfortable as she walked down the path to the beach. She knew that if she cut out junk food and exercised more, she'd probably lose the weight. Over the summer, she planned to be more active by riding bikes and walking all over the island.

AFTER A FEW HOURS on the beach and lunch on the screened porch, Ellie took a quick shower to wash off the sand, sunscreen, and salt water. Her cell phone was ringing when she turned off the water, and she hurriedly wrapped a towel around herself before darting into her room to answer it.

"Hey, Olivia, where are you?" she asked, seeing her friend's name pop up on caller-ID when she answered.

"Hello! I'm in North Charleston. The GPS says I should be there in about thirty minutes, if traffic doesn't get backed up."

"Okay, great! I'll see you soon then!"

"See you soon."

A FEW MINUTES before Olivia was supposed to arrive, Ellie was still struggling to decide what to wear. She had purposely picked out one of her more stylish outfits, but it felt shabby in comparison to the clothes Olivia typically wore. Ellie had always envied Olivia's figure and the trendy clothes she wore; everything seemed to have been tailored for Olivia's specific body shape. The girls were only a few months apart in age, but Ellie had hit puberty first, and her awkward phase had seemed to go on forever. During those years, nothing seemed to fit her changing body, and she felt gawky and frumpy almost all the time. Olivia, on the other hand, blossomed from a gangly girl into an elegant young woman almost overnight and never experienced an awkward phase.

Ellie was still studying herself critically in the mirror when gravel crunched in the driveway outside. She glanced out one of the upstairs windows and couldn't help but notice that her friend was driving a new SUV. Ellie shook her head, smiling to herself. No doubt, the new car was yet another of Daniel's extravagant gifts. Olivia was lucky, Ellie thought to herself as she hurried down the stairs to greet her friend.

"Hello!" Ellie called down joyfully from the back porch. "I'm so glad you're here."

Olivia climbed out of the driver's seat, smoothing her yellow sundress. "Me too! That drive took forever!"

Ellie hurried down the steps and greeted her friend with a warm hug, squealing with delight. "It's been way too long since I've seen you!"

"I know! It's been months," Olivia agreed. "When did our lives get so busy?"

"I know, right?" Ellie stepped back and admired Olivia's pretty dress and fresh, dainty appearance. Her dark hair was swept up into a perfect, messy bun, and diamond earrings sparkled in her ears. Olivia looked as if she were spending her summer in the Hamptons rather than in the South Carolina Lowcountry.

"Let me help you with your bags," Ellie offered. "We can get you something cold to drink and get you unpacked, and then maybe we can go out for an early supper."

Olivia nodded. "That sounds good to me. I had a greasy fast-food burger for lunch, and I could definitely use something more substantial for supper."

"So how is everybody?" Ellie wanted to know as they carried Olivia's suitcases up to her room. "How's Daniel? And your parents? I haven't seen them in a long time, either."

"Everybody is doing really well. Charlie's eager to come visit while we're here—you know him. He wouldn't miss this for the world!"

Ellie plopped down on the end of Olivia's bed and pulled her knees to her chest, laughing nervously. "Oh Charlie!"

Olivia giggled. "He always wants to see you. He's never quite gotten over his crush on you."

Ellie blushed and bit her lip nervously. "I know. We talked about it when he came to visit me a couple weeks ago."

Olivia whirled around and stared at her friend in disbelief. "What?"

Ellie and Charlie, Olivia's brother, had dated for two years of high school, but their romance had fizzled out when she left for college, at least on her end. But even though Ellie had dated several different people since then, she and Charlie still kept in touch.

"He came and stayed with me for a weekend." Ellie covered her face with her hands, shaking her head.

"What does this mean?" Olivia threw herself across the bed, propping up on an elbow. In an instant, they were back to their teenage days, sharing secrets. "Are you two really going to get back together this time?"

"I don't know!" Ellie groaned loudly and buried her face in the bedspread. "He called me and we started talking, and somehow he ended up coming to spend the weekend. We hung out with all my friends, and then we spent hours talking about whether or not we should get back together."

Olivia's green eyes widened. "Wow! What did you decide?"

"We didn't really decide anything," Ellie said. "We're both taking a little time to think things over, but he's already hinted several times that he wants to come visit this summer."

"I don't even know what to say." Olivia shook her head, frowning. "What about all the reasons you two broke up in the first place?"

"Nothing has changed." Ellie flopped onto her back, stared up at the ceiling, and watched the fan spin lazily.

"So if nothing has changed, what is there to think about?" Before Ellie could speak, Olivia held up her hands as if surrendering. "Just so you know, I would *love* it if you and my brother could make things work, but let's be honest, El. You have so many plans and dreams for your life, and we both know that Charlie is content to stay in our hometown forever. He has no desire to see the Eiffel Tower or the pyramids of Egypt or even go on a cruise!"

"I know you're right," Ellie admitted. "But it's Charlie! We're so comfortable with each other. He knows everything about me, and I know everything about him. It's easy, you know?"

"I know, and you know that I love my brother, but I think you really need to consider everything before you get back together with him. If nothing has changed, how will the relationship be any different?"

"You're right." Ellie smiled and took a deep breath. "Now, enough about me! How's Daniel?"

"He's good," Olivia said, picking at a piece of lint on her dress. Then, she stood up and unzipped her suitcase.

"I'm surprised he didn't mind your being gone for a few weeks," Ellie added. "He probably won't know what to do without you."

"I'm sure he'll be fine," Olivia said, reaching into her suitcase and pulling out a stack of shirts, smoothing them neatly. "Besides, it's healthy for couples to spend some time apart every now and then."

Ellie laughed. "Good, because I would have been so bummed if you hadn't come."

"Daniel's mom said she would have him over for dinner a few nights a week so he won't starve," Olivia explained. "And I wouldn't have missed this trip for anything! I'm in desperate need of some girl time, and it really has been way too long since we spent more than a weekend together."

"Yes, it has." Ellie grinned, tucking her legs up under her. "I don't have anything planned for us really, besides tanning and riding bikes and being shamelessly lazy."

"You have no idea how wonderful that sounds."

"I also have a stack of books to read," Ellie went on, playing with the ends of her hair. "But we have endless options. We can ride bikes, go explore downtown, shop on King Street, get manicures—whatever we want."

Olivia nodded, pleased with the suggestions. "All of that sounds good to me." She twisted her wedding ring back and forth on her finger, frowning for a moment.

"Don't worry—I don't have that much money to spend either, so we won't do anything too frivolous," Ellie hastened to assure her friend, concerned that Olivia was worried about cost. "Aside from buying food, we actually don't have to spend any money in order to have fun. And I know for a fact that Uncle Jim has paddleboards and kayaks underneath the house, so we should definitely take advantage of those."

"Yes, that's a good idea. Daniel and I are trying to save money." Olivia hung several sundresses and her classic little black dress in the closet and then she turned back to Ellie. "I know you've been super busy with school, but I am excited to have a chance for us to spend some time together. I really have missed our long talks."

"Me too," Ellie told her. "But we're here now, and it's just the two of us. We can stay up late talking every night if we want to."

"I would really like that."

For the next couple of hours, the girls sat on the screened porch, catching up on everything that had happened since they'd last seen each other. Ellie griped about her finals and then talked about how excited she was to begin her final year of college. Olivia shared some juicy bits of gossip about two of their childhood friends who were constantly feuding and then described the new sectional couch she had recently purchased for her living room. She also told Ellie about her decision to apply for the dental hygiene program at the local technical college near their hometown. Ellie could easily picture Olivia as a hygienist, wearing cute scrubs to work every day and calming the nervous patients; she encouraged her friend to submit the application.

Finally, around five in the afternoon, Ellie and Olivia drove the golf cart to Home Team for supper. Even though she'd eaten there the day before, Ellie didn't mind going back, and Olivia was craving it. The island was buzzing with activity—people were leaving the beach, loading up their cars to head home for the day. Several neighbors were outside in their yards, firing up their grills, and the smell of burning charcoal and cooking meat drifted along with the ocean breeze.

When they were finally seated, Olivia picked up a menu and studied it intensely. "It feels like forever since I've been here."

"Well, it has been several years," Ellie pointed out. "Y'all haven't come to the beach with us since you and Daniel started dating. The first year y'all were dating, I think you went to the beach with his family."

Olivia rolled her eyes. "Yes. Ugh, that was the worst trip ever! We went to Panama City, and the beach was so crowded. We stayed in this condo on the twelfth floor, and it wasn't nearly as much fun as staying in a beach house.

"Staying here is definitely a treat," Ellie agreed, putting down the menu when she'd made up her mind. "There aren't a lot of places like Sullivan's Island."

The waitress arrived and took their order. While they waited for their food, Ellie and Olivia planned out how to spend the next couple of weeks. Ellie wanted to go paddle-boarding, Olivia wanted to shop at some local boutiques that she'd passed on the way to the beach house, and they both wanted to eat at some of the colorful local restaurants.

AFTER SUPPER, they drove the golf-cart around the island, admiring the beautiful beach homes. Finally, they parked on the southernmost point of the island and watched as the sun sank over Charleston, the sky over the harbor awash with vibrant shades of pink and orange.

"Once it gets darker, I'm going to walk on the beach," Ellie said as they drove back to the house.

Olivia's face lit up with excitement. "Oh yes!" she exclaimed. "The Lights Out Club! You're planning to go on patrol tonight?"

"And every night I'm here."

"Oh good! I'd love to come with you."

Ellie stared at Olivia. "Seriously?"

"Yes. We used to have so much fun roaming the island at night. I can't even remember why I stopped going with you in the first place."

"Well, I think I always loved the turtles more than you and Charlie." Ellie parked the golf cart underneath the house and removed the keys from the ignition.

"I'm sorry we stopped going," Olivia apologized, the corners of her mouth turned down. "I know it hurt your feelings. The whole Lights Out Club seemed a little childish, and everyone acted as if I was growing up, so I felt like I had to do grown up things."

Ellie nodded, struggling to understand why aiding the sea turtles was childish. "I was a little hurt," she admitted truthfully. "But eventually, I made my peace with being the lone beach patroller."

"I'll never forget how it all started," Olivia went on as they walked up the back steps. "When you marched up on that doorstep for the first time, I thought you were going to get shot!"

Ellie laughed. "I was a little worried about that, too."

"I've always admired how disciplined you were about your nightly patrols. Even when you were sunburned or not feeling well, you still went."

Ellie nodded. "Yes, I did."

"I might not walk with you every night while I'm here—I'm not as dedicated as you are—but if you don't mind, I would like to go every now and then."

A smile spread across Ellie's face, and she nodded slowly. "I'd really like that."

ONCE DARKNESS ENGULFED the island and the lights-out ordinance took effect, Ellie and Olivia set off down the beach. They wore tennis shoes and bug spray, and Ellie carried a small, lightweight shovel to fill in any holes they found. To most people, leaving a crater in the sand might seem insignificant, but a loggerhead turtle might waste energy crawling around or over it when coming ashore to nest. She might even change her mind and go crawling back into the ocean.

"One day, I want to actually *see* a loggerhead, and I don't mean at the aquarium," Ellie remarked as they made their way back towards her uncle's house. They had walked nearly a mile before turning around. All the houses on the beachfront were dark, so Ellie didn't need to make any house calls. Olivia didn't respond to her friend's remark, and Ellie glanced over at her. Olivia's eyes were shining, full of tears, and Ellie heard her inhale a shuddery breath.

"What's wrong?" She stopped and faced her friend, putting a gentle hand on Olivia's shoulder.

Olivia wiped the corners of her eyes, trying to stop the tears before they fell. "I didn't really want to get into it tonight, but I can't help it."

"What's going on? Talk to me," Ellie encouraged gently.

"I'm scared to say it aloud because that will make it that much more real." Olivia twisted her hands together nervously.

"Olivia, whatever it is, you can tell me."

Olivia nodded, finally allowing a tear to slide down her cheek. "Okay, I'll just say it." She took a deep breath, and then her face crumpled.

"Oh Ellie, I think my marriage is over!"

CHAPTER FOUR

Olivia had managed to hold it together all afternoon and through supper, but as they walked along the beach, her emotions reached a tipping point. She couldn't keep her secret any longer, and the words began to spill out. In less than fifteen minutes, Olivia filled Ellie in on everything that had happened since the wedding, including Daniel's official diagnosis of Asperger's. Ellie nodded occasionally, listening silently until Olivia finally paused for breath.

"Wow," Ellie said softly, shaking her head. "I had no idea. You and Daniel always seem so happy—like the perfect couple."

Olivia sniffed loudly. "Only because I talk about the good parts. I don't want anyone to know what it's really like."

Ellie pushed a shell out of the sand with her big toe. "How bad is it really?"

"It's pretty rough." Olivia shivered in the cool ocean breeze. "Can we talk back at the house?"

IN THE KITCHEN, Olivia sat at the bar and wiped her eyes and nose with a tissue while Ellie pulled a package of Oreos out of the pantry.

"Why didn't you tell me about all of this sooner?" Ellie wanted to know, reaching into the fridge for the gallon of milk.

Olivia shrugged, her chin trembling. "I don't know. I guess I was embarrassed and confused and..." she shook her head. "We had this big, expensive wedding, and everyone was so happy for us. I couldn't admit that it wasn't the fairytale everyone had imagined."

"That's a silly reason," Ellie said quietly, pulling two glasses out of the cabinet. "I'm your best friend. You can tell me anything."

"I know." Olivia nodded and then dissolved into tears again. After she had kept everything squashed down inside for so long, it was a welcome relief to get everything out in the open.

"How did you bring Asperger's up to Daniel?"

Groaning, Olivia balled up one tissue and grabbed another one from the box. "It wasn't easy, but I found this test with dozens of questions, and it's supposed to be a really good indicator of whether or not someone has AS or not. So one night, while we were watching TV, I sorta made it into a game. For the first ten or fifteen questions. Daniel wasn't taking it seriously, but then the questions started getting more intense, and I had to explain."

Ellie's eyes widened as she imagined what Daniel's reaction must have been. "Was he angry?"

"No, actually." Olivia sniffed loudly. "Oddly enough, Daniel is very aware that he's not quite like other people. Once I explained the quiz to him and how I had stumbled on it, he took it really seriously. And when we were done, the quiz results told us that Daniel likely has AS."

"Wow." Ellie shook her head slowly. "What did you do after that?"

"I found a doctor for him to see. It took a long time for us to get an appointment, but we finally got in. The doctor did all these different tests—so many tests. And they asked us a ton of questions. Some of them were really personal. In the end, all the results were unanimous."

Ellie bit into a cookie, chewed slowly, and then swallowed. "So what happens now? How did y'all leave things?"

"Not good." Olivia frowned again, reaching for the cookies. "The doctor recommended we see a counselor who is specially trained to deal with adults who have AS, and we went together. They told us that many people who have AS manage to maintain healthy, successful relationships."

"Well that's good news, right?" Ellie asked.

Olivia poured herself a brimming glass of milk. "It is, but now Daniel is refusing to go to any more counseling. He doesn't really see a problem with how things are between us, and no matter how many times I explain my point of view, he doesn't get it! And he doesn't even try to see it from my perspective! Ironically, some counseling might help him with that."

"That's a little selfish of him," Ellie remarked, her expression sour.

Groaning, Olivia dipped her Oreo into the milk. "I just want to know how I missed it, you know? Why did he act relatively normal while we were dating, and how did I not see that something was different? Was I *that* blinded by love?"

Ellie pulled her friend into a warm hug. "I don't think anyone who knew you two together would have thought that Daniel had Asperger's, Olivia. I know I didn't! Daniel seemed like the perfect guy for you. A little awkward at times and maybe not the best conversationalist, but I never would've suspected something like this."

"I know! I want *that* man back! The one who was fun and adventurous and devoted to making sure I was always happy."

"What does he say exactly? When you tell him how

unhappy you are?" Ellie asked, patting her friend's back comfortingly.

"He seems to think that I'm making a mountain out of a molehill—that the behaviors I say are damaging our relationship are insignificant. He says I should be happy because all of my basic needs are met—a house, a car, clothes, food—but I'm not."

"Having stuff doesn't necessarily make a person happy," Ellie agreed. "Oh, Olivia, I am so sorry. I had no idea you were going through this! I wish I could say that would make it better."

"You don't need to say anything. The only thing that could make it better is if Daniel changes his mind about counseling, and we start to work through some of our problems."

"So I guess this explains why you were so eager to get away for a while, huh?"

Olivia twisted her wedding ring back and forth on her finger, watching the diamonds sparkling under the kitchen lights. "Yeah. I saw it as a good opportunity to get away from Daniel and think about what I want to do. What I need to do. It's going to be a really tough decision."

"You know I'll stick with you no matter what you choose, Olivia, but I do think that you deserve to be happy."

"Me too. So I'm going to think long and hard before I decide if I really want to file for divorce or not." Olivia almost choked when she used the "d-word", something she had avoided for weeks.

"Well, stay here as long as you want. The house is mine all summer long, and this island is a perfect place to clear your head and make good decisions. I know from experience."

"Thanks." Olivia smiled sadly at her friend, grateful that Ellie was so understanding. "I know we haven't talked much lately, and a lot of that was my fault. I didn't want to talk to you because you know me better than anyone else, and I knew you would figure out that something was wrong."

"Probably."

"You're my best friend, and I would really love to spend some time doing all the things we used to do when we were kids. I want to feel like that girl again—carefree and happy."

"Definitely!" Ellie smiled and hugged her friend again tightly. "We'll get you through this, okay?"

"I hope so." Olivia nodded, sighing wearily. "I really hope so."

CHAPTER FIVE

*E*llie slipped out of bed quietly the next morning. After talking until well past midnight, she and Olivia had both fallen asleep in her bed. Ellie figured her friend needed the rest, so she pulled on her robe and tip-toed downstairs, leaving Olivia to sleep in peace. In the kitchen, Ellie rubbed her tired eyes while she filled the coffee pot with water. When the first cup of coffee had finished brewing, she poured it into her waiting mug and walked out onto the screened porch. The sun was barely peeking over the horizon, and only a handful of people were walking along the beach. Ellie took a seat on the wicker couch and tucked her feet beneath her, pulling out her phone to check her social media accounts.

It was well past eight when Olivia finally came down the stairs. Her long hair was disheveled, and her eyes were red and puffy from crying so much the night before.

"Good morning," Ellie greeted her. "You look like you could use some coffee."

Olivia nodded in agreement. "I'll pour a cup and then come out here with you."

. . .

"I've felt exhausted the past couple weeks," Olivia remarked when she returned with the hot beverage. "Some days it just feels like I have no energy at all."

"Well, you have a lot on your plate, and I'm sure that takes a toll on you."

"Probably," Olivia agreed.

"If you aren't too tired, how would you feel about a bike ride after breakfast?" Ellie suggested, wrapping her fingers tightly around the warm mug in her hand.

"That sounds good. I think some exercise would really do me good."

"Me too." Ellie looked down at her waistline and frowned. "I could stand to lose a few pounds this summer, so I'm trying to be more active this summer."

"Don't be silly. You look great," Olivia assured her friend.

Ellie snorted, almost almost spilling her coffee. "Yeah, right!"

Frowning, Olivia tilted her head to the side. "What do you mean, 'yeah, right?' You *do* look great."

Ellie groaned and rolled her eyes. "I've gained weight in the past year, and I feel so unattractive. No wonder I haven't had a date in months."

"I think you're being too hard on yourself," Olivia said. "You have a great figure. I wish I had your curves. You have what millions of women pay a lot of money to have."

Again, Ellie wrinkled up her nose, glancing down at her chest. "I hate how big they are. I want to have a breast reduction, but mom says that's something I can look into when I'm older. That's why I want to be more active while I'm here. I want to try and lose a few pounds."

"Okay, we can definitely do that," Olivia said, offering an encouraging smile. "But I still think you're being way too critical of yourself. You really do look good, and I'm not just saying that because I'm your friend."

"Thanks, Liv. That means a lot."

. . .

BOTH GIRLS WERE silent for a few minutes, and Ellie found herself staring out at the Atlantic Ocean. In the distance she could see two cargo ships easing into the harbor, one closer to shore and the other much farther out to sea. A pilot ship was speeding towards them, and Ellie wondered faintly where the massive ship was coming from and what sort of cargo its many containers carried.

"This is a really nice way to start the day," she commented.

"I was thinking the same thing." Olivia inhaled deeply and closed her eyes. "It's so peaceful."

"It really is."

"Something about this house is so comforting," Olivia went on. "I swear it's exactly the same as the last time I was here." She ran her fingers along the seam of the soft, faded cushion on the back of the couch.

"Uncle Jim rarely changes anything," Ellie said, "and there is something nice about that." She stared down at the grounds that had settled to the bottom of her cup, wondering if she should have a third cup as her mind moved to other subjects. She had spent most of the hour before Olivia woke processing her friend's announcement, and she felt foolish and immature for harboring jealousy for so many years. How many times had she wondered how Olivia had been so lucky to find a husband like Daniel? How many times had Ellie cried herself to sleep, lonely and certain that she'd never find someone with whom she would be equally as happy? Hadn't she cried when she saw Olivia and Daniel's Christmas card from the year before, thinking that she'd never reach a point in her life where she could send out a Christmas card with someone? Ellie felt guilty of her jealous thoughts, but she couldn't seem to get rid of them.

What bothered her now, though, was how awful Olivia's situation seemed. It was so unfair that her twenty-one-year old friend was married to a man struggling with such a relationship-altering condition! Ellie knew it wasn't as though Daniel could help having Asperger's, but for Olivia's sake, she wished that he would agree to the counseling.

AFTER EATING a quick breakfast of scrambled eggs and peanut-butter toast, both girls changed clothes and headed downstairs in search of bikes. They found a few older beach cruisers wearing years of inevitable rust from being stored in the salt air, but in otherwise good condition. Ellie smiled knowingly when she saw the new tires and freshly-greased chains; her uncle knew how much she loved to ride bikes all over the island, and she suspected he'd had them tuned up for her.

"It's getting hotter out here by the second," Ellie said, wiping sweat off her forehead with the back of her hand. "This might have to be a short ride."

"We'll have to start getting out earlier." Olivia climbed on her bike and nodded at her friend. "Which way should we go?"

OVER THE YEARS, Sullivan's Island had been untouched by the hands of time or commercialization. The tiny beach town consisted of a handful of restaurants, a post office, a doctor's office, several churches, and a one or two small shops. The lone gas station on the island provided fuel, ice, and a few snack items, but for anything more substantial, residents and visitors had to return to the mainland.

Ellie and Olivia rode through town, heading north towards Isle of Palms, the next barrier island up the coast. They pedaled up and down the streets, admiring several beach houses. Olivia appreciated the newly constructed homes, but Ellie preferred the older ones like her uncle's with more character and personality. She especially admired the houses with large screened porches. In Ellie's opinion, a beach house wasn't truly a beach house unless it had a screened porch.

"I'm still in shock over what you told me last night," Ellie finally said when they turned back and pedaled towards home. "You said Daniel isn't affectionate anymore and doesn't care about sex, but when you two were dating, he couldn't keep his hands off you. How does that make sense?"

"I don't know!" Olivia shook her head, frustrated. "He just doesn't need the physical aspect of a relationship to be fulfilled, I guess. I thought he would be a passionate husband because he was such a passionate boyfriend and fiancé, But, people with AS watch what other people do and imitate them. I guess that's what Daniel did for all those years."

"What do your parents say?" Ellie wanted to know. "What does Charlie think?

"Charlie is upset about it, but he and Daniel are still friends, so it's tough for him. My parents are really upset. Mom cries whenever we talk about it. She won't tell me what she thinks I should do. She says I'm the only one who can decide whether or not I want a divorce." Olivia winced, the ominous word thudding loudly as she spoke. "Charlie says he wouldn't have to think about it at all. He says I should find a lawyer and go ahead and file."

Ellie didn't want to voice an opinion, but she was inclined to agree with Charlie's view. "What about Daniel's family? What do they say about all of this?"

Olivia sighed wearily. "That's a whole other story. You know I *love* Daniel's family. They are so good to me, but they don't seem to understand that the Asperger's is a big deal. They seem to think it's something that I can cope with—like an allergy or something."

"Do they know all the details?"

"Most of it, yeah. They have really encouraged us to go to

marriage counseling with a special counselor, but Daniel's adamant that we don't need to do that."

"That sucks." Ellie wasn't sure what else to say, and she hated the awkwardness.

"Yes, it does. And I don't want to be angry with them, but they're making it tough. They're convinced that we're having newlywed trouble, and I can't make them see any different."

"That has to be frustrating."

"It really is." For a moment, her bottom lip trembled, and her voice broke slightly. "And you wanna know the worst part?"

"What?"

"I still love Daniel. I still love the idea of being his wife. But unless something major changes with him—meaning he decides that he needs some help in order to make our marriage work—I don't know what choice I have. Daniel's the only man I've ever loved, and the idea of not being married to him breaks my heart. At the same time, I don't know if I can handle a lifetime of the way things are right now."

"I wish I knew what tell you, Olivia, but I think I agree with your mom."

"What do you mean?"

"This is a choice you have to make."

Olivia smiled tearfully. "I know I do. Right now, it's good to be here and not stuck at home, wondering what happened to all my happy plans. I know I have a choice to make, but I want to enjoy myself for a few days and try not to think about it."

"In that case, should we hit the beach? I could stand to work on my tan."

"The beach sounds perfect."

CHAPTER SIX

*M*onths had passed since Olivia had felt as relaxed and carefree as she did on the island. She could finally breathe deeply again. She could make simple, mundane decisions without worrying about how it would affect Daniel. She could sleep in or rise early, depending on her mood. She could order takeout if she didn't feel like standing over the stove and cooking. Something about driving across the long causeway and crossing the old swing-bridge provided a sense of separation from the outside world of the mainland, and Olivia savored the feeling. She knew that she couldn't stay forever—eventually she would have to return home—but she dreamed of a reality where she never had to leave the island.

Olivia was shocked when she woke up one morning, glanced at the date on her phone, and realized that a week had passed already. She and Ellie had fallen into the comfortable routines of seasoned beach bums. Each morning, they exercised for almost an hour, often riding bikes or walking a couple miles. Midmorning, they would don their swimsuits and head to the beach to soak up as much sunshine as they could. Within a few days, they could both see a difference in their complexions, and when she showered, Olivia could see tan lines starting to appear. They ate lunches on the screened porch, never bothering to change out of their wet suits. For the most part, they wore bathing suits and cover-ups all day, every day. Olivia read magazines, took naps, and allowed herself to forget about applying makeup and styling her hair every day. Every day after supper, Ellie patrolled the beachfront, and Olivia joined her most nights. When they returned to the house, they stayed up late watching rom-com movies or giggling in the dark like silly teenage girls until finally falling asleep in the early morning hours.

AFTER SHE LOOKED at her phone, Olivia rolled back over in the bed, savoring the feeling of the cool sheets against her skin. The first rays of sunshine were pouring through the window, and she knew it was going to be another beautiful day. A dream about Daniel had awakened her well before sunrise, and she hadn't been able to fall back asleep since. Her dream had been a vivid reenactment of the day she left for the beach. Daniel had carried her luggage out to the car reluctantly, still mumbling about the fact that she was leaving and that she was taking so many bags. Olivia had ignored his comments all morning, but when she finally picked up her keys and purse and headed for the door, her temper had reached a boiling point. He was about to say good-bye, but she stopped him.

"I think you should know," she said firmly, "I'm going on this trip to spend time with Ellie, but I'm also going to do some think-ing. I'm going to use this time apart to decide whether or not I want to stay married to you. You should know that I am seriously considering filing for divorce."

. . .

OLIVIA SAT up in bed and moaned quietly. She felt sick to her stomach as she recalled that particular moment. She would never be able to erase the look of bewilderment on Daniel's face when she slammed the door behind her. His expression had been one of genuine confusion, and she had heard him call from the porch just as she shut the car door.

"I don't understand," he had said.

And she had driven away without a word.

Olivia sat up in the bed, running her fingers through her long hair and then beginning to braid it absently. He didn't understand. She genuinely believed that he didn't understand why she was so upset and conflicted; his brain couldn't comprehend why she was unhappy.

Finally, when she heard Ellie moving around across the hall, Olivia crawled out of bed. Her stomach still felt a bit queasy, but she chalked it up to stress and headed downstairs. Ellie was standing at the kitchen counter, scooping coffee grounds into the coffeemaker.

"Morning," Ellie greeted her. "Sleep okay?"

"Not really," Olivia admitted. "I woke up thinking about Daniel and everything else, and it has my stomach tied up in knots."

Ellie frowned. "I'm sorry. That sucks."

Olivia nodded. In lieu of coffee, she decided to make a cup of hot ginger tea in hopes of calming her churning stomach. "Daniel doesn't understand, you know. When I told him I was going to decide whether or not I still wanted to be married to him, he looked so puzzled."

"You did say his brain is wired a little differently."

"I know, but it's just so hard for me to understand how he doesn't see all the things that are wrong in our marriage," Olivia said, filling the kettle with water.

"What does he say when he calls you after work every day?"

Olivia shrugged. Daniel called her every day when he left

the office. It was part of his routine. "He doesn't even mention it, and I don't want to bring it up right now."

Ellie stared at the coffee pot, tapping her toe impatiently. "I get that."

"I want to forget about all of it for a little while." Olivia pressed her hand against her stomach, willing it to stop rolling.

"We should do something to cheer you up today," Ellie suggested. "It's supposed to be super hot, I think, so why don't we skip the beach and go shopping? I would love some new things for summer, and we haven't really left the island since we got here."

Olivia nodded. "That seems like a good idea. But let's give it a little while. I want to let my stomach settle first."

"Sure. Also, would you wanna go to Dunleavy's tonight? I saw that they're having a live Irish band, and I'd like to go."

"I wouldn't mind listening to some Irish music."

"Good. It seems like we have a plan for our day for the first time since we got here."

Shopping only took a few hours, and when they returned to the beach house, Olivia could tell that Ellie was in a foul humor. Her friend had struggled to find clothes that fit the way she wanted them to, and Ellie complained over and over that it was the extra pounds she was carrying. Olivia honestly couldn't tell that Ellie had gained any weight. In the end, though, Olivia had convinced her to buy a stylish blue sundress, and she hoped that Ellie would choose to keep the purchase and not return it.

Olivia finished putting her purchases away and then changed into a bikini. They still had the entire afternoon to lounge around before the live music at Dunleavy's, and both of them were eager for a dip in the ocean. Ellie seemed slightly more cheerful when they walked down to the beach, but she was still quiet.

"You okay?" Olivia asked.

"I'm fine," Ellie said. Her tone was clipped, and Olivia knew that she was anything but fine.

"Whew! That sun is some kind of hot today. I'm going for a quick dip first thing." Olivia set down her bag, unfolded her beach chair, and draped her beach towel over the back.

A grin spread across Ellie's face. "Bet I can beat you to the water!" she yelled as she made a dash for the ocean.

"Hey, wait for me!"

ELLIE AND OLIVIA waded out until they were chest deep in the cold, salty water of the Atlantic Ocean. Ellie floated on her back, but Olivia preferred to stand up, keeping an eye on the water around her. She didn't like to think that something could swim underneath her and bite her—sharks, mainly. Even though she loved the ocean, Olivia was secretly terrified of sharks.

"I don't know if I wanna go to Dunleavy's tonight anymore," Ellie said.

"What? You were so excited about it earlier!"

Ellie shrugged. "I dunno. I'm not sure I'm in the mood."

"Is this because you didn't find anything you liked while we were shopping?" Olivia asked.

"I guess so. I'm just so tired of always feeling frumpy and looking like a grandma whenever we go out anywhere."

Olivia eyed her friend sharply. "You're kidding me, right?"

"No." Ellie's lower lip stuck out a little bit, and a tiny part of Olivia wanted to laugh, but she held it in.

"I've never felt more unattractive in my life than I have this summer. No matter what I wear or how much of a tan I get."

"You're being way too hard on yourself," Olivia insisted.

"You're only saying that because you're my friend."

"No, I'm not!"

"Ellie, you're not unattractive. You're so pretty and smart

and funny! You sell yourself short, honestly. I never think you look frumpy. I always think how stylish and trendy you look."

Finally, Ellie smiled a little bit, seemingly comforted by Olivia's words. "Thanks. You're sweet."

"And besides, I happen to know at least one person who thinks you're very attractive."

"Who?"

"Charlie!" Olivia laughed, splashing water towards her friend. "My brother is in love with you, and he's always thought you were the most beautiful girl in the world."

"That *is* a good point," Ellie said, splashing Olivia in return. "That was a good reminder. Thanks."

"And you'll go to the bar tonight so we can listen to the music?"

"Yes, I'll go."

"And you'll wear the dress you bought today?"

"Yes," Ellie nodded, "I'll wear the new dress."

CHAPTER SEVEN

*E*llie lingered in the shower that afternoon, studying her new tan lines. Her arms and legs were growing darker by the day, and the areas covered by a swimsuit were pale in comparison.

The fine hairs on her forearms were bleached even blonder than usual from the sun and stood out in contrast to her now-tawny skin. After spending many long hours in the library earlier in the month, Ellie now felt completely refreshed after an active, sun-filled week. Sullivan's always had that effect on her.

Olivia's pep-talk earlier in the day had cheered her up a little, but she still heard the nagging voice in her head telling her she shouldn't believe her friend. When Ellie emerged from the shower, she stood in front of the mirror for a moment, critically examining her naked body. Ellie had felt self-conscious since she hit puberty and her breasts began developing rapidly. Even now, she thought they were too large and completely out of proportion with her disappointingly flat butt. Ellie thought her face was relatively pretty—round with a dimple in one cheek when she smiled. Her eyes were bright and blue, she didn't have a single complaint about her nose, and her long, naturally blonde hair was shiny. But somehow, despite all that, she still struggled to see herself as physically attractive.

Charlie *did* think she was beautiful, Ellie reminded herself while she dried off and combed the tangles from her long hair. He was also the only boy who had ever seen her naked, and Ellie blushed when she thought about the last time they'd seen each other. Charlie was also the only person Ellie had ever slept with, and he knew every detail about her body, including the mole that was hidden low on her hip. She felt so comfortable with him that she hadn't minded his seeing her naked.

Frustrated with her musings, Ellie leaned over, throwing her hair towards the floor, and made a few passes over it with the hair dryer. She patted her face lightly with mineral powder foundation, applied a coat of mascara, and a swipe of lip gloss. One nice thing about being at the beach was that a little bit of sunshine negated the need for much makeup. Besides, with the temperature outside still in the eighties, she'd sweat off anything she wore before she even reached Dunleavy's. In her room, she slipped into the dress she had bought earlier in the day. Reluctantly, she admitted to herself that the dress did look good—it accentuated her natural waist and showed off her breasts in a tasteful way without showing too much cleavage.

Olivia knocked on her bedroom door. "Are you dressed? Can I come in?"

"I'm dressed."

Olivia pushed the door open, walked into the room, and sat down on the window seat. She was wearing a simple yellow romper and brown sandals, and her dark brown hair was curled loosely and hanging around her shoulders.

"You look pretty," Ellie said.

"Thanks. That dress looks great with your tan. I'm so glad you decided to buy it."

"Me too. I was just trying to decide what jewelry to wear with it."

Olivia stood up and went to look in Ellie's jewelry bag. "Let me choose. You should let me do your hair for you, too. Like when we were kids."

Ellie nodded and grinned. Olivia really could be the sweetest friend, and she always knew how to boost Ellie's mood. "Thanks. I'd appreciate that."

By the time the girls parked the golf cart and walked into Dunleavy's, the Irish pub was growing crowded, and the girls were seated at one of the last two available booths. Even though night was falling, the summertime heat was oppressive, and no one wanted to sit outside. Their waitress, probably only a few years younger than them, brought them menus and took their drink orders, then scurried away. She returned in a few minutes with their sweet teas and complimentary basket of popcorn.

Dunleavy's had been an island institution for as long as Ellie could remember. The wooden walls were packed with old photos and battered license plates from every state in the U.S, and the wide ceiling beams held a collection of ancient beer cans from all over the world. The restaurant housed a few tables and booths, and served classic pub fare to its patrons, many of whom were island residents.

"What should we order?" Olivia wondered, studying the menu intently. "It's been a long time since I've been here."

"I'll probably get a burger," Ellie told her, closing the menu and grabbing a large handful of popcorn to snack on. A bobby-pin in her hair was stabbing her scalp, and she tried desperately to shift its position. Olivia had twisted her hair up into a loose bun on the back of her head, and Ellie was grateful to have her hair off her neck, but all the bobby pins were beginning to drive her a little crazy.

"You can never go wrong with a cheeseburger."

While Olivia debated between two items on the menu,

Ellie's eyes wandered around the restaurant, and her eyes fell on the band setting up in the corner. At first she only saw two musicians, one an older, white-haired man holding a scarred guitar and the other a middle-aged, balding man who was quietly strumming a mandolin. But then she spotted the third member of the Irish trio; he was crouching down in the corner, carefully tuning a fiddle. When he finally stood up, Ellie felt her mouth drop open. He was not the older, wizened man she had expected to see at all. Instead, he was young and handsome—broad-shouldered with a golden tan and dark, curly hair. Ellie's eyes drifted to his hands, noting that they were wide and strong, and they seemed to hold his fiddle casually, yet carefully. His arms were smooth and muscular, and he had at least two tattoos that Ellie could see—one peeking out from underneath a sleeve and the other barely visible above the collar of his gray shirt. He towered over everyone around him, and she noticed that the top of his head nearly brushed the wooden beams in the ceiling. When he took his place between the other two men and cleared his throat, she realized that he was the lead performer of the group. He tapped the microphone, testing it, and cleared his throat loudly.

"Good evening, all," he greeted the restaurant patrons. His accent had a faint, but distinct, Irish lilt, and Ellie smiled when she heard him speak.

"He is really cute," she whispered to Olivia.

"Yes he is," Olivia agreed seriously.

"My friends and I would like to thank you for coming out tonight. We're happy to be here again, playing at one of the oldest Irish establishments around. My name is Pat O'Sullivan, and this old fella here on my left is my grandfather, also Pat O'Sullivan. He's the original, and I'm the third. And on my right is our good friend, Roger Miller, who is not even a wee bit Irish, I'm afraid to say." He paused while several people laughed at his words, and then he winked slyly. "But we try not to hold it against him."

Ellie listened intently, mesmerized by his soft Irish accent and his wide smile. His gaze swept across the restaurant and finally landed on her. She smiled shyly, and he smiled back, his dark eyes crinkling pleasantly at the corners.

"Ellie?" Olivia's voice interrupted the moment.

"Yes?" Ellie looked up and realized that their young waitress was waiting to take her order, tapping her pen on her pad impatiently. "Oh, I'm so sorry. I was distracted. I'll have the burger with American cheese."

"Fries, chips, coleslaw, or pasta salad with that?"

"Fries, please."

"Great." The waitress tucked her pad into her apron and took the menus from them. "I'll put that in for y'all."

As the waitress walked away, the band struck up a tune. The song was an unfamiliar Irish jig, but it was evident that the trio was talented. The handsome young man was a gifted fiddler, and Ellie couldn't tear her eyes away. The beautiful instrument was tucked underneath his chin, and his fingers danced nimbly across the strings. To her further astonishment, he lowered the fiddle and began to sing while the other two men continued to play. Ellie didn't expect him to surprise her again, but when she heard his deep, rich baritone voice, her eyes widened. Many of the bar patrons began to clap in time with the lively tune, and Ellie joined them, impressed by his skills.

"They're really good," she commented to Olivia.

"They really are."

When their first song was over, the group paused to drink water and set up for the next song. "I see a lot of familiar faces out there tonight," the young man continued, "but a lot of unfamiliar ones as well. I'd like to welcome all of you newcomers out there. We really appreciate you being here, and we hope you enjoy our music." Once again his eyes fell on Ellie, and she smiled at him again, more confidently this time. He was, she decided, one of the most attractive men she had ever seen. Maybe the most attractive. She glanced over at Olivia and saw that she, too, was watching him. Suddenly, Ellie's high spirits plummeted. What if the fiddle player hadn't been looking at her? What if he was admiring Olivia? When they were in high school, Ellie had thought several different boys were interested in her only to find out they hoped she would talk them up to Olivia. Ellie felt so stupid. Of course he wasn't smiling at her. He was checking Olivia out. She glanced back up and saw that he was interacting with another section of the restaurant. Who had she been kidding? The fiddle-player was so good-looking that he probably already had a girlfriend. No way was he interested in her.

THEIR FOOD ARRIVED, and Ellie ate without really paying attention to what she put in her mouth. Even though she was sure she'd mistaken his smiles, she kept her eye on the Irish fiddler. She was close to finishing her meal when he announced that after one more song, they would take a short break. For a moment, Ellie imagined him walking by their table and talking to her instead of Olivia.

"We'd like to sing one of our favorites," he said.

He began to sing and Ellie listened, spellbound, as his strong voice rang out throughout the restaurant. It was a haunting song about heartbreak, and the entire audience was captivated, hanging on every note. His eyes swept across the audience and landed on Ellie. She caught her breath sharply, barely even noticing when Olivia slipped out of the booth and headed towards the bathroom. She fully expected his gaze to follow her friend, but instead, he kept his gaze on her. His dark brown eyes shone brightly in the fading evening light, and Ellie suddenly felt as if everything else around her was a blur and only he was in focus. Her heart beat faster in her chest. Her palms were clammy, and she pressed them together tightly. She hadn't even spoken to this man, but she knew she had never been so intensely attracted to any man before, not even to Charlie.

Someone tapped on her shoulder, breaking her gaze. Ellie turned and saw Olivia standing beside the booth. Her face was pale and looked sweaty and at that moment, Ellie feared her friend was going to vomit in the middle of the restaurant.

"I'm sick," Olivia told her, pressing her hands against her stomach. "Can we go?"

Ellie instinctively grabbed her wallet, pulled out cash, tossed it hurriedly on the table, and then rushed after Olivia. Pausing in the doorway, she glanced back at the Irish singer and offered him a disappointed smile. He frowned at her as she pushed the door open and left the restaurant.

"I DON'T KNOW what hit me," Olivia complained weakly, walking up the steps while Ellie unlocked the back door. "I caught a whiff of shrimp, and suddenly I had to throw up."

"Probably a virus or something," Ellie replied, still thinking about the fiddle player.

Olivia headed for the fridge and pulled out a can of ginger ale. "Maybe. Maybe it's all the stress. I've just felt so off lately—nausea, fatigue. Stress can do that."

"Why don't you lie down on the couch, and I'll fix you a glass of ice for your ginger ale."

"Thanks. That sounds good."

WHEN ELLIE RETURNED to the living room with a cold glass of fizzy soda, Olivia was lying on the couch, a blanket covering her legs. Some color had returned to her cheeks, and Ellie was glad to see that her friend didn't look so green anymore.

"You should go back to Dunleavy's," Olivia said, gratefully taking the glass from Ellie. "That fiddle player was definitely checking you out."

"I don't think so," Ellie said, laughing ruefully.

"I think he was. He kept looking at you and smiling."

Ellie shrugged. "I was pretty sure he was looking at you."

"No, he wasn't!"

"He was way too hot to be checking me out," Ellie insisted. "Besides, with a face and a body like that, he's probably already taken."

"You don't know that."

"It's not a big deal."

"Well, I think you should go back. You could be missing out on something great just because my stupid stomach decided that it didn't like shrimp."

Ellie shook her head. "No, it's fine. Really. I'll hang out here to make sure you're okay, and then I'll go on my beach patrol a little later."

Olivia frowned, her eyes narrowing as she watched Ellie. "You're selling yourself short again. I'm so mad at myself for getting sick because I know he was going to come talk to you when they took a break."

"And I think he was going to come talk to *you*."

A COUPLE OF HOURS LATER, long after darkness had settled over the island, Ellie decided to head out on her nightly beach patrol. Once again, all of the beachfront houses were dark, and she had to fill in only one hole. As she walked back to the house, she allowed her thoughts to drift back to the fiddle player. Every detail about him still stood out clearly in her head, and she sighed when she thought about how handsome he was. He probably had a girlfriend who looked like a model, Ellie decided. Despite Olivia's assurances, Ellie was confident that the musician had been watching her friend. She shrugged to herself. They would never know, thanks to Olivia's sudden aversion to seafood. She hoped that Olivia didn't have a contagious stomach virus, and she wrinkled her nose at the thought of getting sick herself.

But the more she thought about it, Ellie realized that Olivia had complained of nausea almost every day since she'd arrived. She had blamed the queasiness and her fatigue on all the stress, but she had also casually mentioned PMS symptoms—breast tenderness, slight cramping, and even a little spotting. And then, at Dunleavy's, the smell of shrimp made her sick to her stomach. Ellie's eyes grew wide, and she gasped loudly.

SHE RAN BACK to the beach house, and when she stumbled inside, she was breathless, sweaty, and nursing a stitch in her side.

"What happened to you? Is something wrong?" Olivia wanted to know, sitting up straight on the couch.

Ellie shook her head, panting and trying to catch her breath. "Liv...is there any chance...you could be... pregnant?"

CHAPTER EIGHT

*O*livia fell back into the couch cushions, stunned. For several moments, she allowed her mind to run wild. She knew that Ellie was watching her closely, trying to gauge her reaction, but she needed a few minutes to process the idea. Finally, she took a deep breath and exhaled deliberately. "Wow! It seems so obvious now."

"There's one way to find out for sure," Ellie said. "We can go to the pharmacy and buy you a pregnancy test."

Olivia stood up and began pacing back and forth around the living room, counting backwards mentally. When she really thought about it, she couldn't remember her last period. With everything that had been going on in her life, she had completely lost track of her cycle, and she hadn't been on birth control in months.

"This is crazy," she said, talking more to herself than Ellie.

"C'mon. If you take a pregnancy test, you'll know for sure. Otherwise, you're just going to sit here and wonder."

Olivia nodded. "You're right. Will you drive me? I think I'm too flustered right now."

Ellie stood up, clapping her hands together. "I'll grab my keys."

THE TEN-MINUTE DRIVE to the nearest pharmacy felt like an eternity to Olivia. She stared straight ahead, her thoughts and recollections of the past couple of months playing out like a movie in her mind. For weeks, she had hoped and prayed for a baby. She had seen her doctor, tracked her ovulation schedule, and done everything humanly possible to conceive, but nothing had worked. Her doctor assured her that she needed to be patient. During that same time, her marriage to Daniel had fallen apart. They had still had sex when she was ovulating, but Olivia had given up on getting pregnant, especially given all the stress she was under. And now that she was contemplating a divorce, she might actually be pregnant. Olivia was overwhelmed by all the emotions that were flooding through her, and she broke her silence.

"We tried for months and nothing!"

"I've heard people say that when you stop trying, that's when you finally get pregnant," Ellie said. "I just didn't realize that y'all were still..."

"Having sex?"

"Yeah."

Olivia shrugged. "Daniel would ask when I was ovulating or most likely to conceive and then insist that we have sex on those days. It wasn't romantic, but I took what I could get."

"Gotcha. I'm sorry, Liv. That doesn't sound like fun."

"That's Asperger's."

Ellie turned into the pharmacy parking lot and pulled into one of the spaces up front. Olivia stared at the entrance but sat frozen in her seat. She swallowed tightly, willing herself to move, to go inside and buy the pregnancy test. But she couldn't find the courage. She was absolutely terrified. When she and Daniel had decided to start a family, it had seemed like a great idea to bring the two of them closer. How had she thought a baby would fix everything between them? As horrible as she felt for even thinking it, Olivia knew a baby would only complicate matters even more.

"Are you okay?" Ellie asked softly. "You're trembling."

"I'm so confused right now," Olivia whispered, gripping her seatbelt tightly. "On the one hand, I've always wanted to be a mother, but on the other hand, I'm scared of what it will mean if I am pregnant. For me and Daniel."

"You mean of how it might affect whether or not you file for divorce?"

Olivia nodded, tears filling her eyes. "I've spent so many hours imagining what it would be like to finally take a test and be confident it was going to be positive, but now I just feel overwhelmed and scared."

"Hey, everything is going to be okay," Ellie assured her friend, squeezing Olivia's hand gently. "No matter when it happens, you're going to be a great mom, but right now we actually have to buy the tests. You could be stressing yourself out over nothing."

"You're right." Olivia wiped her tears away and sniffed loudly.

"C'mon." Ellie turned the car off and unbuckled her seatbelt. "I'll go with you."

"Thanks. I really appreciate that." Olivia offered Ellie a weak smile, grateful for her presence. She looked down at her stomach, lightly pressing her hand against her abdomen. It didn't feel any different, and yet there was no doubt in Olivia's mind; she *was* pregnant.

CHAPTER NINE

*E*llie and Olivia wove their way through the aisles until they reached the Family Planning section. Ellie had absolutely no idea which brand or type of pregnancy test was best, but Olivia seemed confident in her choice when she reached for a three-pack.

"This way, I can be extra sure of the results," she explained.

"Good plan."

"Can you hold them while I go to the bathroom?"

"Can't you wait till we get home?"

"Nope. I need to pee." Olivia pushed the box into Ellie's hands and headed toward the back of the store.

While she waited for Olivia, Ellie wandered through the store, browsing aimlessly. She was studying the box of pregnancy tests intently when she rounded a corner and slammed into a man. She gasped in surprise at their unexpected collision and dropped the box.

"Look out!" he exclaimed, grabbing her shoulders to steady her so she didn't lose her balance.

"I'm so sorry," Ellie was quick to apologize. She glanced up and immediately recognized the handsome young man standing in front of her.

He was the Irish fiddle player from Dunleavy's.

He picked up the box she had dropped and glanced at it briefly before handing it back to her, his expression flickering for only a moment. "Should I be congratulating you?" he asked, his dark eyes twinkling.

Confused, Ellie frowned and shook her head. "Excuse me?"

He glanced down at the box, and she followed his eyes. Realization dawned on her, and she wished she could sink into the floor. She was suddenly aware that she was wearing gym shorts, a ragged old tank top, and a sports bra. Her beautiful bun had transformed into a tangled mess as she walked along the shoreline, and she hadn't bothered to fix it before they left the house. She could only imagine what she must look like through his eyes, and what he must think when he saw her holding a box of pregnancy tests.

"Oh, these aren't mine, I swear! I'm holding them for my friend," Ellie laughed nervously. "I know that sounds like a lie, but I promise it's the truth. She's in the restroom."

The Irishman's smile grew wider as Ellie tried to explain. He was clearly amused by her stammering. "I believe you," he said, extending his hand. "I'm Patrick O'Sullivan. Everyone calls me Pat."

She shook his hand firmly. "I'm Ellie Taylor."

"I recognize you from Dunleavy's. You were there tonight, weren't you?"

Ellie could feel her face growing warm, and she knew she was blushing. "I was. You sounded really good—you and your band."

Pat tilted his head to the side curiously. "But you left so quickly. You must not have enjoyed the music *that* much."

"Actually," Ellie corrected him, "I had to leave unexpectedly because my friend got sick. Which eventually brought us here, buying these." She held up the box.

Pat nodded slowly, digesting her words. "Well I'm glad to hear you liked my music, but I'm sorry your friend got sick. The second half of our set has some of our best songs."

"I came specifically to hear y'all play. I saw the poster on Dunleavy's window earlier this week. I like Irish music."

"We play again in a couple weekends at an Irish bar downtown," he told her.

"Oh yeah?"

Pat grinned, showing off his straight, white teeth. "Yeah, it's an Irish pub called Tommy Condon's. It's a really cool. You should come hear us. The whole set this time, though. Not half of it."

Ellie studied him seriously. He towered over her by at least a foot. "I would really like that."

He stared back at her thoughtfully. "So are you here for vacation, Ellie?"

"Sorta. I'm spending the whole summer on Sullivan's Island, house-sitting for my uncle," she explained. Was he actually interested in her? Had Olivia been right all along? Her thoughts were whirling around inside her head, and she almost felt dizzy.

"The whole summer?" Pat grinned, obviously pleased with that information. "That's awesome."

"Yep."

"So, can I have your number? I can call you and let you know the details of our next show."

"Yes—yes, of course," Ellie stammered. She couldn't believe what was happening. She was standing in the middle of the pharmacy at close to eleven at night, holding a pack of pregnancy tests, about to give her phone number to the cutest guy she'd ever set eyes on.

He handed her his phone, and her hands trembled with

excitement as she saved her phone number in his Contacts folder. "There you go," she told him.

"Thanks. I'll call you soon."

"Sounds good."

Pat turned to walk away but stopped and turned back, winking quickly. "And I hope your friend gets the results she wants from those tests."

Ellie laughed again, not as nervous this time. "Me too."

"Goodnight, Ellie. I'm glad we bumped into each other."

When Olivia finally returned from the bathroom, Ellie tried to hide the grin on her face, but she felt it tugging at the corners of her mouth.

"What are you so happy about?" Olivia wanted to know.

"I bumped into the fiddle player from the Irish band, and he asked for my phone number," Ellie told her as they approached the check-out register.

"See?" Olivia's face lit up. "I told you he was checking you out!"

As soon as they got back to the house, Olivia ripped open one of the tests and hastily read over the instructions. After a few minutes in the bathroom, she emerged, chewing her fingernails.

"I have to wait three minutes now," she said, her voice tight.

Ellie nodded. She had curled up on the living room couch and pulled a pillow against her chest. It had been a long day, and her eyelids were heavy, but she kept herself awake by replaying her meeting with Pat over and over in her head. She wanted to crawl into her bed and dream about him.

"We always talked about having two or three kids," Olivia said, studying her hands. "Here I am, trying to figure out if our marriage is gonna work, and now we might add a child to the equation. I'm realizing now dumb it was to think a baby could fix things."

Ellie nodded sympathetically, forcing herself to pay attention. She was thinking about Pat O'Sullivan. She could still feel the firm pressure of his strong hands on her shoulders, steadying her, and she felt giddy when she pictured herself looking up at his handsome face again. His dark eyes had been so warm and expressive, and she loved how broad his shoulders were.

"I'm sorry. I wish I knew what to tell you."

Olivia's shoulders drooped "I wish I knew what to do. I feel so helpless."

"Whatever happens, it's all going to be okay."

Finally, when three minutes had passed, Olivia went into the bathroom to retrieve the test. She returned to the living room, holding the small stick in her hand and staring down at it.

"So, what's the verdict?" Ellie wanted to know, sitting on the edge of her seat.

"I'm pregnant," Olivia told her. "These two little lines are very pink."

"Congratulations!" Ellie said sincerely, pulling her friend into a hug.

"I'm going to have a baby," Olivia whispered in awe. "I'm going to be a mother."

"Yes, you are! And you're going to be the best mom!"

"Do you really think so?"

"I really do!"

For a moment, all talk of marital problems and divorce seemed completely forgotten. Olivia nodded, tears forming in her green eyes. "I'm pregnant! I can't believe it... I'm going to have a baby!"

. . .

It was past two in the morning before Ellie's head hit the pillow. She and Olivia had spent the last hour discussing baby names for both boys and girls. Ellie had been too tired to wash her face, but she had managed to brush her teeth and remove her contacts. Her pillow had never felt softer as her head sank down into it and she pulled the sheet up over her. Olivia had fallen asleep in Ellie's bed, almost midsentence. The day had taken a mental toll on her, and Ellie moved around the room quietly, trying not to disturb her friend. Before she fell asleep, she plugged her cell phone into the charger and, to her surprise, she had a missed call and a voicemail from a local phone number. She put her phone to ear to listen.

"Hey Ellie, it's Pat O'Sullivan. I know it's late, but I wanted to see if you'd like to go kayaking with me sometime soon. Let me know. Goodnight."

CHAPTER TEN

*O*livia sat on the screened porch, staring out at the beach
and the ocean that stretched to the horizon. The sky
was turning pink where the sun would soon be rising, and the
beach was still quiet, the only sound a gentle breeze rustling the
sea oats and the waves crashing onto the shore. Surprisingly, she
had slept through the night and awakened feeling well-rested.
Ellie was still asleep, and Olivia was grateful for a chance to be
alone with her emotions. The faint nausea—which she now
recognized as morning sickness—ebbed in her stomach, and she
sipped a glass of ginger ale, hoping to calm the churning.

Less than twelve hours had passed since two small pink lines
had showed up on the pregnancy test, and her thoughts were still
reeling. Part of her was thrilled that she was carrying a baby
inside her, but the other part of her was panicking. What did she
do now? If she filed for divorce, she wouldn't simply be divorcing
her husband—she would be divorcing her child's father.

Olivia tapped her chin thoughtfully, imagining Daniel as a
father. She could easily picture him holding the baby and
beaming proudly. Daniel wanted a family, and he had always
been close to his younger siblings. Olivia knew he would be

excited when she told him the news, but she found it difficult to envision him in other scenarios that involved a baby. What would his reaction be when the baby cried at night? When he was forced to change his rigid schedule to adapt to the baby's schedule? When she asked him to watch the baby while she ran an errand or took a shower? Sometimes, she was positive Daniel didn't remember she was in the same house with him, so would he forget about the baby, too? She had read nearly a dozen books about Asperger's and how it affected marriages, but most of them discussed childless couples. Olivia made a mental note to spend some time later in the day researching the topic on the internet.

A baby was something Olivia had dreamed of since the day Daniel proposed. She had always wondered what their child would look like. Would their baby have her dark hair and Daniel's bright blue eyes? Olivia's eyes filled with tears as she pictured a tiny pink face and tiny toes. Even now, she loved the baby growing inside her. She pressed her hand against her stomach, willing the morning sickness to pass. She needed all her energy to deal with the chaos of her life.

"Morning," Ellie greeted Olivia, stepping onto the porch with a mug of coffee in her hand. "How are you feeling?"

"I'm okay," Olivia said truthfully.

"Good. I was worried you wouldn't sleep well."

"Actually, for the first time in weeks, I slept through the night."

"That's good."

Olivia nodded, squeezing her eyes shut as a wave of nausea washed over her. She didn't exactly feel as if she were going to throw up, but she certainly didn't feel like eating breakfast anytime soon.

"Feeling sick again?" Ellie guessed.

"Yes. It sucks."

Ellie wrinkled her nose and took a sip of her coffee. "It's certainly turning out to be an interesting summer."

"I know." Olivia shook her head, laughing quietly. "Before I came, I wondered if we would get bored after a week or two, but I really don't think that's going to happen anytime soon."

"Nope."

"I was sitting out here, thinking about what sort of father Daniel will make."

"Probably a good one," Ellie said.

"I think so, too," Olivia agreed, watching a drop of condensation roll down the side of her glass and drip to the floor. "But I'm not sure how he'll handle all the life changes a baby will bring. Change is really challenging for Daniel, and a *lot* of things will be different with a baby."

"Everything will be different!"

"Exactly."

"Are you still considering divorce, though? Now that you know you're pregnant?"

Fear clenched Olivia's heart, and she swallowed tightly. Ellie always seemed to ask the questions she was avoiding, and Olivia didn't want to admit that the panic she felt was mostly due to the thought of being a single mother. "I don't know what I'm going to do," she finally said.

"Well, I'm no expert, but I think the first thing you need to do is make an appointment to see your gynecologist."

Olivia nodded in agreement. "I can call first thing on Monday," she said. "If he can squeeze me in, that means I have to go home early."

"Aww, I don't want you to leave. I've really enjoyed the time we're spending together."

"Really?" Olivia wiped a tear from the corner of her eye. "You've enjoyed having an emotional disaster interrupting your peaceful vacation?"

"You're not an emotional disaster," Ellie reassured her. "Of course I've enjoyed having you here. You're my best friend, and I love having you here. You could always come back."

Olivia nodded. "Thanks. I'll definitely keep that in mind."

"Have you told Daniel that you're coming home yet?"

"No. He's probably getting dressed for work now, so I'll just wait to tell him when he calls me tonight."

"Gotcha."

The two girls sat in silence for a few minutes, the sound of the waves on the beach the only noise. Olivia dreaded having to pack her bags and return home. All of her problems were waiting at home, and she wasn't ready to face them again. Still, she knew she needed to tell Daniel the news and see her OBGYN.

"I have one more question," Ellie said, smiling.

"Shoot." Olivia shook herself from her reverie and turned to look at her friend.

"Can I be the one to host your gender reveal party?"

ONCE OLIVIA'S NAUSEA PASSED, she and Ellie spent most of the morning and afternoon on the beach. She noticed Ellie pulling out her phone and texting someone occasionally, smiling as she did so.

"What are you grinning about?" Olivia asked, raising an eyebrow at her friend.

"The cute Irish guy is texting me. He called last night and asked me to go kayaking with him."

"You got asked out on a date and you didn't tell me?" Olivia raised her hand and offered a high-five. "That's awesome! See? I told you he was into you."

Ellie nodded. "Yes, you did. He *did* ask me how long I was going to be here for, though, and now I'm wondering if he's just looking for a little summer fling."

Groaning, Olivia threw up her hands. "So what if he is? A summer fling could be fun. Besides, he's hot!"

"I know he is, but I keep thinking about Charlie. I did tell him I'd think about getting back together."

"Just because you're thinking about dating my brother again doesn't mean you have to act like a nun until you make a choice," Olivia pointed out. "Besides, maybe it'll help give you some perspective if you date someone else, even casually."

"You're probably right," Ellie said.

"Go kayaking with him and have a good time. And please bring back a vivid description of what he looks like shirtless. Take pictures if you can." Olivia fanned herself dramatically with her hand.

Laughing, Ellie nodded. "Okay, okay. Deal."

FIRST THING MONDAY MORNING, Olivia called her gynecologist's office, and the receptionist managed to squeeze her into the last appointment slot on Tuesday afternoon. Reluctantly, Olivia began to pack her suitcases, already dreading her return home. Ellie insisted they spend Olivia's last day on the island doing whatever she wanted, so they rode bikes, worked on their suntans, and then ended the day by eating at Fleet Landing downtown and watching the sun set over the Charleston Harbor.

The next morning, Olivia woke early and dressed for her drive home. Ellie packed her a bag with several cans of ginger ale and a sleeve of saltine crackers for the drive and then helped Olivia take her bags down to the car.

"I really wish you could stay," Ellie told Olivia when her stuff was loaded and it was time for her to leave. "I'm going to miss you."

"I wish I could stay, too, but I guess I have to be a responsible adult and go home." Olivia pulled Ellie into a warm hug. "Thank you for everything. You've been such a good friend to me over the past couple weeks."

"If you need anything, call me, okay?"

Olivia nodded, stepping back and wiping tears from her eyes. "I will."

"And if anything changes, you can always come back to the beach," Ellie insisted. "It's just going to be me here for the rest of the summer, unless Charlie comes to visit, so there will always be plenty of room."

"I'll keep it in mind."

"Let me know when you get home, and call me after you see the doctor."

"I will." Olivia climbed into the car and turned the key in the ignition. She rolled her car window down and waved to Ellie. "Bye. Thanks for everything. And don't forget to call and tell me all about your date with Pat."

"I won't."

OLIVIA PULLED out of the driveway, sad to leave her best friend and a beautiful beach house behind. She wanted to stay, but she knew it was important for her to see her doctor. In her rearview mirror, Olivia saw Ellie standing on the back steps, waving and smiling. Her friend's love and support over the past ten days had given Olivia the courage to face her future, and she took a deep breath, gripping the steering wheel tightly.

Whatever happened, whatever choice she made, she knew Ellie would be there for her.

CHAPTER ELEVEN

*E*llie studied her reflection in the mirror, wondering if she should change her outfit again. Clothes were strewn across her bed, and her room was a disaster, but she still couldn't decide what to wear. Kayaking definitely called for a swimsuit, but she wanted to wear something cute over it. Knowing it would be a hot day, Ellie had applied the bare minimum of makeup—only a touch of powder and mascara. She had selected a black one-piece suit, and her long, blonde hair was loosely braided over one shoulder. The logical side of her brain told her it didn't really matter, but she was determined to look pretty for her first date with Pat. Finally, after changing several times, Ellie settled on a classic: denim shorts and a plain white t-shirt. She wished that Olivia was still in the room across the hall so she could ask her opinion.

Pat had offered to pick her up for their date, but Ellie said she would meet him at the Pitt Street Bridge. She didn't know anything about him, and she was a cautious person. If their first date went well and he seemed nice, she might invite him to the beach house. First, she needed to spend some one-on-one time with him.

Olivia had called after seeing the gynecologist to say that bloodwork had confirmed the pregnancy, but Ellie hadn't talked to her since she had told Daniel the good news. She wanted to call, but she knew Olivia was dealing with a lot and would reach out when she was ready. The house had been quiet since Olivia left, though, and Ellie was finally realizing how lonely the rest of her vacation might be.

BEFORE SHE LEFT THE HOUSE, Ellie called her mom to let her know where she was going and when she was supposed to return.

"You've got a date?" Ellie's mom echoed in disbelief. "With who?"

Ellie pinched the bridge of her nose between her thumb and her forefinger. She had known these questions were inevitable. "His name is Pat—well, Patrick—and I met him at the Irish pub here on the island."

"You met him in a *bar?*"

"Mom, it's the Irish pub here on Sullivan's, not some wild, rowdy club. You've been there a dozen times! And he was performing, actually. He's in an Irish band."

"Hmmm."

"Anyways, he seemed nice and he's really, really good look-ing." Ellie rolled her eyes dreamily, picturing Pat.

"Well, be careful," her mom cautioned her.

"I will, but that's why I was calling you. We're going kayak-ing, and we're leaving from the Pitt Street Bridge. He said we'd probably be gone till lunchtime. I'll try to shoot you a text when we get back, but if I don't, call and check on me."

"I'll set an alarm to remind me."

"Good idea."

"Have fun. Do you have sunscreen?"

Ellie shook her head, smiling to herself. "Yes, mom, I have sunscreen."

🐚

ELLIE MET Pat at the Pitt Street Bridge in Mount Pleasant. She saw him pulling kayaks out of his truck bed and pulled her car in to the space in front of his. Her hands were trembling nervously, but she took a deep breath and climbed out of the car.

"Hey," he called. "Glad you made it."

"G'morning," she said, smiling at him. "Need any help with the kayaks?"

Pat shook his head, hoisting the second one out of the truck bed. "No, thanks. You ready to go?"

"Yep." Ellie admired the definition of his muscles under his t-shirt as he lifted the kayak out of the truck with ease. "I brought some bottles of water. Is there a way for us to carry them?"

"Sure. I've got a waterproof bag I strap to the front of my kayak. We can put them in there."

Pat hauled the kayaks down to creek and slid them into the water. Ellie swallowed tightly as she pulled her shirt over her head and shimmied out of her shorts, self-conscious about the weight she had gained recently. As she handed the bottles of water to him, their fingers brushed for the briefest moment, but that was all it took for Ellie's heart rate to speed up.

"Have you kayaked before?" he asked.

"Yes, but it's been a while though."

"Gotcha." Pat offered his hand to her. "Want some help getting in? It can be a little wobbly."

Ellie took it and sighed inwardly. His fingers might be able to dance nimbly across the strings of a musical instrument, but his grip was strong, and he had rough calluses on his palms. When she was safely seated and holding her paddle, Pat gave her kayak a firm shove, pushing her away from the muddy bank. His movements seemed so easy and natural as he secured the waterproof bag to the back of his vessel and then eased into his seat before pushing away from the bank himself.

"I thought we could paddle out in the harbor," he said. "We'll stick close to the shore so we don't have to deal with the current as much."

Ellie nodded, trusting his judgment. She dipped the blade of her paddle into the water and pulled it back towards her. Immediately, she felt resistance, and she knew her arms and shoulders were going to pay for the exertion later.

"You seem to know what you're doing," Pat remarked as they settled into a steady rhythm.

"I've vacationed at my uncle's house on Sullivan's every summer for almost my whole life, and we used to kayak and paddleboard a good bit. I never could quite get the hang of paddleboarding. I don't have the balance for it, I guess."

"Is your uncle from here?" Pat asked, the Irish r's rolling delightfully across his tongue.

"No, but he bought the house on Sullivan's about twenty years ago, and we've been coming here ever since."

"And you're house-sitting for him this summer, right?"

"Yep. He's in Europe till August."

"Sounds like he leads an interesting life."

"For him, it's perfect. He's a bachelor—always has been and probably always will be—and he dotes on his only niece—me." Ellie winked at Pat, grinning.

The duo paddled steadily, the conversation never ceasing. Ellie learned that Pat held dual citizenship between Ireland and the U.S. because his father was Irish and his mother was American. Pat's mother had met his father while spending a year abroad after college, and after their marriage, she had opted to live in Ireland for the next fifteen years. Pat had been raised there until he was in middle school when his parents moved back to the states to be closer to his mother's family.

"After my parents lived here a couple years, they finally were able to bring my granddad over. He didn't really want to leave Ireland, so he keeps a small flat there and goes back every now and then."

"It must have been hard to leave the country you grew up in and come here," Ellie remarked, wondering what it would have been like to move to a different country during her middle school years.

Pat shrugged. "It was challenging, yes, but we had visited my grandparents in Charleston a lot when I was a kid, so I knew the area already."

"And you've kept your accent a little, too." Ellie enjoyed listening to him talk, waiting for those moments when his Irish accent slipped out.

"Aye, though when I'm around my American family, I tend to lose it more. But when I'm around my granddad or I go back to Ireland for a visit, it gets very strong. So strong that you'd probably have a hard time understanding me," Pat laughed. "Now, enough about me. Where did you grow up?"

"Born and raised in Georgia, in a town called Warner Robins." She rested her paddle across her lap and took a moment to wipe the sweat off her brow. "I'm an only child, and I'm working towards my Bachelor's in Public Relations at the University of Georgia. Only one more year to go, and then I'm done!"

"What do you want to do after you graduate?" Pat asked, putting his paddle down, too.

"I would really like to work in public relations," Ellie laughed quietly. "Actually, I really do want to be like a spokesperson for a company or maybe a city or a police department. I've got an internship in the spring semester, and I'll be working with the police department in my hometown. I'm pretty excited."

"So you'd write press releases and go to news conferences and stuff?"

"Yes, exactly. I'd also likely work with social media and different outlets like that."

"How did you first get interested in that field?"

Ellie shrugged. "Well, I've always been good at public speaking, I guess. And then I took an Intro to Business class trying to figure out what area I wanted to study. The class briefly touched on PR, so I decided maybe I'd check it out. After the first class, I knew it was right for me."

"That's cool."

"What do you do?"

"I'm a Project Engineer for a local construction company."

"That sounds interesting. What do you do exactly?"

Pat kept paddling further inland, away from where they'd put the kayaks in the water, and the muscles in Ellie's arms and shoulders ached in protest. She didn't want to admit that she was tired, so she encouraged him to talk about his job, trying to keep her mind off the pain. Pat told her about at typical day on his job and how he hated being confined to an office and preferred to work on the actual jobsite, overseeing the construction. He explained that he had grown up playing with Legos and how that had led to his using real tools and building bigger things.

"And you like living in Charleston?"

Pat nodded enthusiastically. "Oh yes. It's got all the perks of a big city, but it's really just a small town."

"I love it here, too," Ellie agreed. She leaned forward and stretched her shoulders. She dropped one hand into the creek, and she trailed her fingertips in the cool water. "We've been coming here for so many years it feels like a second home to me."

"Does your friend always come with you?" Pat asked,

glancing over at her. "The one who was with you at Dunleavy's?"

Ellie could tell that he was studying her, but she didn't let on. "No, not always. One summer, we invited her family to come with us to Sullivan's. They fell in love with it, so we started this tradition of coming together for a week every summer. My uncle travels a lot during the summer when it's so hot, so his house is usually empty."

"Nice." Pat steered his kayak into one of the narrow marsh channels.

Ellie followed him, praying he knew where he was going. "Oh yes. Olivia, Charlie, and I—Charlie is Olivia's older brother —have explored every square inch of the island. We've spent hours playing on the sandbar up near Station 28, and we've walked the shoreline hundreds of times on our nightly patrols."

Pat's eyebrows furrowed together. "Nightly patrols?"

The words slipped out before Ellie realized it, and she hoped she could explain without sounding silly. "I'll tell you, but you have to promise you won't laugh."

Pat rested his paddle across his lap and folded his arms across his chest. "I promise I won't laugh. Now, tell me what you're talking about," he said in his deepest Irish accent.

She recognized that he was trying to charm her and eyed him sharply. "When we were young, the three of us were on the beach one morning, and we met one of the Island Turtle Ladies. She told us about the sea turtles and schooled us on filling in holes on the beach at night and protecting the nests during the incubation period. She stressed the importance of keeping our beaches clean and, most importantly, keeping the lights out on the beachfront at night so the turtles don't get confused. She was a natural-born teacher, and I have never forgotten how passionate she was, so I decided to do my part to protect the turtles. Later that night, the three of us were on the beach, and I noticed this house with the lights still on, so I marched up to their front door and asked them to turn off their lights."

"Seriously?"

"Yep. And that's how the Lights Out Club was born. From then on, I have gone on beach patrol every night I'm on Sullivan's unless I'm sick or sunburned, which has only happened a couple times."

"What did you patrol for exactly?" Pat wanted to know, processing the information slowly as they paddled along.

"It depends," she explained. "Sometimes, I go before dark and pick up any trash that I find and fill in holes. And then some nights, I walk after dark and look for houses with lights on."

"And how long did you keep this up? How many summers?"

Ellie thought for a moment as she counted in her head. "Over ten years. This is either the tenth or eleventh summer."

"Wait! You still do it?" Pat's mouth fell open and he stared at her with a mixture of wonder and respect. Ellie's cheeks felt warm, and she looked down at the water shyly.

"Yes. Every night that I'm here. Sometimes I only walk a few blocks, but some nights I'll walk a mile or two."

"That is some serious dedication!" Pat continued to stare at her, and she glimpsed admiration in his eyes.

Ellie shrugged casually. "Over the years, Olivia and Charlie have stopped coming with me, but I still go."

"Not a lot surprises me, but that does."

"Should I take that as a compliment?"

"Yes, you should. I'm impressed."

As the morning wore on, the duo maneuvered their kayaks further back into the narrow channels of the marsh. Pat pointed out herons and egrets hiding among the reeds, waiting to catch a fish. All around them, tiny fiddler crabs crawled into the grass, escaping the watchful eyes of human intruders. Several blue crabs swam underneath their kayaks, and Ellie studied their bright, vibrant colors closely.

"It must be amazing to live here year-round," Ellie said as they finally turned and headed back. The sun was almost directly overhead, and sweat trickled down the back of her neck.

"If you can adapt to the relentless summer humidity, the threat of hurricanes, and a large population of mosquitos, then yes, it's great," Pat laughed.

"I'm used to that already," Ellie pointed out. "Except that we don't get many hurricanes in Georgia. At least not where I'm from."

Up ahead, two dolphins breached the surface of the water and then ducked back down, out of sight. Ellie squealed with delight. "I love dolphins. Actually, I love almost all sea creatures." She turned to Pat. "Have you ever seen a sea turtle? Like out in the water?"

Pat thought for a moment and then shook his head. "No, I haven't. They don't typically come up this far into the harbor, I don't think. Besides, there are so many boats coming in and out of there that it would be dangerous for them."

Ellie sighed, gratefully accepting the bottle of water that Pat had handed to her. "I want to see one in person. At least once in my lifetime."

"You've never seen a sea turtle up close? Not even after all these years of trying to make their lives a little easier?"

"Nope. I mean, I've seen them in captivity, but I want to see one in its natural environment. I'd love to see a loggerhead on the beach, laying a nest, or maybe see one hatching. One day, I hope."

By the time they got back to the Pitt Street Bridge, it was well past lunchtime, and Ellie's stomach was gnawing with hunger. Pat suggested they grab sandwiches at a local deli, and Ellie followed him there in her car. By the time they reached the restaurant, she could feel the stabbing pains of a migraine behind her left eye. Ellie was prone to severe migraines, and she wondered if the bright reflection off the water was the cause. She had a prescription medication that she was supposed to take as soon as she felt the first twinge behind her eyes, but it as back at the house. Groaning, Ellie climbed out of the car and headed into the deli, trying to ignore the pain.

"So, what do you have planned for the rest of your summer?" Pat asked while they waited for their food. He had chosen a table outside of the crowded restaurant where it was quieter.

"Spend a lot of time on the beach working on my tan, of course," she told him, thoughtfully resting her chin in the palm of her hand. "I also have this huge stack of books that I want to read. And I want to eat lots of good food, ride bikes, and basically be an overall beach bum."

"That doesn't sound too much like a beach bum to me."

Ellie shook her head. "I guess not. But when I'm at school, I always have a million different things to do. Here, I only do what I feel like doing when I feel like it."

"And what about your friend? Is she staying the whole summer?" Pat wanted to know.

Before Ellie could answer, a server arrived with their sandwiches and after unwrapping hers and taking a bite, she answered him.

"She actually left yesterday. She's dealing with a lot right now, so she ended up going back to Georgia about a week early."

"That sucks. I hope everything's okay."

Ellie shrugged, swallowing a mouthful of food. She didn't want to discuss Olivia's private business with a man she'd met a few days ago. "I think it will be, but some things take time."

THEIR DATE ENDED in the parking lot of the deli, and Ellie was a little disappointed when Pat didn't kiss her cheek or even try to hug her. Instead, they exchanged friendly farewells, and he promised to call her soon. Ellie sat in her car for a few minutes, analyzing the time they had spent together. Once again, she wished Olivia was at the beach house so they could discuss the details.

He had been friendly, but not overly flirtatious. His interest in her felt genuine, but Ellie still couldn't figure out why he would be interested in her. Pat was not the type of guy who usually expressed any attraction to her. He was a triple threat—attractive, intelligent, and athletic—and he oozed charm. She groaned, massaging her temples. The pounding in her head was worsening, and she knew she needed to go home and try to sleep off the migraine that was building.

THE NEXT DAY, Ellie woke up with a full-blown migraine. She pulled the curtains over the windows and stayed in bed all morning, the sheets pulled up over her head. The stabbing pain behind her eyes was impossible to ignore, and every hint of light that slipped through the curtains made the throbbing worse.

Around lunchtime, she showered in the hottest water she could tolerate, hoping to relieve some of the tension. Afterwards, she curled up on the couch and pulled a blanket over her head, blocking out any unnecessary light. She was so nauseated that she skipped lunch and instead sipped on some ginger ale, chuckling ruefully to herself when she thought about the amount of ginger-ale she and Olivia had consumed in the last couple of weeks.

Pat texted her mid-morning to say hello and that he'd enjoyed their date. She told him she'd had a good time, too, but that she was sick with a migraine. Staring at the bright screen made her eyes ache, so she put her phone away after telling him she didn't feel well. As the afternoon wore on, Ellie dozed on and off, always hopeful that the next few minutes of sleep would ease her headache. Finally, sometime midafternoon, she fell asleep on the couch and slept heavily for a two hours. When she woke up, her head was still aching, but the nausea had passed, and her stomach was gnawing with hunger. She stood up slowly, swaying slightly. Her migraines made her head feel heavy, a sensation similar to dizziness.

Opening the fridge, Ellie propped her hand against the door and stared at her options. Her choices were deli meat or leftover pizza, but neither option appealed to her. Her stomach growled loudly, and she sighed, wishing the island had a fast food restaurant. She had a sudden craving for a greasy cheeseburger and an ice-cold Coke, but she tried to avoid driving when her head was pounding, especially when she felt the slightest bit dizzy. Grumpy and still hungry, Ellie retreated to the couch. She went searching for her phone, hoping to find a local place that would deliver, and found it buried beneath a pile of throw pillows. When she unlocked the screen, she saw a text message from Pat.

PAT: *Feeling any better?*

Ellie: A little.. At least I don't feel sick to my stomach anymore. Now I just want a greasy cheeseburger.

Pat: Seriously??

Ellie: I know, it's weird, but greasy food makes me feel better.

Pat: Interesting...

Ellie: Like I said, weird.

Pat: Are you going to get food?

ELLIE FROWNED, trying to decide. As hungry as she was, she knew that she needed to eat the leftover pizza. She had driven with a migraine before, and she knew how much it affected her reflexes. She typed out a quick response to Pat, explaining how she didn't think it was wise for her to get behind the wheel. She expected that he would respond as promptly as he had before, but fifteen minutes went by with no response, so she set her phone down and forgot about it.

HALF AN HOUR LATER, Ellie's phone rang, and she answered it without glancing at the screen to see who was calling.

"Hello?"

"Ellie? It's Pat."

Instantly, Ellie was alert. "Hi."

"Listen, I'm on Sullivan's Island. I brought you a cheeseburger, but when I got over here, I realized I have no idea where you lived."

"Are you serious?"

"Yes ma'am."

"Bless you!"

ELLIE GAVE Pat the address to the beach house, and in a few minutes, he came bounding up the back steps, holding a large brown paper bag.

"You said greasy food would make you feel better, so I here I am."

Ellie's face lit up. Her headache was agonizing, and her eyes ached so badly already, but now she thought she might cry. "This might be the sweetest thing anyone has ever done for me," she told him. Her eyes welled up, and she forced herself to blink back the tears.

"I'm just here to drop it off," he said, handing her the bag. "I'll let you get your rest, and I hope you feel better." He moved past her towards the door, but she caught his hand gently.

81

"Wait," she stopped him. "Can you stay for a few minutes at least?"

Pat grinned, evidently pleased. "Sure."

ELLIE LED Pat out onto the screened porch, and they sat down on the ancient wicker couch. Ellie opened the bag and gasped; Pat hadn't just ordered a cheeseburger. He had ordered a burger, popcorn chicken, a chili dog, onion rings, French fries, and even mozzarella sticks.

"This is really, really sweet of you," she repeated, shaking her head as she carefully set everything out on table in front of them. Her first choice was a mozzarella stick, and she took a bite hungrily. "Oh my gosh, this is exactly what I needed!"

Pat made himself comfortable on the couch and stretched his long legs out. "Well, I figured you must be feeling pretty rotten if you didn't feel like leaving the house, so I swung by the closest fast food restaurant."

"It's like you read my mind."

Shrugging, Pat draped one arm across the back of the couch. "I didn't know what you liked, so I tried to get a little bit of everything."

"Thanks." Ellie glanced down at her mismatched outfit. "Sorry I look like such a bum. I've been sleeping most of the day."

Pat shrugged. "I think you look fine."

"Did you work today?" she asked, changing the subject and reaching for the cheeseburger she'd been craving.

"Sure did. Spent the whole day on my job site downtown. I'm exhausted, but it was a good day."

Taking a huge bite of the cheeseburger, Ellie sighed dreamily. "This is so much better than I imagined. I am in your debt forever, Pat O'Sullivan."

"I'll be sure to collect sometime soon."

They sat in comfortable silence for a few minute while Ellie ate. Soon, her stomach was full, but her head was still hurting. She leaned back against the pillows wearily, exhaling slowly.

"I can't thank you enough for bringing me food," she told him again. "I've never seen a sight as beautiful as you standing on the back porch, holding up a grease-soaked bag. It has given me the energy for beach patrol tonight."

"You're gonna go even though you feel so rotten?" Pat asked, surprised.

Ellie nodded. "Yes, I made myself promise that I wouldn't let anything—aside from being really, really sick—keep me from going. And besides, the ocean air will be good for my headache."

"You're certainly an interesting woman, Ellie Taylor," Pat laughed, shaking his head. Then, he stood up reluctantly. "I wish I could go with you, but it's been a long day, and I desperately need a shower."

"I understand." Ellie smiled and stood up, too. She suddenly realized how close they were standing to one another, and she detected the faint hint of sweat emanating from his skin. As he towered over her, she looked up into his dark brown eyes and noticed hints of amber flecks in the brown. She spotted a few white hairs already sprinkled in with his dark, curly hair, and she realized that the more she studied him, the more handsome she found him. She wondered what it would be like to kiss him.

"I'll see you around." Pat turned and headed for the door.

Disappointed, Ellie forced herself to smile warmly as she walked him to the screened door. Something about him was so intriguing, and she longed to spend more time with him. "Thanks again," she added, lingering in the doorway.

Pat turned back to her quickly. "I hope you feel better soon, because I'd actually like to take you out again this weekend."

"I'm sure I'll be back to normal by tomorrow," she assured him. "And I'd like that."

A smile lit up Pat's handsome face, and his eyes crinkled at the corners. "Good. I'll talk to you tomorrow." Then he leaned in and pressed a light kiss to Ellie's lips. Stunned, she barely had time to realize he was kissing her before he pulled back, winked, and then bounded down the stairs.

"Bye, Ellie," he called back over his shoulder.

Ellie leaned against the doorframe, touching her lips lightly. The kiss had been so brief she wondered if she'd imagined it. "Bye!"

When Pat had pulled out of the yard and driven away, she walked back to the couch and sank back down into the cushions, pressing both hands to her chest, completely stunned.

"I have to call Olivia!"

CHAPTER TWELVE

*O*livia stared at her suitcases. They had been sitting beside her closet for several days, ever since she returned home, but she hadn't unpacked them. She sat on the edge of her bed, trying to find the energy to take her clothes out and put them away. Typically, Olivia unpacked the same day she returned from a trip, but something was holding her back.

On Tuesday, she had driven home from the beach and seen her OB/GYN, who only confirmed what the three pregnancy tests had already indicated; Olivia was eight weeks pregnant. She'd heard the baby's heartbeat, which had brought on a fresh onslaught of tears. Fortunately, the sonogram technician had been a sweet woman who was comfortable with an emotional, pregnant woman.

That same night, she'd shown Daniel the sonogram photos and told him that she was nearly eight weeks along in her pregnancy. His reaction was exactly what she had expected; he was thrilled that they were going to be parents, but once the initial excitement wore off, she found him bent over the kitchen table, researching how much boxes of diapers and cases of baby formula cost. He was lost in his own world of numbers, and

Olivia finally went to bed without him. The next day, she and Daniel told their parents the news, and the future grandparents were overjoyed at the prospect of a New Year's baby. But behind her parents' happy congratulations, Olivia sensed hesitation. They knew how unhappy she was in her marriage, and she was certain they were wondering why she'd chosen to start a family with a man she was thinking of divorcing.

During the days following her return, Daniel never mentioned what she had said the day she left for the beach. Instead, he seemed to have forgotten it, and their lives fell back into the same routines they'd had before Olivia left.

EVERY PART of Olivia wanted to return to Sullivan's Island. She missed the calm, soothing mood of the island. Ellie had called the day before to talk about her date with the Irish guy from the bar and how he'd brought her food when she'd been sick with a migraine. He had even kissed her before he left. Olivia longed to be back on the island with her friend, eating supper on the screened porch and riding around the island on the golf cart. And, truth be told, Olivia thought she might go crazy sitting around the house all summer with nothing to do besides read baby books and plan the nursery décor.

Why shouldn't she go back to Sullivan's? Ellie said she was welcome, and Olivia needed the relaxation. Stress, the doctor had told her, wasn't healthy for the baby. She still had a choice to make—divorce or no divorce—but she didn't think she could make the decision while living in the same house with Daniel. She bit her lip nervously, but picked up her phone and called her husband. After a few rings, her call went to voicemail; she'd known it would because Daniel never answered his cell phone during work hours.

"Hey, it's me. Listen, I'm still trying to figure everything out with us, especially now that we're going to have a baby. I need time to think and process, so I'm going back to the beach with Ellie. I love you, but I'm still unhappy with the way things are between us. I'll talk to you soon. Bye."

Olivia let out a deep breath when she finished leaving the message. A weight had been lifted from her chest, and she knew she had made the right choice. Emboldened, she called Ellie next. Unlike Daniel, Ellie answered on the third ring.

"Hey Liv, what's up?"

"Does your invitation still stand? For me to stay with you?"

Ellie didn't hesitate. "Of course. You're welcome anytime. Is something wrong?"

"Nothing new," Olivia told her. "But I can't stay here right now and make this decision. I need distance from Daniel more than ever."

"Then come back," Ellie told her. "Honestly, I've been so lonely since you left."

Olivia stood up, determined. "I'll be there by suppertime tonight."

"I'll be here."

AFTER LOADING her suitcases and eating a quick snack, Olivia hit the road. While she was driving, she called her mom. She didn't know what her mom would think when she heard the news, but she knew her parents were hoping for a miracle between Olivia and Daniel, and when she finally spoke to her mother, Mrs. Tanner let her opinion be known.

"How are you supposed to work on a marriage when you're in a different state?"

"I need some time and space to think, Mom."

"But you're pregnant. What about your appointments? And what if you need anything while you're over there?"

"Don't worry," Olivia said. "I already called my doctor's nurse, and she says he knows a great doctor in the Charleston area that I can call if I have anything urgent to talk about. And I'll come home for my appointments."

"I just don't know if it's such a good idea..."

"Mom, I'm an adult, and I'm going to the beach with my best friend. I'm going to do my best to relax and keep my stress levels low, which will be good for the baby. I'm sorry you don't think it's a good idea, but I'm going. I'll check in with you regularly, I promise. I love you, mom."

"I love you, too, sweetie. Let me know when you get there, please."

THIS TIME, the drive to Sullivan's Island didn't seem so long and miserable. Olivia listened to the latest country songs on the radio, even singing along a little bit. Her troubles and problems were still present in her mind, but she managed to push them to the back. She found herself looking forward to supper at Poe's, the Edgar Allen Poe-themed restaurant on Sullivan's Island, and a ride around the island on the golf cart afterwards. It was nearly six o'clock in the evening before she finally crossed the Ben Sawyer Bridge, and Olivia called to let her mother know she'd arrived. As she pulled into the yard, her phone rang. Daniel called every day when he left work, and she knew it would be him even before she glanced at the Caller ID.

"Hello."

"I got your voicemail. You went back to the beach?"

Olivia pressed her lips together tightly. "Yes, I did."

"Oh. I didn't know you were thinking about doing that."

"I was, but I didn't say anything about it."

Silence echoed between the phone lines for a moment, but Daniel finally spoke again. "Okay. Well, have fun. Maybe I'll find a weekend I can come visit."

"You don't like the beach," Olivia reminded him.

"No, I don't."

"I have to go now. I just pulled in, and Ellie's waiting on me for dinner, so..."

"Bye, then. I love you."

Olivia hesitated for a moment. "I love you, too, Daniel. We'll talk soon. Bye." She hung up quickly, concerned she might start crying if she talked much longer. The hardest part about wanting to divorce Daniel was that she was still in love with him. Daniel was thoughtful in the ways many men weren't; he knew her favorite flowers, he remembered every birthday and anniversary, and he knew how to buy the perfect gift. Olivia owned diamond earrings, a pearl necklace, and a designer handbag with matching wallet—all gifts that other women envied. She turned the key in the ignition, switching her car off. Her decision would be much easier if she didn't love Daniel.

THE GIRLS WAITED MORE than half an hour for a table at Poe's, but they were finally offered two seats on the porch, overlooking Middle Street and the patio.

"I'm so glad you came back," Ellie said after they'd ordered.

"Me too. I couldn't bring myself to unpack my bags, and I knew there was a reason."

"How were things at home?"

Olivia wrinkled her nose. "Like I expected, I guess. Daniel is so excited about the baby, but he immediately started crunching numbers. By the time I went to bed, I think he had already opened a college fund account."

Ellie laughed. "That's sweet, though."

"It is, but he takes things to the extreme, you know. But I don't want to talk about it anymore. I want to spend the next couple weeks relaxing and enjoying myself. I need to take care of me." Olivia shook her head, taking a sip of her ice water. "Are you going back out with Pat again soon?"

"Yes, tomorrow night." Ellie twisted the paper wrapper from her drink straw around her index finger. "I can't help but wonder if he's looking for a summer fling. I don't want to be someone he tells his buddies about, you know?"

"I think you need to stop thinking that way," Olivia told her. "You don't give yourself enough credit. He might not be looking for anything serious, but you'll never know unless you put yourself out there."

"That's true." Ellie admitted grudgingly.

"So stop second-guessing yourself and go out when he asks you. I'd be willing to bet that he likes you because you're beautiful and smart—not because he's looking for a quick fling." Olivia put her arm around her friend's shoulders.

"I'll try."

"Good. And no matter what happens, have fun," Olivia encouraged her. "If worse comes to worst, you've had a few meals paid for and been out with a very good-looking guy. You'll have something fun to tell all the girls at school when you go back."

Ellie laughed, finally smiling. "You're absolutely right. See? This is why I was so glad when you said you were coming back. I need my best friend with me."

"I needed my best friend, too."

CHAPTER THIRTEEN

"*S*o, where are we going?" Ellie buckled her seatbelt and turned, looking expectantly at Pat.

"Have you ever been on a sunset cruise on the Harbor before?"

"No, I haven't. Is that what we're doing tonight?"

Pat nodded. "Yep. I know one of the guys who runs that catamaran cruise out of Shem Creek, so I thought that would be a fun way to spend the evening."

Ellie clapped her hands together in delight. "That sounds awesome! I've always wanted to go out on that boat, and the sky over the harbor is beautiful at sunset. I'm so excited!"

PAT PARKED on one of the side streets near Shem Creek, and he and Ellie walked down to the waterfront. The Palmetto Breeze, a catamaran sailboat, departed from the docks along the historic creek every evening. The deck was already filled with passengers, and Ellie and Pat were two of the last people to board. Pat greeted his friend who worked on the crew, and the two of them spent a few moments catching up before Pat introduced Ellie.

"Hi Ellie, I'm Sam," Pat's friend said, shaking her hand. "He's told me a lot about you."

Ellie raised her eyebrows and glanced over at Pat. "Did he?"

"Yep. I think he's smitten."

"Shut up, man," Pat laughed, playfully punching his friend in the arm.

"We're about to shove off, so y'all go up front and enjoy," Sam said. "I think we're gonna have a great sunset tonight."

PAT AND ELLIE wove their way through the other groups of people until they were standing at the front of the boat. Ellie leaned against the metal railing on the side, her eyes scanning across Shem Creek. Years ago, before Ellie was born, Shem Creek had been a hub for shrimpers and fishermen; these days, though, Shem Creek boasted a vibrant nightlife scene. Dolphins often popped up, playfully circling kayakers and paddle-boarders who moved up and down the creek.

"You know, it occurred to me that we kayaked on our first date and now we're on a sailboat. I never asked you if you liked being out on the water," Pat said.

"I love being out on the water!" Ellie pulled her long hair back into a loose ponytail. "And I would've told you if I didn't."

"I bet you would have!"

"I take it you really enjoy spending time on the water."

Pat nodded, pushing his baseball cap back a little. "Yep. Most of my friends bought boats before they bought cars, and somebody was always taking one out. Eventually, I had my own boat, and I started fishing almost every weekend. I used to bring home blue crabs and shrimp and all kinds of fish to my Mama, and she'd cook 'em for me."

"You know, you might talk like you're half Irish, but you're really a Lowcountry boy at heart, aren't you?"

"I think so," Pat said. "I love Ireland, but I'm most at home in Charleston."

Ellie inhaled deeply and closed her eyes, the ocean breeze blowing the tendrils of hair that curled around her face. "I am, too, I think. I'm most myself when I'm on Sullivan's Island."

"What do you mean?" Pat took a step toward her, leaving less than a few inches between them.

"I feel at home on the beach, you know? I love wearing a swimsuit everywhere and not worrying about styling my hair or putting on makeup. I feel a sense of freedom but also a sense of belonging." Realizing that Pat was staring at her, Ellie blushed and looked away. "That probably sounds silly, huh?"

"Not at all." Pat reached out and took Ellie's hand, squeezing it tightly. "I think it makes total sense."

The Palmetto Breeze slipped out of Shem Creek and into the Charleston Harbor. Passengers on the boat milled around leisurely, talking and drinking, but Ellie and Pat stayed at the bow. They talked quietly, completely focused on each other as their conversation drifted from topic to topic. The sun dipped lower and lower, and the sky was awash with shades of pink and purple. Ellie pulled out her phone to snap several photos, and Pat asked Sam to take one of the two of them together. When she turned her attention back to the sunset, Pat slipped his arm around her waist and she snuggled a little closer to him.

"It is so peaceful out here," she whispered. "You sure do know how to plan a good date."

In college, Ellie had dated a few guys—never anyone very seriously—but not one of them had planned something as exciting as a sunset cruise. Charlie had been a model boyfriend, but even he had never thought to take her somewhere so romantic. Ellie studied Pat closely while they stood together. A tattoo was peeking out from underneath the collar of his shirt, and she tilted her head to the side, trying to see what it was.

"What are you looking at?" Pat wanted to know.

"I was wondering what your tattoo is."

He pulled his collar down a little to show her. The design looked as if someone had slashed his skin deeply, revealing an Irish tartan beneath his skin. "What do you think?" he asked.

"I love it!" Ellie stood on her tip-toes to examine it closer. "It's really well done."

"Thanks. I got it as a reminder that my Irish blood runs deep. Not that I could ever forget," Pat laughed. "Kinda hard when you play in an Irish band almost every weekend."

"Do you go back to Ireland often?" Ellie asked, brushing her fingertips over the tattoo. "And is this the tartan of your family's clan?"

"Aye. I wouldn't want anyone else's colors."

Ellie giggled. "You *really* know how to turn that accent on, don't you?"

Pat winked. "Aye, tha' I do, lass."

"It's definitely charming."

The daylight dimmed quickly once the sun dipped behind the horizon, and the temperature dropped several degrees within a few minutes. The sea breeze blew steadily across the harbor, and Ellie shivered, wishing she'd thought to bring a light jacket.

"Are you cold?" Pat asked pulling her closer. He wrapped both arms around her and held her against his chest.

"No," Ellie sighed. "Not anymore."

WHEN THEY MADE it back to Shem Creek, Ellie was reluctant to leave the catamaran. They walked across the street to have supper at a nearby restaurant. They ordered burgers and fries and lingered at their table long after the check had been paid. Ellie found herself telling Pat about her college roommates, her favorite professors, and her upcoming internship. The longer they sat and talked, the more Ellie believed Olivia; Pat wasn't asking her out just so that they could have a brief summer fling. He seemed genuinely interested in her life, and nothing about him struck Ellie as insincere. She found him even more attractive when she realized that he'd never once stopped to check his phone. Instead, his attention was focused solely on her. He talked about his childhood in Ireland and about his family who still lived there, and she listened, mesmerized by the soft lull of his Irish accent. When they finally left, Ellie couldn't believe that it was nearly eleven o'clock.

Pat drove her back to the beach house and walked her to the door. The lights were still on inside, and Ellie knew that Olivia was still awake—probably hoping to hear all the juicy details of the date.

"I had a really, really good time tonight," she told him, stopping at the door and rummaging in her purse for the house keys

"Me too." Pat shoved his hands into the pockets of his shorts. "Are you busy tomorrow?"

"Olivia and I are going to the beach for most of the day. Wanna join us?"

Pat nodded. "I'd like that. It's been a while since I've had a beach day."

"Great. We usually get down there around ten-thirty or eleven, so come whenever you're ready."

"I will." Pat stepped in closer and rested his hands lightly on her waist. He leaned down and kissed her. Nothing about their second kiss felt rushed, and Ellie sank into Pat, her hands resting lightly on his chest. When they broke apart, Ellie swayed and Pat caught her, his arms around her waist.

"Wow," she breathed, leaning against him for support.

"Goodnight, Ellie," Pat said, backing away and heading down the stairs. "I'll see you tomorrow!"

"That sounds so romantic."

"It really was. And when he kissed me..." Ellie fanned herself with her hand. "It was amazing!"

It was past midnight, but Ellie and Olivia were conducting a nightly beach patrol. As they walked, Ellie filled her friend in on the details of her date with Pat.

Olivia sighed, looping her arm through Ellie's. "What a great second date. This guy is really setting the bar high. If Charlie still thinks he has a shot, he better hurry over here and turn on the charm."

Ellie was quiet for a minute, allowing the old familiar doubt to creep in. "I really like Pat, and he does seem very nice, but how do I know this isn't some elaborate plan to get me into bed?"

"You don't. You need to trust your instinct. What is it telling you?"

"It's telling me that Pat is a truly good guy who, for some inexplicable reason, is interested in me."

"The reason is *not* inexplicable," Olivia insisted. "And I wish you'd stop saying that."

"Well!" Ellie said, as if that was an explanation. "Growing up, the only really cute guy to show any interest in me was Charlie, and you know that's true. Everyone else just wanted to be friends with me."

"But that was a long time ago. You're so different from when we were in high school."

"You really think so?"

"Yes, I do."

"I'm definitely hanging out with him again," Ellie finally said. "He's coming to the beach with us tomorrow."

"Great. Use the time to talk to him more and get to know him better. I'm going to run to the bookstore in the morning, so that'll give you two some time alone before I intrude and become the third wheel."

Ellie wiggled her eyebrows and grinned suggestively. "Oooo... I'll have him at the house all by myself. That *does* sound like fun!"

CHAPTER FOURTEEN

The next morning, Olivia left the beach house a few minutes before Ellie expected Pat to arrive. She drove into Mt. Pleasant, to the nearest bookstore, and headed straight for the Parenting & Family section. Several of the more popular, well-known books caught her attention right away, but she decided to buy one or two others. On her way to the register, Olivia spotted the Relationships section of the store, and she recognized several of the books she had read when Daniel was first diagnosed with Asperger's.

WHEN THEY'D RECEIVED the diagnosis, Olivia had been surprisingly upbeat and positive about the situation. Their problems had a label—Asperger's. Millions of people had AS, and the doctors assured them that many of those people maintained healthy, successful marriages. Olivia had ordered half a dozen books off the internet, eager to find what solutions might work best for her and Daniel. She didn't expect him to read any of them, so she wrote pages of notes and highlighted huge chunks that she deemed applicable to them. She had done her homework, and sometimes she even read sections aloud to Daniel.

At first, he didn't seem bothered by her research. In fact, for a few weeks, she thought he seemed relieved to know that his brain worked differently from most. His attitude had changed when she made their first appointment with a marriage counselor, however. As the days passed leading up to their counseling session, Daniel retreated further within himself. He barely spoke, and Olivia couldn't figure out what was wrong with him.

He was uncomfortable talking about their marriage with a counselor, Olivia learned during their first session. He didn't want to discuss the problems they were having. In fact, he couldn't really acknowledge that they were having problems. Daniel admitted, reluctantly, that he was glad he had been diagnosed because it explained why he wasn't like most men his age. He didn't understand how it was affecting Olivia, though.

Furious, she'd driven home from that counseling session and then screamed and cried to an empty house. Olivia's eyes brimmed with tears as she slowly scanned the living room filled with photographs and memorabilia from their engagement and wedding. She hardly recognized the deliriously happy, head-in-the-clouds girl in those photos. That girl had been transformed into a resentful, angry, bitter young woman. *It's not fair,* Olivia had screamed at the photos. When she'd stood at the front of the church before two hundred of their closest family and friends, Olivia had seen her whole life mapped out in front of her. She would finish school and work for a few years before they started their family, and then she'd be a stay-at-home-mom until their children were old enough for school. Daniel would continue to work at his father's accounting firm, and they'd take family vacations every summer. They would have three kids—maybe four, depending on their financial situation—and at least one dog.

Olivia would cook delicious meals, keep her house clean, and decorate for every holiday.

OLIVIA PAID for her books and then sat down in the bookstore café. She ordered herself a smoothie and a muffin, grateful that her morning sickness had passed for the moment. While she waited for her order, she opened one of her books and began to read, but her thoughts soon drifted to her life back in Georgia. In hindsight, Olivia decided she had been too young and naive to get married. She hadn't truly known what to expect from marriage. Her parents, who had been married for over thirty years, made it look so simple and easy. Olivia *had* been young, and many people had been surprised that she was marrying at barely twenty, but Olivia had no doubts about her love for Daniel when she said "I do."

Even now that she was aware of Daniel's true shortcomings and flaws, Olivia knew that a big part of her was still in love with him. He was the first and only boy she'd ever loved, and she knew it wasn't his fault that he had Asperger's. He hadn't chosen to be born with it, and he had never deliberately tried to hurt her in their marriage. His brain was wired differently—it was as simple as that. But no matter how many books she read, Olivia couldn't seem to find a way through to him. She had continued to see the counselor on her own, but it didn't seem to be helping. She had tried so many of his suggestions, but nothing improved her relationship with Daniel. Olivia tried desperately to look at their marriage from Daniel's point of view, but she struggled with it daily. Her frustration festered until she lost her temper, and he shut down when she yelled at him.

OLIVIA HAD BEEN SERIOUSLY CONSIDERING RETREATING to her parents' home when Ellie invited her to Sullivan's Island,

and she had seen it as an answered prayer. If she moved back in with her parents, people would notice. People would talk. People would know that she and Daniel were having problems, and she wasn't ready to face the gossip of a small town. In Warner Robins, Olivia's family knew almost everyone, and she could easily imagine what the rumor mill would produce. Going on a long, leisurely vacation with her closest friend wouldn't raise any questions, Olivia decided, and when she'd told Daniel she was leaving, she could've sworn he was relieved. She couldn't blame him. The tension in their house was bordering on unbearable, and she suspected he was working longer hours every day to avoid her.

OLIVIA SIGHED and sipped her drink slowly. Before she came to the beach, she had been almost certain she wanted to file for divorce, but everything had changed since then. She had a baby growing inside her—a new life that was her responsibility. Whatever decision she made in the coming weeks would affect the life of her baby, and she hated the idea of a child growing up with divorced parents. Would it be fair for a child to be raised by two parents who were unhappily married, though?

Her cell phone rang, snapping Olivia out of her reverie. She checked the Caller ID; her brother Charlie was calling, and she answered with a smile on her face.

"Hi."

"Hey, sis! How's the beach?"

"It's great. I'm at the bookstore right now, though. Ellie's at the beach."

"Oh yeah? How's she doing? I haven't talked to her in a couple days."

Charlie's tone was nonchalant, but Olivia sensed he had ulterior motives for asking. She wondered if Ellie had mentioned her dates with Pat to Charlie. "She's good. She still patrols the beach every night, and I've been going with her most nights."

"Good for y'all! I'm jealous, you know. I'd love to be relaxing on Sullivan's right now."

He's not very subtle, Olivia thought to herself. "Charlie, do you want me to ask Ellie if you can come stay for a few days?"

"That would be awesome! You don't mind doing that?"

Olivia rolled her eyes. "No, I don't mind."

"Great! Let me know, okay? I don't have anything planned for the next couple weekends."

"I will call you as soon as I talk to her."

"Sweet! Have fun at the bookstore, then. I'll talk to you later."

"Bye, Charlie."

OLIVIA TUCKED her phone into her purse, shaking her head. She knew Ellie wouldn't object to Charlie visiting, but she wasn't sure how her brother would react to the presence of a certain local named Pat O'Sullivan. Olivia knew Ellie better than anyone else, and she knew that Ellie was smitten with him. She also knew that Ellie was conflicted about her feelings for Charlie and the future of their relationship.

Laughing quietly to herself, Olivia began to unwrap her breakfast pastry. If Charlie came to visit and learned that Ellie was dating someone else, she didn't know what he would say or do, but she did know that it would make their summer much more interesting.

As if it weren't eventful enough already.

CHAPTER FIFTEEN

*W*hen Olivia left for the bookstore, Ellie showered hastily. She normally showered at night to wash off the sunscreen and sand from the day, but she wanted to look her best for Pat. She braided her long, damp hair and pulled on a new swimsuit she'd never worn before. It was a red two-piece that showed more of her skin and cleavage than she typically wore, but Ellie smiled when she saw it lying in her drawer. A beach day with Pat, she decided, was the perfect day to step out of her comfort zone and wear the bikini.

She was in the kitchen, filling a small cooler with snacks and drinks, when Pat knocked on the back door. She opened it and invited him in.

"Good morning," he greeted her, leaning in to kiss her quickly on the cheek.

"Good morning."

"I'm not too early, am I?"

Ellie shook her head. "No, you're right on time. I was about to grab my towel and head down to the beach."

Pat glanced around at the house. "Your uncle has a great

place. Not many of these older beach houses are left on the island anymore."

"I know." Ellie's eyes swept around the kitchen and living room. "When he bought it, he said it was one of the nicest homes on this street. But over the years, the island has changed a lot, I guess."

"It really has. Even in the last ten years, I've seen a lot of change."

"I have some snacks and drinks to take with us," Ellie said, hoisting the cooler off the kitchen counter and reaching for her beach tote. "I didn't know what you liked, so I packed a little bit of everything."

"I'm easy to please."

"Good." Ellie smiled. "Let's go."

PAT CARRIED chairs for both of them, but they chose to leave the umbrella at the house. The sun was shining brightly, and Ellie didn't see a cloud in the sky. The shoreline was already dotted with tents, chairs, and umbrellas belonging to other beachgoers, and she couldn't help but notice the envious stares when she and Pat walked down the private boardwalk from the house. Many people drove to Sullivan's for day trips, coming from inland towns to spend their summer days on the beach, and Ellie never took for granted how lucky she was to stay in a house only a few yards from the water's edge.

"Tide's low," Pat remarked.

"Yep. Look how many people are out on the sandbar," Ellie said, pointing to the large, exposed shelf of sand. "I used to find the biggest seashells out there. I would take them home and make them into jewelry dishes or Christmas ornaments."

"Well let's go, then." Pat set the chairs down in the sand and dusted his hands off. "I told you I have trouble sitting still."

"Yes, you did."

. . .

ON THE NORTHERN end of Sullivan's Island, low tide exposed a wide sandbar. Some days, the water receded so far from the shoreline that it was ankle-deep between the beach and the sandbar. Dozens of people would cross the channel to explore. Boats anchored in the deeper water on one end of the sandbar, and the boaters would bring coolers and chairs onto the exposed sand—sometimes even portable grills. They would spend a few hours on the sandbar, drinking beer and enjoying summertime until the tide turned and covered the sand once more.

The water in the narrow channel was knee-deep, and Ellie and Pat walked across with ease. They had almost reached the bank of the sandbar when the water deepened suddenly. It was up to Ellie's waist in a moment, and they found themselves swimming towards the sandbar.

"It's so cold," she squealed. Pat grabbed Ellie's hand, and together they scrambled up onto the beach. Ellie stood up and gazed across the wide expanse of the sandbar. Waves crashed on the far side of it, and when she glanced back at the island, she felt as though she were miles away from the house.

"It's so serene out here," she said softly.

Pat nodded, looking around them. "When we were in college, we used to come out here all the time on somebody's boat and hang out until the last bit of sand disappeared with the high tide."

Suddenly, Ellie realized she was still holding Pat's hand, and she squeezed it tightly. "C'mon!" She pulled him towards the distant waves. "I want to play in the surf."

THEY LAY on the beach and allowed the waves to crash over them again and again. Ellie laughed merrily, enjoying the childish behavior. Pat sat beside her, scooping up handfuls of sand and letting the grains fall through his fingers.

"I feel like a mermaid," Ellie said.

Pat laughed. "You look like a mermaid right now."

"Good."

"Do you and your friend have plans tonight?"

Ellie sat up, thinking. "Not that I know of. Why?"

"My roommate, Ben, and I were planning to go out tonight for dinner and drinks. We usually go out to Shem Creek at least one night every weekend. Y'all should come."

"That sounds good to me," Ellie said as Pat pulled her to her feet. "Even if Olivia doesn't want to come, I'd love to tag along."

"I was hoping you'd say yes."

"So TELL ME," Ellie asked as they walked along the sandbar, "when you're not working or playing Irish music in local pubs, what do you do?"

"Nothing out of the ordinary," Pat told her. "Obviously, I enjoy being on the water, and I live for college football season. I like being outdoors, I guess."

Ellie bent down to pick up a cockle shell as big as her hand. "I found one!"

"That's a good one. Not broken at all."

"Do you play other instruments besides the fiddle?"

"Are we playing Twenty Questions now?" Pat laughed, adjusting the baseball cap on his head.

"Maybe." A smile twitched at the corners of Ellie's mouth, and she stared up at Pat, a hand planted firmly on her hip.

"Cause if we are, I'll ask you some, too."

"Fair enough." Ellie pushed her wet hair out of her face. "Ask me whatever you want."

"I play the guitar and the mandolin," he told her. "Now I've got a question for you. You don't have a boyfriend waiting for you back at school or anything, do you? Cause I'd hate to think someone's going to show up and kick my butt for taking you out."

Though the question caught her off guard for a minute, Ellie laughed at the idea of anyone beating up Pat. He was taller and stronger than most men she knew. "No, I don't have a boyfriend. I promise. I've actually been single for more than a year."

"I find that hard to believe."

Ellie shrugged, storing his subtle compliment away. "I don't always fit in with people my own age, I guess. I enjoyed my first two years of college, and I did my share of partying, but I'm over that phase now. I still like to have fun, but I've settled down and focused on my schoolwork. A lot of my fellow classmates still seem to be stuck in the partying phase."

"Yeah, it's easy to get stuck in that part of life. I did for a while, till my Dad told me I had to bring my grades back up or I could come home and get a job." Pat shook his head ruefully. "I didn't like the idea of living with my parents again, so I made some changes."

"How old are you?"

"Twenty-five. You?"

"I'll be twenty-two in August."

They walked in silence for a few minutes until Ellie mustered enough courage to ask another question that had been nagging her since Pat first asked her out.

"Do you usually date girls like me? You know, girls who are only here for the summer." Ellie faced Pat, wanting to gauge his reaction.

Pat didn't hesitate to answer. "When I was a teenager, I hit on a lot of summer girls. It was easy—they were here for only a week or two, and I had fun showing them a good time. During high school, I worked summers over at Wild Dunes on Isle of Palms, and I met a lot of different girls." Pat frowned looking down at his feet. "They wanted something to tell their friends back home about, and I took advantage of that."

Ellie scrutinized Pat's body language. "And do you still do that? Am I just another one of your summer flings?"

"No, no, no!" Pat assured her, reaching out to hold her hand. "That was a long time ago, and I've moved past that phase in my life."

"Good. Cause I don't want to be someone you tell your friends about."

"I respect that," Pat insisted. "I know you haven't known me for long, so you have no reason to believe me, but I promise you I'm not that guy. Not anymore."

A slow smile spread across Ellie's face, and she took a step closer to him so that their bodies were almost touching "I believe you." She turned to keep walking, but then stopped again. "I guess I should tell you about Charlie."

Pat's smile flickered. "Your friend's brother?"

"Yes. The three of us grew up together, and then Charlie and I dated through most of high school and my first year of college. We broke up, but we're still good friends. And he..." Ellie hesitated, twisting her hands together. "He would like for us to get back together. And before I came here this summer, he and I actually talked about that possibility."

"And are you going to?" Pat asked, his face betraying nothing.

"If you had asked me that question a couple weeks ago, I would have said yes, but now..." she shook her head, embarrassed. "Now, I'm not so sure. I hope that doesn't scare you."

Pat shook his head. "No, it doesn't. I appreciate your letting me know I have a little competition, though."

"And you should also know that Charlie will probably come visit sometime this summer. Soon, actually."

"I can handle that."

Ellie let out a deep breath. "Good. I just wanted to be upfront with you."

"I appreciate that."

. . .

AFTER SPENDING THE MORNING TOGETHER, Ellie and Pat walked to Home Team for lunch. While they ate, they were interrupted several times by friends of Pat who stopped to chat with him. He introduced Ellie to each one, but she knew she would never remember their names.

Pat was unlike anyone Ellie had ever met. The more time she spent with him, the more she liked him. Every detail she learned made him more appealing, and she felt as if she could sit and talk to him for hours. She found herself studying his tattoos and noticing the way that one dark curl hung down in the middle of his forehead.

She hadn't meant to tell Pat about Charlie or that she was considering a relationship with him again, but the words had slipped out. To her surprise, he hadn't seem spooked by her honest words. Instead, he'd held her hand as they walked along the sandbar. When something had brushed against her foot as they'd waded back to the beach and she'd squealed, Pat had picked her up and carried her the rest of the way. So much of her bare skin had touched his bare skin, and her heart had beat wildly in her chest. Her hands had rested on his shoulders, and she could feel the muscles rippling beneath his skin. Something stirred deep within her, and her entire body hummed with desire.

ONCE THEY FINISHED LUNCH, Ellie and Pat returned to the house. Olivia's car wasn't parked in the driveway, and Ellie silently thanked her friend for giving them privacy. Ellie yawned as they walked in the back door. She was sun-soaked and sated from their meal—two factors conducive to an afternoon nap.

"I'm so sleepy all of a sudden," she said.

Her yawn was contagious, and Pat covered his mouth to stifle his own. "Me too. It's funny how a few hours on the beach can make you so drowsy."

"I think naps are an essential part of a beach bum's life."

"Oh yeah?" Pat laughed. "You should know, I guess, since you are a self-declared beach bum this summer."

"Did you know," Ellie asked him, lowering her voice to a seductive whisper and leaning in close, "that the hammock on the porch is the best place to take an afternoon nap."

"I did not."

"Well, it is," she told him, staring at his lips and thinking about how much she wanted to kiss him. "How do you feel about an afternoon nap?"

"If you're asking me to join you, I feel good about it." Pat closed the space between them and pressed his warm mouth against hers.

THEY CURLED up in the hammock with the ceiling fan spinning lazily overhead. Pat wrapped his arm around Ellie's shoulders, and she nestled her head against his chest. She could feel his heart beating steadily beneath her palm, and her breath hitched slightly. She *wanted* Pat, more than she'd ever desired any man. It was one thing to find a man attractive, but Pat was different. Her intellectual attraction to him only intensified her physical attraction.

"This is nice," she said, her eyelids drooping. Pat's body was warm and strong against hers, and she forced herself to resist the temptation to run her fingertips along his arm.

"Mhm," Pat mumbled. He nestled his head on top of hers, and within a few minutes, his breathing slowed into a soft, steady rhythm.

OVER AN HOUR LATER, Ellie woke up feeling refreshed and

relaxed. Pat was still asleep, his breathing slow and steady. Ellie knew something had awakened her, and she listened carefully. Then Olivia called out to her again from inside the house.

"Ellie! Are you here?"

With difficulty, Ellie rolled herself out of the hammock without waking Pat up. She allowed herself a quick moment to study his face while he slept, and she sighed to herself, certain that she was dreaming and would soon wake up to find that Pat was a figment of her imagination.

PAT WOKE up about a half hour later and spent a few minutes chatting with Ellie and Olivia before he headed back to his apartment.

"See y'all tonight," he called as he closed the door behind him.

Olivia turned to Ellie, her brows bunched together. "What's he talking about?"

"Oh yeah, we're going to dinner on Shem Creek tonight with Pat and his roommate."

"What?" Olivia's eyes widened. "That sounds like a double date to me."

"Well it's not, cause you're married." Ellie grinned nervously, hoping her friend wouldn't back out.

"Have you met his roommate?"

"Nope, but evidently Pat has known him for years, and they're best friends. Please come! I think we'll have fun. It's a good excuse to wear a cute outfit and actually put on some makeup for once this summer."

"Does this roommate think it's a double date?" Olivia asked.

Ellie shrugged, shaking her head. "I'm sure he doesn't. I told Pat you're married, so I don't think it'll be awkward at all."

"You and Pat will be in your own little world, and I'll be

stuck with the roommate. What if he's weird? What if he thinks that we're on a date?"

Ellie threw up her hands in frustration. "Fine, don't come. I'll go by myself." She slipped off the barstool and walked to the fridge.

"No, I'll come," Olivia caved. "But if it feels like a double date, I'm calling an Uber to take me home."

Ellie clapped her hands together. "Yay! I love that we have plans!"

Olivia shook her head as though she were a little sorry she'd agreed to go. "Just please don't make me feel like a third wheel."

"I will do my best," Ellie promised.

"What's this guy's name anyway?"

"Um..." Ellie struggled to pull the name from memory. She knew that Pat had mentioned it a couple of times, but she never remembered names. Then, it dawned on her. "Ben! His name is Ben."

CHAPTER SIXTEEN

livia couldn't believe she'd let Ellie convince her to go out. What business did she, a married woman—and pregnant, at that—have going out with her friend and two local guys? She should've told Ellie she wanted to stay home and read her new books, but she couldn't resist the chance to spend a couple of hours at Red's, one of the most popular spots on Shem Creek. So she was applied a little makeup and told herself she was primping simply because her Southern mama had always taught her to at least wear a little lipstick and mascara when she went out in public or even if she were just going to be at home all day, for that matter. "You'll feel better if you look nice," was her motto. For a brief moment, Olivia even considered curling her hair, but she didn't want to give Pat's roommate the wrong impression. If she showed up looking as if she'd spent an hour or two getting ready for dinner, he might think *she* thought it was a double date. Choosing an outfit was a seemingly impossible task. Everything seemed a little too short or too low-cut, so she finally chose a simple sheath dress and a pair of sandals. As she stood in front of the mirror, she wondered why she felt guilty for going to dinner. She wasn't cheating on Daniel, so why did it feel as though she were breaking some unspoken rule?

ELLIE DROVE them to Shem Creek in her uncle's car. He had left her with strict instructions to drive it occasionally over the summer, and both girls enjoyed riding in his luxurious sports car. She parked in the garage near Shem Creek, and they walked through the parking lot to the restaurant.

Red's, a waterfront bar and grill, was busy all year long, but especially during the summer. Boaters docked in front of the restaurant, tied up, and ate dinner while overlooking the creek. Red's also boasted the best view of any establishment on Shem Creek with its rooftop bar. From up there, patrons could see all the way across the marsh and out to the Charleston Harbor.

Ellie spotted Pat standing at the bar with his roommate and pointed them out to Olivia.

"There they are!" Ellie said, "C'mon."

Reluctantly, Olivia allowed herself to be led through a collection of sunburned boaters, tourists, and seasoned locals until they reached the bar.

"Ellie!" Pat called out, waving when he spotted them. He slipped his arm around her waist, pulling her to his side, and Olivia felt an odd twinge of jealousy. She missed the romantic early days of a relationship—the honeymoon phase.

Pat turned back to the guy standing at the bar and tapped him on the shoulder. "Ben, I want you to meet Ellie and Olivia."

When Pat's roommate turned around, Olivia's eyes widened. She wasn't sure what she had been picturing, but Ben looked nothing like what she expected.

"Hi, I'm Ellie Taylor, and this is my friend Olivia Blakely," Ellie introduced them, shaking Ben's hand with a confidence Olivia envied.

"Nice to meet y'all," Ben said, turning to Olivia and extending his hand. "I'm Ben Billhorn."

"Billhorn?" Olivia repeated. "What an unfortunate last name!"

❀

As soon as the words left her mouth, Olivia realized how rude they sounded. She hadn't mean to say them—they'd just popped out.

"I'm so sorry," she apologized hastily. "That came out wrong."

Ben cleared his throat and shifted his weight slightly. "Okay... I've never been told that before, but I guess there's a first time for everything."

"We should get y'all something to drink," Pat said to Ellie and Olivia, clearly trying to break the awkward silence. "I have a tab open. What would you like?"

"I'll just take a Sprite," Olivia said.

"Sweet tea," Ellie added. Then, she turned back to Ben. "I'm glad to finally meet you. Pat's told me all about your wild summers growing up together in the Lowcountry."

Ben laughed. "That sounds about right. We've definitely got a lot of stories."

"I bet."

Pat called Ellie's attention to something on the TV over the bar, and Olivia found herself face-to-face with Ben.

"Again, I'm sorry," she said, laughing nervously. "Billhorn is *not* an unfortunate last name. I meant to say it's an unusual last name, but the words just didn't come out right."

Ben offered a kind smile, and Olivia felt the warmth of it all the way down to her toes.

"It's nice to meet you, too, Olivia," he told her. "But I'll never forget that I have an 'unfortunate' last name."

Olivia's cheeks burned, and she wished she could sink through one of the cracks in the greasy wooden floors of Red's. More than ever, she wished she had stayed at the beach house. Truthfully, she thought Ben's last name was both unusual *and* unfortunate, but she wasn't about to tell him that.

"So Pat tells me that you and Ellie are staying out on Sullivan's this summer," Ben said, taking a long sip of his beer. "Where's home for y'all?"

"We're from Georgia. A town called Warner Robins, actually, which is pretty much in the middle of the state. Ellie's uncle asked her to take care of his beach house on Sullivan's, and she asked me to come stay with her."

Ben let out a low whistle. "Damn! That's pretty lucky! People pay top dollar to stay out there for a week or two during the summer."

"Oh yes, we're very lucky," Olivia agreed, wishing she had somewhere to put her hands as she talked with Ben. He seemed so comfortable and at ease, but she had never felt so awkward in her life. She wished that the bartender would come back with the drink Pat had ordered for her. She also wished Ellie would stop batting her eyelashes at Pat long enough to join in the conversation between her and Ben.

Ben didn't look anything like the men that Olivia normally found attractive. She liked tall men, and Ben was only an inch or two taller than she was. In fact, he almost stood eye-to-eye with her. She quickly decided that he had a sweet face, covered in only the slightest hint of a five o'clock shadow, with a dimple in his right cheek when he smiled.

"What about you?" Olivia finally asked. "Are you from here originally?"

"Yup. Born and raised."

"What do you do? Do you work in construction like Pat?"

"Oh no," Ben assured her, chuckling. "I work for a software development company here in Charleston. I'm in sales."

"Nice!"

"What about you? What do you do?"

"Well, I'm actually in school right now," Olivia explained. "I'm studying to become a dental hygienist." She reached up and tucked some hair behind one ear, and she saw Ben's eyes land on her left hand. More specifically, on her sparkling wedding ring.

"You're married?" A hint of surprise rang in his tone.

Olivia nodded. "Yes."

"That's great," Ben said sincerely. "What about your husband? Is he coming out tonight?"

"No, no," Olivia said, shaking her head. "Daniel is at home in Georgia. It's hard for him to get away from work."

"That's a shame. He's missing out on all the fun."

A smile spread across Olivia's face, and she finally felt herself beginning to relax. "You're right. He *is* missing out!"

THE BARTENDER RETURNED with drinks for the girls just as the table buzzer Pat was holding began to vibrate. While Pat closed out his bar tab, the hostess showed Olivia, Ellie, and Ben to their table. She left them with menus and a promise that a waitress would be over shortly.

Olivia studied the menu intently, debating about what she wanted to order. She had been to Red's before, but it had been a long time ago.

"I think I was a teenager when I last came here," Ellie said, as if she could read her friend's thoughts. "But I definitely want to order some of their shrimp skewers. They're wrapped in bacon and basted in barbeque sauce! It doesn't get much better than that."

"Those are definitely a good choice," Pat told her, taking his seat beside her. "I get the Lowcountry Boil here. It's pretty good."

"And all their sandwiches and burgers are good, too," Ben added. "I'm thinking a shrimp po'boy sounds good tonight."

When the waitress arrived, Ellie ordered two different appetizers for everyone to share, and then they each ordered individual entrees. The waitress scribbled their orders down and then dashed away, stopping by her other tables to refill drinks and pick up checks. The restaurant was crowded, as were all three of the bars in the downstairs section.

"Have y'all made any big plans for what do with the rest of your summer?" Pat wanted to know, draping his arm loosely over Ellie's shoulders.

"Eat lots of seafood," Ellie said.

"Work on our tans," Olivia added cheerfully. She doubted that Pat and Ben would be interested in hearing about her marital problems or unexpected pregnancy.

"Maybe do some shopping, visit some of the local tourist sites."

"Basically work on becoming professional beach bums."

"So just more of what you've already been doing," Pat laughed.

"Pretty much."

Ben nodded. "That sounds like a great summer to me."

"You're not totally lazy, though," Pat reminded Ellie. "You do your nightly turtle patrols."

"Turtle patrols?" Ben echoed. "Oh, please don't tell me you're one of those sea turtle nuts!"

Olivia winced and shook her head, knowing Ellie wouldn't appreciate that remark.

"I don't like to think of myself as a 'sea turtle nut' as you put it," Ellie said, her words clipped. "But yes, I do my part to help the sea turtles."

Ben rolled his eyes, shaking his head at her. "Oh boy. Another turtle lover!"

"You say that like it's a bad thing!"

"Ellie works hard to make sure the beaches are as safe as possible for the sea turtles," Olivia piped up, determined to stick up for her friend. She wasn't as dedicated as Ellie, but Olivia knew that her friend's efforts had the potential to make a real difference.

"You'll have to forgive Ben," Pat said, trying to hide his laughter. "He's resentful of the turtles. In fact, I think it's safe to say he hates the sea turtles."

"So you have an unfortunate last name *and* you hate sea turtles. What is wrong with you?" Ellie's eyes flashed, and Olivia cringed when her friend brought up her earlier slip. Olivia had really hoped that they would all forget about that.

Sighing, Ben leaned in closer so that his voice could be heard over the din of the crowded restaurant and explained how one of the nearby islands had commissioned a beach re-nourishment project one summer when he was in high school. When the project wasn't finished by the expected completion date, the dredge boat continued pumping sand from the ocean floor onto the beaches well into tourist season.

"I had a job that summer working at the resort on Wild Dunes. I was the guy who carried chairs and umbrellas down onto the beach for the resort guests. For most of the summer, the beach was covered in this black, sticky mud that was pumped in off the ocean floor, and I had to spend hours washing it off the chairs at the end of every day."

"But that doesn't really explain why you hate the sea turtles," Olivia pointed out. "Where do they tie in to this story?"

"So the beach re-nourishment project was approved for two reasons. One was that the beach had eroded after several big hurricanes, but the second was to rebuild the beaches so that the sea-turtles could continue nesting. Ever since that summer, I've just really hated all the crazy stuff people do to protect the sea turtles. I mean, c'mon! Let nature take its course!"

As he was finishing his story, the waitress arrived with two orders of the bacon-wrapped BBQ shrimp, and everyone dug in quickly, except for Olivia, who wasn't too sure about eating shrimp at the moment.

"Mud on the beach," Ellie finally said after taking a bite of her shrimp kebab. "Mud on the beach is why you hate the sea turtles."

"It wasn't just on the beach," Ben reminded her, wiping his hands on a napkin. "It got all over everything on that beach, and the stuff didn't wash off easily."

"Well that's silly," Olivia told him. "Really. I was expecting something much more dramatic like, oh I don't know, maybe you were bitten by a turtle or something wild like that."

"No, it's nothing like that." Ben studied Olivia shrewdly. "Are you a turtle nut, too?"

"Ellie has always been more dedicated, but I used to walk the beach with her every night when we were kids. It was our thing. Her uncle dubbed us the Lights Out Club because we were known for asking people all over the island to turn their lights out for the sea turtles."

"You walk every night?" Ben turned to stare at Ellie, his eyes wide. "I gotta say, that's pretty dedicated."

"Thanks." Ellie sat up a little straighter and smiled when Pat winked at her.

"Ellie hasn't missed a night in a really long time. She goes no matter how late it is or what the weather is like," Olivia said proudly, patting Ellie on the back.

"Okay, *that* might make you a bit of a sea turtle nut," Ben told Ellie.

"I'm okay with that."

As the evening wore on, Olivia realized that she hadn't once thought about calling an Uber to take her back to the beach house. While they waited for their entrees, Pat and Ben regaled the girls with tales of growing up in the Lowcountry. The girls laughed till tears streamed down their cheeks as Ben described Pat as a lanky, acne-riddled teenager who tried to impress girls by doing back flips off the old Pitt Street Bridge into the water, where he often met the sharp end of an oyster shell.

"We grew up on the water," Pat told them. "Our dads taught us to fish and crab and how to cook everything we caught."

"I would love to have grown up here," Ellie said wistfully. "Spending lots of time during childhood summers was great, but not the same as living here."

"Summers *were* the best," Ben told them. "Before we were in college and our parents insisted we get summer jobs, we would roam this town all day, every day. We'd leave early in the morning and be gone all day. As long as we didn't drown or get arrested, our parents really didn't worry about what we did or where we were."

"That's how our parents were when we would come to Sullivan's," Olivia said. "It's a different way of life over here."

"It really is," Ben agreed.

🍥

SOON AFTER THEY FINISHED EATING, a band cranked up inside the restaurant, and the noise became deafeningly loud. The waitress brought their checks, and all four of them paid quickly and left. After saying their goodbyes in the parking lot, the girls headed back to the car.

"Pat's going to come do beach patrol with me tonight," Ellie told her as they walked through the parking garage.

"Ooooo! Is he going to spend the night?"

Ellie blushed, answering Olivia's question. "Yes, I think so. Oh, he also told me that he and his band are playing a last-minute gig at an Irish bar in downtown Charleston tomorrow night. Do you wanna come with me to hear them?"

"After what happened the last time you tried to hear him play, I think I owe it to you to be your wingman again," Olivia laughed. "I'd love to come."

ELLIE WAS ABOUT to shift the car into reverse when her phone and Olivia's chimed at the same time. Olivia looked at the group message they had received.

"It's from Charlie," she said.

"*Surprise*," Ellie slowly read aloud, "*I'm tired of waiting for an invitation. I'm coming to the beach house when I get off work in the morning. Can't wait to see y'all.*"

"Ellie, he doesn't have to come if you don't want him to," Olivia said, turning to her friend. "He called me today and asked if I'd mention his visiting to see what you would say, but I never thought he'd just invite himself."

"No, it's fine." Ellie tucked her phone back into her purse. "We'll have a good time, I'm sure."

"What about Pat?"

Ellie eased the car out of the parking spot, and Olivia couldn't believe how calm her friend appeared. "Pat knows that Charlie and I have talked about getting back together."

"And?"

"And Charlie has some serious competition."

AN HOUR LATER, Olivia was lying in her bed when she heard Pat and Ellie leave the house for nightly beach patrol. She sighed, pulling the sheets up over her. Their evening out had been fun—exactly what she needed to take her mind off everything. Her mind had only drifted to her marital issues once or twice all night, and she felt more relaxed than she had all summer long. She had been so reluctant to go and meet Ben, and even after her embarrassing honesty when they first met, he had turned out to be... Olivia sighed again. She wasn't exactly sure what she thought about Ben. He was handsome, but he certainly wasn't the type of man that Olivia typically found attractive. He was polite and well-mannered, but what she had appreciated the most about him was that he listened attentively when she talked, focusing all of his attention on her. Ben had a good face, Olivia decided, rolling onto her side and tucking her arm under her pillow. Aside from the fact that he hated the sea turtles, Olivia couldn't think of a single thing she hadn't liked about him.

In fact, she thought to herself with a guilty smile, she hoped she would have an opportunity to see Ben again. And the next time she saw him, she would remember to keep her big, fat mouth shut.

CHAPTER SEVENTEEN

*W*hen Ellie woke up the next morning, it took her a moment to remember where she was. Pat was still sleeping soundly beside her, and she took a good, long look at him. He was shirtless, sleeping in nothing but his briefs, and the sheet was scrunched down around his waist. Ellie smiled, thinking about how they'd fallen sleep facing one another. They hadn't had sex; they'd simply fallen asleep together, and Ellie appreciated that Pat hadn't expected anything more. She watched the gentle rise and fall of his chest. She noticed the way his dark lashes brushed the tops of his cheeks. Once more, desire pooled in the pit of her stomach, and she exhaled slowly. She reached out and traced the lines of his tattoo with her fingertips. He stirred beneath her touch but didn't wake up.

Half an hour later, Ellie heard Olivia's bedroom door open across the hallway. Ellie was still lying beside Pat, reluctant to leave the bed. She wished he would wake up, but she also wanted to let him sleep. Finally, she threw back the covers and crawled out of the bed, yawning and stretching. She and Pat had walked the beach until after one in the morning, and she already knew she would need a nap later in the afternoon. She ducked into the bathroom quickly to comb the tangles from her hair and brush her teeth. When Pat did wake up, Ellie certainly didn't want to greet him with morning breath.

DOWNSTAIRS, Olivia was in the kitchen, filling the coffeemaker with water. She had given up caffeine since she discovered she was pregnant, but she still brewed a pot if she was the first person awake.

"Late night?" Olivia asked, glancing at the clock when Ellie came downstairs. "It's unusual for me to wake up first."

"We were up pretty late," Ellie said. "We walked the beach a long way, talking."

"Yeah? What did you talk about?"

Ellie shrugged, sliding on to one of the bar stools and rubbing her eyes sleepily. "Nothing. Everything. It was amazing."

Olivia nodded. "I'm glad. I take Pat is still upstairs? I saw his truck in the yard."

"Yep. He's still sleeping." Ellie yawned again.

"Did y'all... you know?"

Ellie shook her head firmly. "No. I want to, though, but I think we should spend more time together before we take it that far."

"Good idea." Olivia pulled two slices of toast out of the toaster and spread butter across them.

As soon as the first cup of coffee had brewed, Ellie poured it into her waiting mug. "I'm gonna need several cups this morning," she said. "Otherwise it's going to be a long d—"

Ellie's words were interrupted by a knock at the back door. She glanced at Olivia questioningly, but Olivia shrugged.

"Who could that possibly be?" Ellie muttered, walking towards the door. "Charlie!" she exclaimed with surprise when she saw him standing on the back porch, grinning at her. She opened the door for him, and he pushed past her with his duffle bag over his shoulder. She hadn't expected him to arrive so early —certainly not before nine o'clock.

Charlie dropped his bag. He gave Ellie a quick but tight hug. "I got off earlier than I thought I would. Hope I'm not too early."

"Umm..." Ellie's thoughts were racing too wildly for her to form a coherent sentence. Pat was sleeping upstairs, and Charlie was standing in the entryway grinning at her. He was enjoying her surprise, she realized.

"What time did you leave Warner Robins?" Olivia asked in amazement.

Charlie shrugged. "I got off work at midnight and slept for a few hours. I left around four o'clock or so to surprise y'all. Figured I could get in a full beach day."

"You definitely surprised us," Ellie said, laughing nervously. She glanced up the stairs, wondering when Pat might come down. She hadn't had a chance to tell him Charlie was coming, and she wasn't sure how either man was going to react to the other. Pat, she thought, would be polite and civil because he knew about Charlie, but Ellie had barely talked to Charlie since she'd arrived on Sullivan's.

"Whose truck is that in the yard?" Charlie asked, walking into the kitchen. He made himself right at home, pulled a mug from the cabinet, and poured himself a cup of coffee. "Has Uncle Jim got somebody working on the house? A few of the boards are starting to rot, I noticed."

"No, no one is working on the house," Ellie said slowly. She balled up her fists and then relaxed them. She and Charlie had only *discussed* the possibility of dating again, so he shouldn't have any reason to be angry. Should he?

Charlie stopped mid-pour, the carafe suspended mid-air. "Whose is it?"

"It belongs to Pat."

Ellie's words hung in the air. Charlie hesitated for a moment before he finished pouring his coffee.

"Who is Pat?" he wanted to know, turning to face her.

"He's a guy I met," Ellie explained. "We've been out on a few dates."

"Must be more than just a few dates if he's staying the night already."

"Please don't fight," Olivia pleaded with them. She was standing at the kitchen sink, looking back and forth between both of them.

"We don't have anything to fight about," Ellie said.

"Nope. Nothing at all," Charlie returned.

"Right." Olivia rolled her eyes. "You two really can be so frustrating sometimes, you know?"

"So where'd you meet this guy?" Charlie asked, ignoring his sister completely.

"At Dunleavy's," Ellie said, folding her arms across her chest defensively. Charlie's presence was interfering with what had been a pleasant morning.

"Oh yeah? At a bar?" Charlie chuckled, taking a long sip of his coffee. "Cool."

"When Pat comes downstairs, please don't be rude," Olivia said, putting a hand on Charlie's arm. "He's really a nice guy."

Charlie's face was the picture of innocence. "Me? Be rude? Never!"

Footsteps echoed on the floorboards overhead, and Ellie froze. Pat was awake, and he was about to walk into an awkward situation with absolutely no warning.

"We didn't agree to be exclusive," Ellie reminded him gently. "We talked about it, but we didn't decide anything specific."

"I know." Charlie drained the rest of his coffee. "I wanna meet this guy, though. He must be something special if you asked him to stay over."

"Fine." Ellie sat down at the bar and waited for Pat to descend the staircase. Charlie poured himself another cup of coffee, and Olivia left her toast untouched.

. . .

ELLIE HAD KNOWN Charlie since she was a child. She had grown up alongside him and Olivia, and he'd been in her life for as long as she could remember. For a period of their childhood, Charlie had delighted in teasing and tormenting Ellie and Olivia. In high school, however, Charlie had transformed into a handsome teenager, and Ellie found herself daydreaming about him during her English and History classes. Though he was only a year older, Charlie seemed more mature and experienced, and Ellie had a serious crush on him.

Dating him seemed so natural and easy. Ellie's parents knew Charlie well, and they were comfortable with Ellie's spending time alone with him. They started going out during Ellie's sophomore year and quickly became one of the most established couples in their high school. Everyone predicted they would be the high school sweethearts who stayed together forever, and Ellie believed it, too.

Their relationship remained free of conflict up until Charlie's senior year. Ellie, who was combing through college catalogues and scheduling campus tours as an eleventh-grader realized that Charlie had no interest in attending college. He wasn't lazy or unintelligent; in fact, Charlie was a hard worker and on track to graduate near the top of his class, but he had no desire to pursue higher education. For years, he'd been working for his dad during the summer, and he told Ellie he planned to stay in their hometown and work for his dad full-time following graduation.

Ellie didn't mind Charlie's choices, but when he suggested—multiple times—that she also stay in Warner Robins, live at home, and attend a local college, it dawned on her that she and Charlie wanted different things in life. Ellie had already been to Europe once with her uncle, and she planned to travel there again, hopefully with a study abroad program.

They'd held their relationship together by a thread for the first half of Ellie's freshman year at the University of Georgia. She came home almost every weekend, but Charlie rarely came to visit her. Eventually, Ellie's friends began urging her to stay in Athens on the weekends and enjoy college life. When she chose to stay at school several weekends in a row, Charlie was unhappy, and he wasn't shy about telling her. Gradually, Ellie realized that she and Charlie weren't a good match anymore. Their relationship no longer made sense. She wanted to attend football games and use her fake ID at the bars in downtown Athens, and Charlie wanted her to come home. Every other conversation they had turned into an argument, and Ellie finally couldn't handle it anymore. During her freshman year, she had learned that Charlie had no real desire to travel the world—not even if he was with her. He was content to stay in their home-town, still spending every Friday and Saturday night doing the same things he'd done during high school.

Over Christmas Break, Ellie and Charlie had fought endlessly. Even Olivia thought they should break up, and she told Ellie as much. Finally, the night before she returned to school, Ellie broke off her relationship with Charlie. She knew it would cause an uneasiness between their families, but she was unhappy, and she didn't want to spend any more of her college experience feeling as if she needed to be at home with Charlie.

Their breakup had actually cleared the air, and everyone around them could see they were happier as friends. Ellie was surprised and relieved that she and Charlie were still able to maintain their friendship. Deep down, though, she knew that Charlie still loved her, at least a little bit. She had simply chosen to ignore it for the last two and a half years.

When Pat stepped into the kitchen, Ellie saw his eyes lock on Charlie. Somehow, she realized, he knew who Charlie was.

"Good morning," he said, his voice a little gruff first thing in the morning.

"Good morning." Ellie smiled warmly, trying not to betray her internal distress.

"Do I smell coffee?"

"I'll get you a cup," Olivia said, hurrying to the cabinet for another mug.

"You must be Pat," Charlie said, stepping around the counter and extending a hand. "I'm Charlie Tanner, Olivia's brother."

Pat nodded slowly, and Ellie was certain she saw him sizing Charlie up.

"Pat O'Sullivan." Pat took Charlie's hand and shook it. "I'm a friend of Ellie's."

Charlie smirked. "Yeah, I got that."

Olivia handed Pat his coffee, and he smiled at her, but it wasn't the carefree, relaxed smile that Ellie found so charming.

"Charlie texted us late last night to say he was coming to visit today," she explained. "And then he surprised us by showing up super early."

"Nice."

"Couldn't let you two have all the summer fun," Charlie said, putting his arm affectionately around Olivia's shoulders. "Besides, it'll be just like old times."

"I should probably head out," Pat finally said after they spent a few minutes making idle conversation. He set his empty coffee mug down on the counter and then slipped his arm around Ellie's waist. She was sure she saw Charlie's body tense visibly, but she chose to ignore him and looked up at Pat instead.

"We'll see you tonight," she told him. "What time will y'all start playing?"

"I'd say around nine or so, but I recommend getting to

Tommy's around eight or eight-fifteen. You'll have a better chance of getting a table up front."

"What's happening tonight?" Charlie asked Olivia.

"Pat's Irish group is playing at a pub downtown, and we're gonna go," she told him.

"Ben'll be there," Pat said. "Maybe you can save a seat for him at your table. He was excited when I told him y'all were coming."

"We can definitely do that," Ellie said.

"I'm shocked he'd want to see me again," Olivia said, shaking her head. "After I insulted his last name."

Pat shrugged. "He got over it pretty quickly." Then, he leaned down and kissed Ellie lightly on the lips. "Bye. I'll call you later."

"Bye." Ellie found herself staring up into his brown eyes, and she sighed. He had such warm, kind eyes, she decided. She hoped she had the opportunity to study them more closely.

WHEN PAT WAS GONE, an uneasy silence filled the room. Ellie wasn't sure what to say or if she should say anything at all.

"So, it looks like you two have been busy making friends," Charlie said, taking a deep breath. "Anyone else gonna pop up that I should know about?"

"Nope, don't think so," Olivia said. "Now take your bag upstairs to one of the spare rooms, and let's get ready for the beach."

"CHARLIE JUST SHOWED UP UNEXPECTEDLY?" Ellie's mom was incredulous when she called to check in.

"Yep. He's down at the beach right now with Olivia." Ellie was standing in the cupola on the third floor of the house, looking out over the beach. She could see her the two of them sitting side-by-side in their beach chairs, clearly locked in a deep conversation. "But to be fair," she added, "he texted to tell us he was coming, but then showed up about four or five hours earlier than expected."

"That was a little inconsiderate."

Ellie thought about telling her mother just how inconvenient Charlie's timing had been, but she wasn't about to admit to her mother that a man had stayed over. Her mother wouldn't hesitate to voice her disapproval and disappointment.

"I think he thought it would be fun to surprise us. We were still in our pajamas."

"Sweetie, I know it's really none of my business, but are you and Charlie... are you starting to date again?"

"No," Ellie said, her voice sounding small and childish. "But we have talked about it."

On the other end of the phone line, Ellie's mother sighed. "What brought that on?"

"I don't know," Ellie shrugged. "He came to visit me at school before finals, and it was just so good to see him. I've been single for so long, and I started thinking that maybe I made a mistake breaking up with him."

"Do you really think that, or are you just lonely, Ellie?"

Somehow, Ellie's mother always managed to ask the right questions. She was intuitive, and Ellie loved that her mother knew her so well. "Loneliness might be a small part of it," she said. "I do care about Charlie, but..."

"...but nothing has really changed, has it?"

"No. He's still so set in his plan for life, and I still have all of my big dreams that don't involve me living in Warner Robins."

"There's nothing wrong with staying in your hometown," Ellie's mother reminded her, "but you two had bigger issues than that. He wanted to *keep* you here, and you're just too adventurous for that, I think."

Ellie sighed. "I think you're right. And I think I need to tell him that."

"Yes, you do."

Before the next words came out of her mouth, Ellie thought about whether or not she should say them. She had mentioned her date with Pat to her mom, but she hadn't told her about everything else, so she briefly filled her in on everything that had happened since the kayaking date. She told her mom how Pat had brought her food when she was sick with a migraine, how sweet and genuine he seemed, and how he had paid for every single one of their dates so far.

"It sounds to me like you really like this boy," her mother finally said. Again, Ellie marveled at her mom's ability to read a situation correctly.

"I really do. And I think he likes me, too."

"Well then, I think you need to talk to Charlie. And you also should spend more time with this Irish boy to see where it goes."

"Thanks, Mom. I will."

After exchanging goodbyes, Ellie hung up the phone and sank into the pillows on the cupola window-seat. Her mother was right about everything, as usual. Ellie needed to explain to Charlie that, though it was tempting because of their history, they didn't need to date again. Neither she nor Charlie had changed at all in who they were and what they wanted out of life, so why should they expect that restarting a romantic relationship would work this time? They would only be putting off the inevitable. No, it was better for them to go ahead and accept now that things would never work between them.

That conversation, Ellie thought to herself, would definitely make his visit more awkward.

CHAPTER EIGHTEEN

"*Tell me everything.*"

Olivia barely had time to sink into her beach chair before Charlie was leaning forward in his, eager to hear about Ellie and the man she was dating.

"I don't really want to get involved," Olivia said.

"Too late. You might be Ellie's best friend, but you're *my* sister, so you have to tell me."

Olivia glared at her brother. "I don't *have* to do anything. But honestly, there isn't much to tell. Ellie has been on a couple dates with him."

"Yeah, but what do you know about him? Do I have anything to be worried about?"

Groaning, Olivia leaned back in her chair and pushed her sunglasses up onto her head. "I don't know, Charlie! Ellie met him about a week after we got here. They went kayaking together, he took her on a sunset harbor cruise, and last night we went to Red's with him and his roommate."

Charlie frowned, scratching his head. "That's gonna be tough to beat."

"Seriously?" Olivia rolled her eyes. "C'mon, Charlie! We

both know that you took Ellie for granted when y'all were dating. You could've planned more romantic dates if you had wanted to."

"Nah." Charlie waved Olivia's words away. "I never took her for granted."

"Yes, you did. Don't even deny it. Everyone knew it except for you."

"That's not the point right now. I'm asking you about this guy. What do you know about him?"

"I really just wish you'd talk to Ellie about it. I don't care what you say—I don't want to get in the middle of all this."

"Fine." Charlie reached into his cooler and pulled out a beer.

"Really, Charlie?" Olivia raised an eyebrow at him. "It's ten o'clock in the morning."

"What? I'm on vacation."

For nearly fifteen minutes, Olivia and her brother sat in silence, enjoying a beautiful morning on the beach. Olivia couldn't be certain, but she suspected that Ellie was lingering in the house, trying to avoid Charlie for as long as possible. Charlie was her brother, but Olivia had always known the relationship wouldn't work. She loved them both, but she realized from the start of their relationship that they functioned better as friends. Charlie had always struggled to treat Ellie like a real girlfriend; he loved her, but he didn't know how to transition from friendship to dating. Ellie was too sweet to see it, but Olivia didn't miss it.

Olivia would have been thrilled if Ellie and Charlie had ended up together. Ellie was already like a sister to her, and marrying Charlie would have simply made it legal. But Olivia had always known that Charlie wanted to live in their hometown after graduation, and Ellie commented several times that she could change his mind. Ellie envisioned the two of them traveling the world together and calling many different cities home, but Olivia had never been able to picture that life for Charlie.

When Ellie finally ended things between them, Olivia had actually breathed a sigh of relief. At one point in the latter months of their relationship, Charlie had talked about proposing, and Olivia knew it wasn't a good idea. Luckily, Ellie broke it off before anything more dramatic happened, and the two of them had managed to remain friends.

FINALLY, Charlie stood up. "I'm gonna walk down the beach," he said. "I get bored sitting here."

"I'll come," Olivia said, tucking her phone back into her beach bag. She hadn't told Charlie that she was pregnant, and she was looking for a good opportunity. If she didn't share the news, he would figure it out soon. After all, the house was littered with her books about pregnancy, and she was almost always sipping on ginger ale or nibbling at a saltine.

"So how are you?" Charlie asked as they walked along slowly.

"I'm okay," Olivia said honestly. "I'm still trying to figure out my next steps."

"You mean whether or not you're going to divorce Daniel?"

Olivia sighed deeply. Charlie was so blunt sometimes, and his words felt harsh. "Yes. That's what I'm trying to decide."

"Seems like it would be a pretty easy decision, if you ask me. If I married a girl and then found out that she had Asperger's or whatever and she didn't try to make things better, I'd divorce her."

"Spoken like a person who has never been married," Olivia muttered.

"What?"

"It's not that simple, Charlie. Divorce is a very complicated thing. Think about all the people who will be affected by my choice. Think about Daniel's family—they're my family now, and I know they would be devastated."

"Yeah, they would, but that can't be the reason you stay married to him."

"I know that!" Olivia tried to twist her wedding ring around on her finger before she remembered that she had left at the house. The engagement ring and wedding band left a semi-permanent mark on her ring finger, though, and her throat ached when she thought about not wearing her beautiful rings again.

"So what is there to think about? You're unhappy, and Daniel's not willing to see a counselor. What choice does that leave you?"

Olivia stopped short and pressed her hand against her stomach. "Charlie," she said, "I have something to tell you."

He glanced at her face and then her hand. His blue eyes widened, and he took a step backwards. "No way!"

"Yep," Olivia nodded. "I'm pregnant."

For a moment, Olivia worried that he wasn't going to be excited for her, but then his face lit up. He engulfed her in a tight bear hug.

"Liv, that's wonderful! I can't believe it. You're going to be a mom! Damn! I'm going to be an uncle!"

Olivia's laughter was mixed with a few happy tears. "I know. It's crazy, isn't it?"

"Does Daniel know?"

"Yes."

"What did he say?"

"He's excited," Olivia said. They turned and continued to walk down the beach. "He's making lots of plans and running lots of numbers. You know how he is."

Charlie rolled his eyes, shaking his head.

"He's the only person I've told besides you. And Mom, Dad, and Ellie of course."

"I'm happy for you, Liv." Then, Charlie frowned and his face darkened. "But what does this mean? Are you going to stay with Daniel because you're having a baby with him?"

Olivia nudged at a shell in the sand with her big toe. It was broken, but it still shimmered in the sunlight. "I don't know. That's what I'm trying to figure out. Being a single mom wouldn't be easy, but I'm not sure raising a child with Daniel will be easy, either."

"Probably not."

"So I'm all confused," Olivia said. "Everything is so complicated. I already love my baby, tiny little peanut that it is right now, but finding out I was pregnant changed everything. My mind was almost completely made up... and then I took the pregnancy test."

"Wow."

"Yeah. Ellie was the one who figured it out. I caught a whiff of some shrimp, and it made me sick to my stomach. She put two and two together, and here we are..."

"Wow," Charlie said again, running his hands through his hair.

"I know. Wow."

Charlie draped his arms over Olivia's shoulders affectionately. "You'll figure it all out. And you know I've got your back, no matter what."

"I know that. Thanks."

By the time Olivia and Charlie meandered back to their chairs, Ellie had arrived. She was lying on a beach towel, slowly turning the pages of a magazine.

"I wondered where y'all were," she said.

"We went for a walk," Olivia explained.

"I got bored when Olivia wouldn't tell me anything about

your new boyfriend," Charlie said, winking at Ellie and tossing a small seashell in her direction. She swatted it away playfully.

"He's *not* my boyfriend," Ellie insisted. "We've only been on a few dates."

Charlie shrugged. "Sure looked like more than a few dates to me. I mean, he stayed the night."

"Now, now, you two," Olivia said, wagging her finger at them. "Charlie, if you're going to stay here, you need to behave. The only reason you and I are here is because Ellie asked us. And technically, she didn't ask you. You invited yourself."

Her words seemed to shut him up, and Ellie smiled gratefully at her. Olivia loved her brother, but she didn't want him to put a damper on her vacation with Ellie. She valued the time she was spending with her best friend, and she didn't want Charlie's presence to affect Ellie's mood.

Charlie opened his mouth to speak, but then closed it again. Olivia shook her head and relaxed back in her beach chair. She had enough to worry about without dealing with drama between Charlie and Ellie.

CHARLIE GRUMBLED about driving downtown to hear Pat and his band play at the Irish pub, but when Olivia finally told him to shut up or stay home, he quieted down and agreed to go. While he was showering, Olivia slipped into Ellie's bedroom. Her friend was lying across the bed, her face buried in the comforter.

"This is a nightmare," Ellie said, her voice muffled.

"It's certainly not ideal," Olivia laughed. "But it'll all be okay."

Ellie sat up, her hair flying in every direction. "Will it, though? Clearly, Charlie's jealous. I guess I should've told him about Pat, but honestly his visit just happened so suddenly. I expected to have more time to prepare."

Olivia sat on the edge of the bed. "I know you did. And it was a little rude of Charlie to show up so unexpectedly. He didn't even give me a chance to talk to you before he sent us that text message."

"It *was* a little inconsiderate," Ellie agreed, frowning. "He should've asked me."

"And you need to stop worrying so much. You and Charlie only talked about getting back together, right? You didn't actually decide anything, did you?"

"No. We just both said we'd think about it until we saw each other again."

"Then you shouldn't feel bad about dating Pat. Get up and get dressed so we can go downtown. You wanna hear him play, right?"

"Yes," Ellie jumped up.

"Okay, then get ready! Your hair is a hot mess. You can deal with Charlie tomorrow. Tonight, we are going to listen to Irish music."

Ellie took a deep breath and then leaned forward to hug her friend. "You always know what to say."

"That's what friends are for."

LEAVING Ellie to dress for their night in downtown Charleston, Olivia walked across the hall to her own room. She opened her closet, studying her wardrobe. Though she wouldn't admit it to anyone, Olivia wanted to look her best when she saw Ben again. She wasn't sure she'd made a good first impression on him, but it was important to her that his second impression improve his opinion of her. His opinion shouldn't matter to her, but it did. He was so different from Daniel—the opposite in almost every way, and she found his company oddly refreshing. Talking to someone who didn't know about all the chaos in her life allowed her to feel a sense of relaxation she hadn't experienced in months.

Olivia pushed some hangers aside, frowning at each possible option. She scolded herself inwardly for wanting to look pretty for another man, but then squashed those feelings down deep. Finally, she chose a pale pink sundress and stood in front of the floor-length mirror, holding the dress against her body. Pink, she decided, was the ideal color to accentuate her new tan and her dark brown hair.

When he saw her, Olivia decided, Ben Billhorn would completely forget that she had ever insulted his name.

CHAPTER NINETEEN

$\mathcal{T}$ommy Condon's was a well-known Irish bar on Church Street, only a block away from the popular Charleston City Market. It boasted a horseshoe-shaped bar and a large indoor and outdoor dining area. The small, raised platform in the corner could hardly be called a stage, but that didn't stop Tommy's from having live music almost every night of the week.

Ellie drove the three of them downtown and parked in a garage across the street from the pub. Charlie trailed behind a few steps as they walked towards the restaurant, but she chose to ignore his reluctance. He had seemed determined to come, but Ellie was equally as determined not to let him ruin her night.

She had chosen to wear her favorite white sundress and a pair of brown espadrilles that added a few inches to her height. Her long, blonde locks had dried naturally in the salty sea air and hung loosely around her bare shoulders. Her skin was tanned, and she had been exercising regularly for the past few weeks. For the first time in months, Ellie felt confident in her appearance as she stepped into the restaurant.

Pat was standing at the bar with a few other guys, but his face lit up as soon as he saw her walk in. While Olivia spoke to the hostess about a table, Ellie greeted Pat with a hug and a quick kiss on the cheek.

"You got here just in time," he told her. "We're about to go on in a few minutes, and I was hoping you'd get here before we started.

"I told you we'd be here," she said.

Pat briefly introduced Ellie to his friends—several of whom had also come to the bar to drink and hear him perform—and then excused himself to tune his instruments. Ben arrived as the hostess was seating Ellie, Olivia, and Charlie, and Ellie invited him to sit at their table.

"Y'ALL ARE IN FOR A TREAT," Ben told them, sitting down next to Olivia. "I know you've heard them play before, but Tommy's is a whole different ballgame."

"How so?" Ellie asked.

"It's all about the audience here. They're always so engaged in the music, and it makes all the difference in the world."

"I'm looking forward to it," Ellie said, picking up a menu and perusing the options. She was starving, and the aroma of food permeated the entire restaurant.

Pat and his bandmates struck up a lively Irish jig that immediately captured the attention of the crowded restaurant. The music was clear and loud, and Ellie's toe began to tap in time with the beat of the song. Several diners even clapped along. When Pat began to sing, Ellie was captivated by his voice—deep and strong with an even thicker Irish accent than normal. He was so unassumingly handsome as he stood in front of a crowded restaurant, his blue jeans and t-shirt so casual, yet well-suited to his figure. His strong hands held his fiddle, and Ellie admired the way his fingers danced across the strings. The more she listened to him, the more she found herself attracted to him. He was such an unusual man—unlike any she'd ever met.

143

Without thinking, Ellie glanced over at Charlie. He was drinking a beer and looked disinterested, but she could see his index finger tapping his glass in beat with the tune. She hid a smile behind her hand and looked back to Pat.

When the first song was finished, an enthusiastic round of applause resonated through the building.

"Welcome everyone," Pat said, grinning brightly. "It's a beautiful summer evening here in Charleston, South Carolina, and we're so happy you've chosen to spend it with us at Tommy Condon's. Now this fella here," he pointed to the older man perched on a stool on his left, holding a guitar, "is my dear granddad Pat, same name as me. And this other fella over here, pickin' on his bass, is our friend Roger." Pat paused to clear his throat and take a sip of water. "A few of our songs tonight will require audience participation, so be prepared." He winked at Ellie as he tucked the fiddle under his chin.

For the next hour, Pat and his band entertained their audience with lively songs and humorous toasts. As the night wore on, more and more people filled the bar, and Ellie was amazed at how they all engaged with the band. The food that Ellie ordered tasted delicious, and she ate her Shepherd's Pie slowly to savor the rich flavors. Then, just when she thought the pub crowd couldn't get any more energized, Pat paused briefly at the end of a song and cleared his throat loudly.

"Alright folks, I want to do a song that I'm sure many of the regulars here will recognize. It's called *Wild Rover*. Anybody here know that one?"

Nearly everyone around them erupted with cheers and applause, some patrons even shouting words of encouragement to the band. Ellie and Olivia looked to Ben questioningly, but he simply smiled and shook his head.

"You'll see," was all he said.

"I'm glad to see I've got a good group in here tonight. I'm going to need your help with this song," Pat said. He briefly explained how the song required the audience to clap in several places during the chorus—first four times, then two times, and then one final clap. Finally satisfied that everyone in the room knew the instructions, Pat gave a quick nod to his bandmates, and they launched into a lively song about a man who spent his life roving free, wasting money on alcohol and women. Ellie had never been to a restaurant or bar where the crowd was as lively and interactive, and she loved that Pat engaged them so easily. Performing the songs of his ancestors seemed to come naturally for him, and she loved watching him sing. When the song reached the chorus, Ellie quickly picked up on the rhythm of the claps. To her surprise, almost everyone in the bar knew exactly where to clap, even Ben. The smile on her face grew wider and wider. She clapped along enthusiastically, swept up with the music, and so did Olivia, Ben, and even Charlie.

It was close to eleven o'clock before the band wrapped up their performance. Olivia was yawning widely, but trying to hide it. Charlie was chatting with some locals at the bar, and he'd been downing drinks with them for the last hour. Ellie was surprised that Ben chose to sit with them all night. He talked to both of them, but Ellie could see his attention was focused on Olivia, who looked unusually pretty. Any awkwardness from barely knowing each other had vanished, and the two of them talked quietly throughout the night.

After spending a few minutes talking with different restaurant patrons, Pat collapsed into the chair Charlie had vacated.

"What did you think?" he asked.

"I loved it!" Ellie exclaimed. "Y'all are so good!"

"You really are," Olivia added. "I've never been to Ireland, but this is what I imagine live music in an actual Irish pub would sound like."

Pat shrugged nonchalantly but beamed proudly. "Thanks. I'm glad y'all came."

"So are we." Ellie leaned in closer. "You have such a good voice."

"Thanks. And thanks for staying so long. I figured y'all would've left earlier."

"Nope. I told Olivia and Charlie that I planned to stay as long as you played, so they did have the option of driving separately."

Pat glanced over at Charlie, who was watching them closely from the bar. "Yeah, I bet Charlie didn't want to give us too much time alone."

Ellie's smile faded. "I'm sorry he surprised you this morning. He texted us late last night that he was coming and—"

"Ellie, you don't have to apologize," Pat told her, putting his hand over hers. "I believe you."

"Thanks."

"I know you have history with him, but you should know that I won't give you up without a fight."

Pat's expression was so sincere and earnest that Ellie felt it all the way to her core. No one had ever told her that he would fight for her, and she thought they were the most romantic words anyone had ever said to her.

"I don't think you'll have to fight," she said softly, her cheeks warm. She looked down at her lap, biting her lip nervously. Vulnerability made her anxious, and she worried that Pat might balk.

"Yeah?"

"Yeah." Ellie looked back up at him, losing herself in his dark eyes. "I don't want to get back together with Charlie."

Pat leaned in close, his tone low. "I'm really glad to hear that."

ELLIE, Olivia, and Charlie finally made it back to the beach house around midnight. Olivia immediately went to bed, and Ellie went upstairs to change into something more suitable for a late-night beach patrol. When she walked back downstairs and passed through the screened porch, Charlie stepped out of the shadows, taking her by surprise. She gasped and took a step back.

"Sorry, didn't mean to scare you," he apologized.

"It's fine. I just thought you had gone to bed, too."

He shook his head. "No, I knew you would be going out on the beach, and I wanted to go with you."

"Oh." Ellie twisted her hands anxiously. She sensed that an uncomfortable conversation was coming. "Okay, well let's go."

AS THEY STROLLED DOWN the boardwalk in the moonlight, Ellie pressed her lips together into a thin line. She wasn't sure how to tell Charlie that she didn't want to get back together. Earlier in the summer, when she'd first arrived on Sullivan's Island, she had been almost certain that she wanted to try dating him again. Now, even though she and Pat had been on only a few dates, she already felt a stronger connection with him than she had ever felt with Charlie or anyone else. She knew she was falling fast for him, which terrified her. She didn't know what the rest of the summer would hold for them, but she wanted to find out. She couldn't do that if Charlie was sulking in the corner all summer long.

Ellie knew she should never have invited Charlie to visit her at college. All his visit had done to was stir up old emotions and feelings for both of them, and she felt bad that she had reached out to him in moment of loneliness. She had only gotten his hopes up.

"So, should we just go ahead and discuss the elephant in the room?" Charlie finally asked, shoving his hands into the pockets of his cargo shorts.

Ellie sighed. "I guess so."

"Judging from the way you were looking at the fiddle player, I'm guessing you're *not* interested in dating again, huh?"

"Oh Charlie, I wish things were different between us, but nothing's really changed since we broke up, so what's the point of us getting back together?"

"I've changed," Charlie insisted, his dark brows furrowed together. "I've grown up a lot in the last couple years. I've got a good job, and I'm looking to buy my own house next year."

"In Warner Robins?"

"Yeah?"

"See?" Ellie turned to Charlie, her hands clasped earnestly in front of her. "Charlie, you want to stay in our hometown for the rest of our lives, and I don't want that. I didn't in high school, and I don't now."

"What's so wrong with our hometown?"

Groaning, Ellie threw her hands up in the air. "Nothing! I love Warner Robins. It's my home, but I want to see the world. I want to live somewhere else—a big city, maybe."

"Charleston?"

Ellie couldn't help but notice the snide way in which Charlie suggested she might want to live in the Charleston area. He was considering proximity to Pat, no doubt. "Actually," she told him, "I started looking for job opportunities in Charleston earlier this year, so yes, maybe."

Charlie rolled his eyes, turning away, but Ellie caught his arm.

"You know I'm right about this, Charlie," she said. "I don't think we would be happy—at least not for very long."

"Why? Why do you think that?"

"Because we want different things!"

"Nah," Charlie shook his head. "You're wrong."

"I really don't think I am."

"Then how come everyone says we were great together?" Charlie picked up a piece of driftwood and hurled it into the surf.

"Because in some ways, we are great together." Ellie's expression softened, and she exhaled deeply. "Charlie, you and I know everything about each other. We grew up together. We've been friends for almost as long as I can remember, so of course people think we'd be great together. But it's not up to everyone else. It's up to you and me."

"Well, I think we're great together!"

Ellie tilted her head at him sharply. "Really?"

Charlie shrugged. "We weren't a perfect couple, but who is?"

"Charlie, do you not remember the last year of our relationship? We were miserable."

"No, I was miserable. You were off at school having a great time."

"Yes. Because I wanted to enjoy my college experience, and you couldn't understand that."

"I missed you. You weren't coming home much."

"And you weren't coming to visit," Ellie reminded him. "I wanted to be at school, to make friends, and try new things, but you were always making me feel as if I should come home."

"Well, you were my girlfriend!"

"And you should have at least *tried* to be happy for me! I got into the University of Georgia, and I was over the moon, but you tried to diminish it. You wanted me to stay home and go to community college."

"What's wrong with that? Olivia's doing it."

"There's nothing wrong with it," Ellie insisted, rolling her eyes. "But it's not what I wanted. Don't you see? That's the problem! You and I want different things! That's why I don't think we need to be together!"

For a moment, Charlie seemed stumped. He turned away from her and stared out at the ocean. She watched him closely, wondering what thoughts were racing through his mind. Finally, he turned back around slowly.

"Fine. Maybe we do want different things. But I really don't think that means we shouldn't be together. We could compromise."

"Oh Charlie, this isn't something we can compromise on! You make it sound like we're talking about which restaurant to eat at. We're talking about our goals, our dreams, our ideas of what kind of lives we see ourselves living!"

Charlie groaned loudly and walked away in the opposite direction, shaking his head. Ellie knew him well enough to know that he needed space. When he was upset, Charlie preferred to be alone and think, so she kept walking down the beach because she could see a house with lights shining brightly across the dunes.

AFTER POLITELY ASKING the residents of the house to turn off their lights, Ellie trudged wearily back towards her uncle's house. She had already been tired before she headed to the beach, but now—after arguing with Charlie—she was mentally exhausted. When she reached the boardwalk back to the house, he was sitting there waiting for her.

"I'll leave in the morning," he told her.

"Charlie, I don't want you to leave."

"Well, you don't want me to stay."

"I never said that," Ellie said. "Charlie, I'd love to have you stay, but as a friend. Nothing more."

He sighed, his shoulders drooping. "Okay, I'll stay." Charlie stood up slowly, brushing sand off his shorts. "But know this— even if you say you're not interested in getting back together, I'm not giving up."

"Charlie..."

"I love you, and I can't just stop loving you. I can't forget about this."

"I know," Ellie said sadly. A part of her wished that she and Charlie could make their relationship work, but she truly didn't feel the same love for Charlie that she once had. Still, only a couple hours ago, Pat had told her that he would fight for her, and now Charlie was basically saying the same.

Ellie trailed Charlie up the boardwalk to the house, her comfortable bed calling to her. When she finally crawled between the cool sheets, she sighed. At the beginning of the summer, she'd been a single woman, but now she had two men competing for her affection. She buried her face in a pillow to stifle another groan. Charlie was her friend, first and foremost, and she didn't want to hurt him; however, she intended to explore the strong feelings that were developing for Pat. She didn't know how long Charlie planned to stay, but she hoped his presence wouldn't create too much uncomfortable tension and awkwardness when Pat was around.

Life had been much simpler when she was single with no one showing interest in her, Ellie thought, but when she remembered the way Pat had held her gaze while he sang beautiful Irish love songs, she was happy that her love life was more complicated than usual. From the start of the summer, she had hoped that each day would hold something new and exciting. So far, she hadn't been disappointed.

A lot could happen in the next eight weeks. Ellie was both terrified and eager to see what the coming weeks would hold. After all, the summer wasn't even halfway over.

CHAPTER TWENTY

*W*hen Charlie left a few days later, Olivia swore she heard Ellie breathe an audible sigh of relief. Olivia wasn't sure exactly what had been said after she went to bed the first night of his visit, but the next morning, Ellie and Charlie had clearly reached a truce of sorts. For the next two days, the three of them spent hours together on the beach, ate at two of Charlie's favorite restaurants in the city, and stayed up late every night, watching their favorite childhood movies. To Olivia, it almost felt as if they were kids again.

"That was a fun visit," Olivia said once Charlie had pulled out of the driveway on his way back to Georgia.

"Yeah, it was." Ellie sipped her coffee slowly.

"How did you and Charlie leave things? You seemed to be getting along well after Saturday night."

"Well, he decided to come on beach patrol with me, and we got into this huge argument. I explained why it wouldn't work out if we got back together, but he didn't want to hear them. He thinks we can compromise on everything."

Olivia sighed. Sometimes, her brother could be so clueless. "What did you say to that?"

"That I don't think compromise is the answer for us. I mean, you were right—ultimately, we both still want different things. That hasn't changed."

"I really hope what I said didn't affect your decision," Olivia exclaimed. "I had no right to offer my opinion."

"It didn't, and you certainly did have a right," Ellie said. "You know both of us so well. What you said really made me think. Well, that and... "

"And a certain Irish fiddle player?"

"Him, too." Ellie smiled to herself. "Meeting Pat was such a surprise. I know we haven't known each other for long, but I feel something different with him."

Olivia smiled, almost sadly, as she watched her friend struggle to find the right words. She knew what Ellie was trying to say. She knew what it was like to fall in love, and she could already see that Ellie was falling in love with Pat O'Sullivan.

"You're falling for him," Olivia pointed out.

"No, I'm not!" Ellie set her coffee down on the table with a decided *thunk*, shaking her head. "That's impossible. We barely know each other!"

Olivia shrugged. "So? That doesn't mean anything."

"Seriously. It's impossible."

"Fine." Olivia put her hands up, palms out, as if surrendering. "Don't listen to me. What do I know?"

Ellie sank into deep thought, tapping her chin with her index finger. After a few minutes, she snapped herself out her reverie. "I was thinking of seeing if Pat might want to come over for dinner tonight. I would cook, of course. That okay with you?"

"Sure." Olivia hesitated for a second. "We could invite Ben, too."

"Do you want me to invite Ben?" Ellie wanted to know, her

eyes narrowing. "Olivia, is there something you're not telling me?"

"No," Olivia insisted. "I just thought it might be a nice gesture, but don't feel like you have to."

"I'll invite him. It would be more fun, anyways. You wouldn't have to feel like a third wheel." Ellie picked up her phone and began typing out a text message.

"Exactly."

Once more, the two girls fell into silence. Olivia wanted to open up to her friend about something that had been bothering her since they went to dinner at Red's with Ben and Pat, but she wasn't sure what Ellie's reaction would be. She bit her tongue, telling herself that she shouldn't bring the subject up, that she should simply keep her thoughts to herself. But, she reminded herself, Ellie was her best friend, and her best friend didn't judge her. They told each other everything, right?

"I think Ben's really cute," Olivia finally blurted out. It felt so freeing to simply say the words out loud. "There! I told you!"

"I agree," Ellie said. "But why do you say it like that?"

"I don't know." Olivia pulled at a loose string on her shorts. "It's just that, well, I like spending time with him. When we were at Tommy Condon's the other night, he talked to me a lot, but when I talked, he listened to me, truly listened. You have no idea how refreshing that was."

"Okay..." Ellie frowned, resting her chin in the palm of her hand.

"I don't know what I'm trying to say exactly. It's just makes me think, I guess. You know, I don't even think Daniel would care if I had an affair."

"Olivia!" Ellie gasped and sat up straight. "Are you serious right now? Is that why you want me to invite Ben over for dinner?"

"No! Maybe! I don't know!" Olivia buried her face in her hands. She knew she should have kept her mouth shut.

"Are you going to try to seduce him?"

"Of course not," Olivia snapped. "I shouldn't have said anything about an affair. I promise that's not what I meant. All I meant was that it feels really good when someone seems interested in me, you know?"

All the panic drained from Ellie's face and she nodded. "Yes, I know how that feels. It is nice," she admitted begrudgingly.

"I'm not saying I want to have an affair with Ben. All I'm saying is that it would be nice to spend more time with him."

OLIVIA WAS BEING COMPLETELY honest with Ellie; she didn't really think she'd ever have an affair with anyone. Of course, she had never had the opportunity, but in some of her darkest moments of unhappiness, she had thought about it. All Olivia wanted was someone who would make her feel desirable and beautiful, and when a man flirted with her or smiled at her, it made her feel almost unbearably lonely. Her marriage vows weren't something she took lightly. Olivia knew how strong the bond of marriage was, and she never wanted to betray Daniel. She simply wanted someone who would pay attention to her and fulfill her physical needs. Ben was kind and friendly, and Olivia really didn't want to be the third wheel at dinner with Ellie and Pat. She wanted someone to talk to through dinner, and though she tried to convince herself she wasn't doing anything inappropriate, but she was struggling with guilt. While Ellie went to the store mid-afternoon to pick up groceries, Olivia stayed at the house to nap, but she tossed and turned on the bed. Finally, she climbed the stairs to the cupola. The small room was warm from the sunshine streaming in, so Olivia switched on the ceiling fan before she took a seat. She had her book, but she found herself reading and re-reading the same sentences over and over again. Frustrated, she tossed the book aside and folded her arms across her chest.

She was attracted to Ben. There. She'd finally admitted it to herself. Was it wrong? Maybe. Was she going to act on her attraction? Probably not. And yet, she already found herself wondering what she should wear when he came over later that evening for supper. That, she decided, was inappropriate.

Would Daniel even care if she had an affair? Olivia really couldn't picture his reaction, but she guessed he would use logic to make sense of it because that's how his brain worked. He was so caught up in his own world that he might not even notice, Olivia mused. But, when she really thought about it, she didn't *want* to have an affair with anyone. She simply wanted Daniel to be the husband he'd promised to be, but it was beginning to sink in that he would never be able to fulfill those promises. What made Olivia even sadder was that she knew he wasn't intentionally trying to hurt her, but the knowledge that Daniel's brain worked differently didn't comfort her.

Olivia buried her face in her hands, shedding the first tears she'd cried in over a week. Some days, she longed to be eighteen again. If she had known that Daniel had AS, she wasn't sure she would have married him at all. She decided she probably would have ended the relationship altogether. What if she had dated other guys besides Daniel? What if she had gone away to college like Ellie? What if she had left him in their hometown and never looked back? *What if?*

Olivia knew they were questions that would never be answered, but she still wished she knew. She was certain about one thing, though. If she hadn't married Daniel, she wouldn't be pregnant right now, and she placed a loving hand over her stomach. She already loved her baby, tiny as he or she was, and she didn't want to trade her baby for any number of hypothetical answers. She had chosen to marry Daniel, knowing he was a little quirky, just like she had chosen to conceive a baby during a rough patch in her marriage. Her choices had led her to where she was, sitting in the cupola of a beachfront home on Sullivan's Island, trying not to fantasize about having an affair.

❦

ELLIE DECIDED to make lasagna for supper using her mother's recipe, and Olivia helped. First they cooked the lasagna sauce, and the aroma of the herbs and tomatoes permeated the entire house. While the sauce cooled, Ellie boiled the lasagna noodles, and Olivia sliced mozzarella cheese. Together, they assembled a large casserole dish of lasagna, and then set it in the fridge until it was time to bake.

When they were finished in the kitchen, the girls quickly cleaned the house. Neither one of them was especially messy, but the house needed a certain amount of upkeep before Ellie would deem it presentable to guests. Around three o'clock, they took their chairs down to the beach for a couple of hours of sunshine.

"PAT SAID they'd come over around six-thirty," Ellie said, relaxing back in her chair.

"That'll be good," Olivia said, rubbing sunscreen on her face and chest. Even though both of them were deeply tanned, she didn't want to risk burning, so she always wore sunscreen.

"Pat said Ben was really looking forward to it."

"Oh yeah?" Olivia tried to sound casual, but she wasn't sure she succeeded.

"You know, it's none of my business what you do," Ellie said hesitantly. "I hope I didn't sound too judgmental this morning when you asked if we should invite Ben."

"You didn't."

"I just want you to be careful. You've already got so much going on in your life, and I'd hate to see something with Ben complicate it even more. Plus, he does seem like a nice guy, and I don't want to see anyone else get hurt."

Olivia hadn't considered that she might give Ben the wrong impression if she flirted with him or showed too much interest. "You're right. One hundred percent. I hadn't really thought of it that way."

"But," Ellie continued, "I think you deserve friendship, and there's nothing wrong with being friends with Ben, right?"

"I don't know," Olivia admitted. "Is there?"

Ellie shrugged. "I don't know, really. Neither one of us has ever been in a situation like this, so it's uncharted territory."

"You're telling me!"

"I would just hate for anything to happen between you and Ben and then somehow your family find out..." Ellie's voice trailed off. "I'm afraid they would blame me for not stopping you. And I know that sounds silly."

"No, it really doesn't." Olivia pushed her toes into the sand and sighed. "You know, we're talking about all of this as if Ben has even expressed interest in me, and he hasn't. I don't even know if he likes me!"

"Who wouldn't like you?" Ellie laughed. "You're irresistible to men!"

Olivia laughed, too. "No, I'm not."

"Yes, you are. And trust me, if Ben is excited to come over tonight, it's probably because he's interested in you—not because he thinks that my cooking is going to be great."

Staring down at her feet, Olivia decided she needed to repaint her toenails before supper. "There's something he doesn't know about me that would probably change his opinion of me, even if he were interested," she said soberly, swallowing tightly.

"What's that?" Ellie asked, her brows furrowing together.

"Ben doesn't know that I'm pregnant."

CHAPTER TWENTY-ONE

*H*er lasagna smelled delicious when she pulled it from the oven, and Ellie served hearty portions to Pat, Ben, and Olivia. The four of them ate supper on the screened porch as the sun sank low in the west, painting the sky over the ocean an array of oranges and pinks. Ellie watched the interaction between Olivia and Ben for the first part of the evening, trying to determine if Ben was showing any romantic interest in her friend. He was tough to read, and she couldn't tell if he was friendly or flirtatious. He and Olivia discovered their shared interest of a particular TV series that neither Ellie nor Pat had ever seen, and they launched into an in-depth discussion. Ellie noted that Olivia seemed to come alive around Ben. She transformed into the girl Ellie had grown up with—vibrant, charming, and subtly flirtatious.

After supper, Pat helped Ellie put away the leftovers and tidy up the kitchen. It was a beautiful summer night, though almost unbearably humid for late June, and Olivia suggested they drive the golf cart down to Middle Street for ice cream. Sweat trickled down the back of Ellie's neck as she drove, and she sighed; no matter how hard she tried, it was impossible for her to look as neat and polished as Olivia did when it was eighty degrees outside. Pat didn't seem to mind, though. He rested his arm around her shoulders as she drove, and they laughed and joked all the way to the ice cream shop. Ellie was reminded of a similar trip to Sullivan's Island nearly four years prior when she and Charlie were an established couple, and Olivia and Daniel had just started dating. They were vacationing with their parents, but the four of them spent almost all of their time together. Ellie remembered riding around the island on the same golf cart. Charlie had insisted on driving, and Ellie had held his free hand tightly. Olivia and Daniel had been snuggled up together on the back seat of the golf cart, lost in their own world, as they almost always were. During that trip, Ellie would never have predicted that life would take the twists and turns that it had. Back then she thought she and Charlie would be together forever, and yet here she was now, sitting next to a completely different man whom she cared for in a very different way and Olivia was in the back, flirting with someone who was *not* Daniel.

"You seem far away," Pat said quietly. "You okay?"

Startled from her reverie by his voice, Ellie turned her face away slightly and answered pensively. "Just thinking about old times."

He kissed her cheek affectionately. "You look beautiful tonight."

Ellie smiled, squeezing his hand. "Thank you."

ONCE THEY HAD ice cream cones in hand, Ellie drove them back to the house, taking the long way so they could admire houses. Ben pointed out one that belonged to Stephen Colbert, which sparked a discussion of all the famous people who owned homes in the Charleston area. It was completely dark outside by the time Ellie pulled the golf cart back into the yard. Ben yawned and glanced at his watch.

"Is it your bedtime?" Olivia teased him. "It's only nine-fifteen."

"I have a meeting at seven tomorrow morning," he said. Then, he looked at Pat. "We should probably head out soon. I need to do a little bit of preparation for the meeting tonight."

Ellie frowned. She had hoped they would stay long enough for Pat to walk the beach with her, but he and Ben had driven to the house together, which meant that if Ben needed to leave, Pat would have to go too.

"Sure. I'm ready if you are," Pat said. Then, he turned back to Ellie. "Can you wait half an hour or so for beach patrol? I can take Ben home and then come back to go with you."

"I have an idea," Olivia piped up. "I can drive Ben home, and you two can go on ahead with your beach patrol."

Ellie could've hugged Olivia. Her best friend seemed to have read her thoughts.

"Works for me. Does that work for you, man?" Pat looked at Ben, waiting for an answer.

Ben smiled at Olivia, and Ellie suspected he was equally as pleased with the plan. "Yeah, that works for me. I really appreciate it, Olivia."

OLIVIA HURRIED upstairs to get her keys and wallet and when she and Ben left, Pat immediately looped his arms around Ellie's waist and pressed a searing kiss to her lips.

"I've been wanting to do that all night," he told her when they broke apart, his voice husky.

"Me, too." Ellie took his hand and pulled him towards the screened porch. He sat down on the wicker couch and she snuggled up against him, amazed by her own newfound confidence. They kissed deeply, his hands roaming over her body and finally coming to rest on her hips. The porch was completely dark—Ellie believed in turning the lights out for the turtles earlier than the town ordinance commanded—and she didn't care what they did in the semi-privacy of the porch. No one could see them, and she found it wildly exciting.

She wasn't sure how, but she found herself tugging at the hem of Pat's shirt, and he sat back for a moment, allowing her to pull it over his head. She tossed it aside quickly and leaned back in, kissing him again. When he pulled at her tank, though, Ellie almost froze. She wasn't sure she was ready for Pat to see her undressed—even if it was only half undressed—but she reminded herself that they were sitting in the dark, and he wouldn't really be able to see much of her body. Taking a deep breath, she raised her arms up, and Pat pulled the tank top off quickly. His hands seemed to hover over her, his fingertips brushing her skin lightly. Ellie closed her eyes, savoring his touch.

"You're so beautiful, Ellie," he said softly.

His voice had the same husky tone as earlier, and Ellie recognized it for what it was: desire. She pressed her forehead against his and felt the rise and fall of his chest against hers as they breathed in and out together.

MORE THAN ANYTHING, Ellie wanted to lead Pat upstairs to her room, but she stopped herself. Despite the connection she felt with him, Ellie had known Pat for barely a month. She wanted to be certain that he wasn't spending time with her so she would sleep with him, even though she was gradually beginning to believe that Olivia was right—Pat really did like her for *her*.

"I don't want us to go too far," she said softly, holding her breath and hoping that he wouldn't mind. "Not yet."

Pat nodded, holding her face between his strong hands. "I understand."

"But soon." She nestled closer to him. "For now, I'm happy right here. I just want to spend as much time with you as possible."

A smile spread across Pat's face. "Me, too."

PAT TOOK Ellie's words literally. For the next two weeks, she saw him almost every day. If he didn't come to the beach house after work, she met him downtown for lunch. They grabbed coffee before he went to work, spent the weekends at the beach with Olivia and Ben, and explored downtown together. Pat introduced Ellie to several local restaurants she had never tried, and she experienced Charleston from an entirely different perspective.

With every hour they spent together, Ellie fell harder and harder for Pat. A part of her kept screaming at herself to be logical and rational, but the romantic in her kept charging ahead, giving him bigger and bigger pieces of her heart. She opened up to Pat about so many topics that she had kept buried down deep, told him embarrassing stories about herself from her childhood, and welcomed him into every area of her life.

DURING THE MONTH OF JULY, Dunleavy's had booked Pat as a solo act every Friday night. He parked his truck at the beach house and ate supper with Ellie and Olivia before Ellie drove him to Dunleavy's around seven-thirty. She took a seat at the end of the short bar and even though she had already eaten, she ordered a sweet tea and small plate of nachos while she watched Pat tune his instruments. Several locals were sitting at the bar, and the tables and booths filled up quickly as people crowded in off the beaches, many of them tourists. Ellie made small talk for a few minutes with some of her fellow bar-mates and then spent a few minutes on her phone, checking her social media accounts until Pat finally struck up a lively tune on his fiddle.

Ellie nibbled at her food lazily, happy to sit and listen to the music. She didn't think she would ever tire of hearing Pat sing, even if she had already heard most of the songs. His voice was so rich and deep, and he sang the unfamiliar words so clearly that she easily imagined she was walking through the lush, green hills of Ireland.

Nearly halfway through the set, Pat traded his fiddle for a guitar and sat down on a tall stool. "I'd like to slow it down a bit here, folks," he told the restaurant patrons. He strummed his fingers lightly across the strings, and Ellie felt a chill run down her spine. He liked to run his fingers down the back of her spine until she arched against him, and she blushed when she thought about it.

"This song is about a young man who stole food to save his starving family and was sentenced to exile in a foreign land," Pat explained, his Irish accent unusually strong as he spoke. "It's called *The Fields of Athenry*." He cleared his throat loudly and then began to play softly, his fingertips tugging lightly at the strings.

"*By a lonely harbor wall, she watched the last star fall, as the prison ship sailed out against the sky. Sure she'll wait and hope and pray for her love in Botany Bay. It's so lonely round the fields of Athenry.*"

The words of the song were simple and sorrowful, and tears filled Ellie's eyes as she listened to the haunting story Pat told with his music. She watched him closely, noticing the way he seemed to disappear into his music, oblivious to everyone else around him. Her heart ached as he launched into the final chorus, and in that moment, Ellie knew.

She *knew*.

She had always heard people say that she would know when she had found the one, and Ellie knew that she had found the one.

"Low lie the fields of Athenry, where once we watched the small free birds fly. Our love was on the wing, we had dreams and songs to sing. It's so lonely round the fields of Athenry."

As the last lyrics of the song fell from his lips and his fingers strummed the final chord on the guitar strings, Ellie's mind was made up. When she left Sullivan's Island at the end of the summer, she wanted to continue a long-distance relationship with Pat. She didn't know what that meant for her future, but she knew she wanted to see where their relationship might lead. Pat wasn't just some local boy to have fun with; he was a unique man who cared about her and made her feel more beautiful than anyone ever had.

Ellie didn't know the depth of Pat's feelings for her, but she prayed that he felt the same. Why else would he make a point of seeing her every single day? He went out of his way to make her happy, and she believed his feelings for her were strong. Vulnerability terrified Ellie; she knew she was risking heartache if Pat didn't return her love, but she had to take a chance. She had to put herself out there and hope that Pat was falling in love with her, too.

IT WAS close to ten-thirty when Pat's show wrapped up. When they returned to the house, Ellie noticed that while most of the lights in the house were already out, Olivia had left the back porch light on for them.

"I guess Olivia's already in bed," she said.

"Is it beach patrol time?"

Ellie yawned and stretched her arms over her head. "Yes, but not for too long. I'm tired."

Pat nodded. "A short walk then?"

"Yes, a short one."

"And then bed?"

Taking a deep breath, Ellie nodded nervously. Pat had already planned to spend the night, but Ellie was finally ready to take their relationship further. "And then bed."

DURING THEIR BEACH PATROL, Ellie and Pat filled in two large holes, and she spotted one house with lights on downstairs, so she walked up and politely knocked on their door. The occupants, who turned out to be renters and unaware of the Lights Out For The Sea Turtles initiative, listened politely to Ellie and then agreed to turn off their lights.

Ellie and Pat walked farther than she had intended, and her heart was pounding in her throat. She avoided eye contact with Pat, busying herself with scooping sand into the deep holes in the beach. After they finished filling in the second one, Pat caught Ellie's hand and pulled her to him.

"Are you ready to go back in?" he asked her. "We've been out here a while."

"In a minute," Ellie told him. "We can walk a little far—"

"Ellie," Pat interrupted her. "Is something wrong?"

"I wanted us to, you know..." her voice trailed off, and she blushed.

"Tonight?" Pat asked quietly.

Ellie nodded solemnly, unable to look him in the eyes.

"I wasn't expecting anything, so it won't bother me if you change your mind. I mean it."

"I *do* want to," she whispered, her words so soft that they were almost lost on the breeze. "But I'm scared."

"What are you scared of?" Pat wanted to know, staring straight into her eyes. "Tell me honestly."

Ellie hugged her arms to herself shyly. "I don't know. You

seeing me completely naked, I guess. I know I'm not the skinniest person, but—"

Pat put a finger over Ellie's lips, stopping her mid-sentence. "Ellie, what are you talking about? Don't you know I think you're perfect just the way you are?" He kissed her lightly.

Her heart pounded harder, but it was different this time. She put her hand over one of Pat's and took it in hers, pulling him back up the beach towards the house. "Let's go," she commanded him gently.

ELLIE LED Pat back to the beach house and up the stairs to her bedroom. He closed the door quietly behind them and then pulled her into his arms, his mouth finding her lips, her neck, and her collarbone. He slipped her shirt off quickly and easily managed the clasp of her bra. Ellie caught her breath when his hands skimmed over her breasts, and she knew she was trembling, but she began unbuttoning his shirt. When it fell to the floor, she loosened his belt and quickly pushed his jeans down. Pat stared at her, lust written in his dark eyes, as he pushed her shorts down until they pooled around her feet.

Even though Ellie had already seen him in nothing but his swim trunks, something about seeing him in just his underwear was intoxicating. She found the smattering of dark hair on his chest that trailed downward from his belly-button and disappeared into his boxers unbelievably attractive. Her eyes followed the lines of his body, studying his handsome face, his broad chest and shoulders, the faint outline of a 'v' shape in the muscles of his lower torso, and his thick, strong legs. He allowed her to admire him before hooking his thumbs in the waistband of his briefs and slipping out of them.

Ellie eyes widened, and she blinked several times. Pat laughed, a deep, genuine laugh at her reaction, and Ellie shushed him quickly.

"You'll wake up Olivia," she told him.

"I really don't care right now," Pat said. He stepped closer to her again, pushing their clothes out of the way with his foot. "Are you sure you want to do this? I'm not trying to push you if you're not ready."

Ellie looked up at him and wrapped her arms around his waist. "I'm sure. I want you, Pat. More than anything."

"Good." With that, Pat lifted her up, and she wrapped her legs around his waist tightly.

An hour later, they lay naked in the bed with the sheet pulled over them. Pat rolled onto his side and propped up on his elbow so that he could look down at Ellie. She was lying on her side, her eyelids drooping with sleep.

"That was perfect," she whispered.

"Yeah?" Pat grinned proudly.

Ellie slapped his arm playfully. "Don't be so smug." She pushed his roving hand away and pulled the sheet to her chest, exposing his naked body.

"Give that back." Pat grabbed for his side of the sheet, but Ellie clung to it, giggling.

"I want to look at you," she teased him. "I don't want you to cover up."

"Same!" With that, Pat jerked the sheet away from her and shoved it to the end of the bed. He pulled her close to him, trailing his fingertips across her shoulder, down her back, and along her spine. Ellie arched against him, catching her breath sharply. Her hands explored every inch of his skin that she could reach, touching. Memorizing.

"Pat, there's something I want to tell you," Ellie said softly, her hands resting on his chest. "I don't want you to think that I do this a lot—sleep with a lot of guys, I mean."

"I never thought you were that type of girl."

She smiled drowsily. "Good."

"Is that all you wanted to tell me?" he asked.

Sleep was beckoning her, and Ellie felt a warm, sinking feeling as if her body was settling deep into the mattress. "Yes," she mumbled, her head falling to his chest. "G'night, Pat."

"Goodnight, Ellie."

CHAPTER TWENTY-TWO

"*W*hen was the last time you saw Daniel?"

Olivia had been on the phone arguing with her mother for the past fifteen minutes. Her mom thought she should be at home instead of staying on Sullivan's Island, but Olivia was determined to stay at the beach house.

"Mom, I don't want to see him!"

"Well, you can't very well work on your marriage and get ready for the baby if you're in a different state, can you?"

Olivia groaned aloud, falling back across the couch. She didn't want to admit that she didn't want to leave the beach because she was having too much fun. She, Ellie, Ben, and Pat were thoroughly enjoying their summer. They were together almost every single night, and Olivia's friendship with Ben continued to develop. For the first time in months, she felt happy and free, and the last thing she wanted to do was go home to Daniel and all the unhappiness she had worked to leave behind.

"Are you even going to try to save your marriage anymore?" her mother wanted to know.

"Why is it up to *me* to save it?" Anger flared inside Olivia, and she sat up straight. "Why is it my responsibility? I can't convince Daniel to see a counselor, so what else can I do? Am I just supposed to accept that my life is forever bound to his now?"

"Sweetie, you and Daniel are having a baby together. That changes *everything*."

"Yes! It means that if I stay with him and have this baby with him, I'll be dealing with a husband who cannot understand my most basic needs while trying to raise a child. I'm not sure I can do that."

"I think you at least need to try."

Olivia stood up and paced back and forth across the living room. When she glanced out the window, she saw Ellie and Pat splashing in the waves. Ben was asleep in his beach chair, his hat covering his face to block the sun. Olivia had walked back to the house to use the bathroom and was just about to walk out the door again when her phone began to ring. Now she wished she hadn't bothered to answer it because the conversation was bringing her high spirits crashing down.

"What else can I try, Mom? I've pleaded—no, begged— Daniel to see a counselor. I've read every single book I can get my hands on, but nothing helps. He doesn't want to change, and I'm not sure how to make this work if he isn't willing to do anything!"

"I just feel like you're too far away from him, sweetie."

Olivia rolled her green eyes, clenching her fists tightly. "I don't want to come home. I'm happy and relaxed for the first time in months. I deserve this." As soon as she said the words, she realized how selfish she sounded, but she didn't care. Anyone, including her mother, who hadn't experienced what Olivia was going through would never be able to fully comprehend the frustration and futility she felt with Daniel.

"You said yourself you've read that lots of people can make marriages work and actually be happy, even when one of them has AS," her mother reminded her. "I'm just asking you to try and make that a possibility for you and Daniel. My first grandbaby doesn't need to be born into all this chaos and stress, so you need to figure this out soon."

"My stress levels are low here," Olivia said, inhaling deeply and trying to calm herself.

"That's not what I meant. You can't run away from your problems forever, Olivia. I know it's fun to retreat to the safety of the island and hide out with Ellie, but you're an adult. You can't avoid reality."

Olivia sighed loudly in response. She hated when her mother was right, and she knew her mother was right. She *was* running away from her problems. She was running away from Daniel.

"What if you invited him to the beach? Y'all could discuss the problems you're having on neutral ground. Would Ellie mind if he came?"

"Probably not." Olivia pinched the bridge of her nose, closing her eyes. Daniel at Sullivan's Island, invading their happy summer, was the last thing she wanted.

"Talk to her about it and then ask him to come," her mother urged her. "I think it's important that you do. People in town are starting to notice that you've been gone for a while."

"So? I don't care!"

"Don't use that tone with me, Olivia. I'm still your mother, and I'm offering my advice. You can take it or leave it. It's up to you, but I'm just offering my two cents."

OLIVIA WALKED BACK to the beach with a dark scowl on her face. She doubted Daniel would even be interested in coming to the beach; after all, he didn't like the beach in general. Still, her mother's words echoed in her head, and guilt washed over Olivia. No matter the state of their marriage, Daniel was still her husband and the father of the child she was carrying. Her shoulders slumped when she acknowledged that her reluctance stemmed at least partly from the time she was spending with Ben. Daniel's visit would mess that up, and she worried that Ben might not want to hang out with her anymore if he were reminded that she was married.

"What's wrong with you?" Ellie wanted to know when Olivia walked down to the water. "You look miserable."

"My mom thinks that I need to spend some time with Daniel because there's no way we'll ever figure everything out if we aren't together. She says I'm running away from my problems."

Ellie nodded. "I mean, you are kinda, aren't you? Isn't that why you were so eager to come? Isn't that why you came back after you went home the first time?"

"I know, I know! She's right, and I'm wrong. But I don't want to go home."

"So what do you want to do?"

"She suggested I invite him here, if you don't mind his coming," Olivia said, halfway hoping that Ellie wouldn't want Daniel to visit.

"That's fine with me," Ellie said, smiling. "It's a good idea, I think. You two can talk about things, and it's such a relaxing place. Maybe you'll both be more at ease."

Olivia sighed, wrinkling her nose. "Fine. I'll ask him when he calls tonight."

"Sounds good to me. We'll have fun. Maybe we can do a double date."

"Ugh." Olivia smacked her forehead with her palm. "This is going to be a nightmare."

To OLIVIA'S AMAZEMENT, Daniel agreed to come to the beach for a weekend. Ellie insisted they would all have a good time, and Olivia's mother seemed somewhat appeased. Somehow, Charlie found out that Daniel was planning to drive over and invited himself back to the beach. Olivia sensed that Ellie was reluctant for him to come back, but Charlie somehow persuaded Ellie to agree. Her brother could be such a pest sometimes and for Ellie's sake, Olivia wished Charlie would give her space. He seemed determined to insert himself into their summer plans.

Daniel and Charlie drove over on Friday afternoon. Ellie already had plans with Pat—Olivia suspected she had made the plans with the intention of avoiding Charlie—and she was gone for the night. At Olivia's suggestion, Daniel had booked a table for them at one of the nicer restaurants on nearby Isle of Palms, and she was trying to psyche herself up for a weekend with him.

When they arrived, Daniel greeted her affectionately, and she wondered if he had missed her. For a brief moment, Olivia remembered why she'd fallen in love with him. He was dressed impeccably in well-pressed khaki shorts, a collared shirt, and dock shoes, and he was carrying a beautiful bouquet of pink roses for her.

"Welcome," she greeted him and Charlie. "Come on in."

"Is Ellie already gone?" Charlie wanted to know, glancing around the house when they walked through the back door.

"Yep," Olivia said brusquely. "I need to put these flowers in a vase."

While Charlie quickly made himself at home, Olivia watched as Daniel studied the house. She knew he was often uncomfortable in unfamiliar places, but he had been to the beach house once before.

"Not much has changed since you were here a few years ago, has it?" she asked him.

"No, not really," he said, a hint of relief in his voice.

"What time is our reservation?"

Daniel glanced at his watch. "It's at seven."

Olivia sighed. Their small talk was awkward, and she

wondered what they were possibly going to have to talk about at supper. It was, she decided, going to be a very long weekend.

AFTER DINNER, Olivia and Daniel returned to the beach house. Charlie was still out—he had some friends in town, and he'd gone to meet them somewhere on Shem Creek—and they had the house to themselves. Olivia suggested they walk on the beach, but Daniel didn't want to get sandy so close to bedtime. He detested the shelly sand that clung persistently to his skin.

Once Daniel shot down her first idea, Olivia asked if he wanted to sit out on the porch. With a shrug, he finally agreed, and she followed him, disheartened. They hadn't discussed much at dinner besides what she and Ellie had been doing for the past few weeks. Aside from a few remarks about the restaurant and food, Daniel hadn't contributed much to the conversation. He hadn't even mentioned the baby except indirectly when he asked how she was feeling. She'd seen his lips moving slightly several times, and she knew he was talking to himself. She hoped no one seated around them noticed.

"I was hoping we could talk," Olivia said once they were seated outside on the wicker couch.

Daniel stiffened visibly. "About what?"

Olivia shifted in her seat, clasping her hands in her lap. "Do you remember what I told you before I left for the beach earlier this summer?"

"Yes," Daniel said after thinking about it for a moment.

"Have you thought about that at all?" Olivia searched his face for some expression, some hint of emotion that might betray his feelings, but she saw nothing.

"Not really. It doesn't really matter anymore, does it?"

"Doesn't really matter?" Olivia echoed, her tone a pitch higher than normal. "Why doesn't it matter?"

"We're having a baby now, so that changes everything,

right?" Daniel blinked blankly at Olivia as if was the most obvious thing.

"It changes a lot, but it doesn't change the issues we're having with our marriage," Olivia exclaimed. "A baby won't fix everything, Daniel!"

As soon as she raised her voice, she saw Daniel begin to shut down. It was as if he was closing in on himself, hiding away in his own body.

"You can't do this alone," he said quietly.

Olivia laughed absurdly. "Oh, you think I can't raise this child on my own? I can if I decide to!"

Daniel shook his head. "You're being irrational."

"So what?" Olivia stood up suddenly and threw her hands up in the air. She began to pace back and forth in front of the couch. "Daniel, I tried to give us some space so both of us could think. I thought that with me gone, maybe you'd realize how serious I am about this. I hoped you would realize that I was right, and that we had some serious issues to work out. But clearly you haven't!"

"We don't have issues!" Daniel insisted, clenching his fists tightly in his lap. "Why do you keep saying that?"

"Because we do!" Olivia was almost shouting now, and she wondered if any of the neighbors were listening. All of her pent up rage and frustration was finally boiling over. "I was miserable at home! And you don't care! You work nearly sixty hours a week, and when you are home, you barely talk to me. You get angry with me if something doesn't go exactly as you planned, and you make me feel as if it's all my fault!"

Daniel stood up stiffly and walked towards the door. "I don't want to argue with you."

"You *never* listen to me!" Olivia called after him. "You avoid the topic. You shut me out and give me the silent treatment when you don't get your way. This is *not* what you promised me when you proposed to me. You're nothing like the person I married. I want *that* man back!"

"I'm going to bed," Daniel said, shaking his head. "I don't understand why you think we're having problems. Everything is fine! I don't understand why you're so angry."

HE TURNED and walked into the house, leaving Olivia on the porch, fuming. She paced back and forth across the wooden boards, listening to the waves crashing outside on the beach. The rational side of her brain told her she needed to calm down because the stress wasn't good for the baby, but she couldn't seem to relax.

Shaking her head, Olivia forced herself to take long, deliberate breaths. A few hours earlier, she had been hoping Daniel might arrive with a newfound devotion and promises to work through their marital problems, but he continued to insist that he didn't understand why she was so unhappy. She knew she wasn't crazy, and that it wasn't all in her head.

Finally she sank back down onto the couch, pulling a pillow against her chest. Olivia had never felt more alone in her life, and her body shook with uncontrollable sobs. She felt as if she was living in a nightmare and calling out for help with no one to hear her. She wished Ellie was home to sit with her and comfort her. Daniel's words played over and over in her head, and the more she thought about them, the more she knew what choice she needed to make. Daniel had deceived her somehow—manipulated her into marrying him by pretending to be someone he wasn't—and then transformed into a total stranger. He didn't think she could handle raising a baby on her own and although Olivia had doubts about her abilities, she could do anything she set her mind to. She sat up a little straighter and rubbed her eyes with the back of her hand. She didn't have her plan all figured out, but for the first time all summer, Olivia knew what she was going to do.

At the end of the summer, when she went home, Olivia was going to file for divorce.

❀

OLIVIA WOKE up in Ellie's bed the next morning. She had refused to share a bed with Daniel the night before, and since Ellie was staying over at Pat's, she decided to take her friend's bed for the night. She heard water running downstairs and the familiar clink of the glass carafe sliding into the coffeemaker. Reluctantly, she crawled out of bed and shuffled sleepily down the hallway to the bathroom.

Ellie was filling the coffee pot with water when Olivia walked into the sunny kitchen.

"Good morning," Ellie greeted her cheerfully. "I was surprised I got home before y'all woke up."

Olivia scooted onto one of the barstools and massaged her temples. "I needed rest. Last night didn't exactly go well."

"Oh no." Ellie set the coffee pot down. "What happened? Did things go badly at dinner?"

"Dinner was fine, but we had this huge argument when we got home, and I ended up sleeping in your room." Olivia started to cry all over again, and she wiped the tears away with the hem of her nightshirt.

"Aww, I'm so sorry. You should've called me. Pat would've brought me home, and I could've..." Ellie thought for a moment. "Well, I'm not sure what I could've done, but I wish you hadn't been alone."

"It's fine. There was no need for that."

Ellie frowned uncertainly. "I had hoped your night went better. Pat and Ben are coming over for brunch and spending the day at the beach."

With that, Olivia folded her arms on the counter in front of her and buried her face in them. "Could this weekend get any more complicated?" she sniffled loudly.

"Sorry," Ellie said, putting the carafe back in its spot on the coffee maker. "Cheer up. We'll have fun."

ELLIE HAD STOPPED by the grocery store on her way back to the beach house and picked up all the essentials for brunch. Olivia's eyes widened when she saw three packs of bacon, pancake mix, fresh fruit, orange juice and champagne.

"You thought of everything, didn't you?" she asked, shaking her head. She would never understand where Ellie found the time and energy to do everything she did.

"Yep. I woke up really hungry, so I decided to cook for everyone."

Olivia glanced at the clock on the oven. "What time will Ben and Pat be here?"

"In about half an hour. They both wanted to get showers first."

Half an hour didn't give Olivia much time to clean up, but she hurried upstairs to change clothes, brush her teeth, and brush some dry-shampoo through her hair. While she hadn't explicitly told her friend not to invite Ben over while Daniel was visiting, she'd hoped Ellie would think of the potential awkwardness it might create. Now Olivia found herself preparing to have brunch with both her husband and the man she'd been flirting with for the last few weeks.

Daniel woke up and showered. He didn't say much to Olivia when he saw her, and she remembered how awful their fight had been. So much for her mom's wish of their working out a compromise on neutral ground.

By the time she went back downstairs, Charlie was awake and nursing a cup of coffee. A few moments later, Pat and Ben knocked on the back door, and the kitchen was suddenly full. For the briefest of moments, Olivia forgot that Daniel was in the house. She immediately began filling glasses with orange juice for mimosas while Ellie tended two skillets of sizzling bacon. But when Daniel's footsteps sounded on the staircase, Olivia was suddenly jolted back to the reality of the situation.

"Good morning, Daniel," Ellie called out cheerfully. "I'm cooking breakfast for everyone." She quickly introduced Pat and Ben to Daniel, and he shook their hands stiffly, his greetings subdued. Olivia watched Ben's face for any sort of reaction when Ellie explained that Daniel was Olivia's husband, but he didn't seem unnerved.

"Alright, who all wants a mimosa?" Olivia asked, holding up the bottle of champagne.

"Me," Charlie said, holding up his hand. "Make it a glass of champagne with just a dash of OJ, will ya?"

At that moment Olivia's gaze met Daniel's. In that fraction of a second, she saw his eyes widen and his mouth begin to open. She knew what he was about to say but was helpless to stop him.

"You know you can't drink champagne when you're pregnant, right?"

CHAPTER TWENTY-THREE

*I*t was still dark outside when Ellie woke up on Sunday morning. Pat was sleeping soundly beside her, and she kissed his cheek before she slipped out of the bed and tip-toed downstairs. Everyone else in the house—Olivia, Daniel, and Charlie—was still asleep, and Ellie jumped at the chance for a brief moment of solitude.

Daniel's visit hadn't exactly gone as Olivia had hoped. Neither he nor Charlie could understand why she was angry that he'd announced her pregnancy the day before, but Ellie knew it was because Olivia hadn't told Ben yet. Ellie had seen the look on Ben's face when Daniel's words sank in, and though he had stuck around for breakfast, he left soon after the dishes were clear, saying he'd forgotten he promised to help his parents with something. Ellie felt sorry for both Olivia and Ben. Yes, Olivia should have been upfront with Ben about her pregnancy, but she hated to see her friend hurting.

Ellie had her own problem to worry about, though: Charlie. She had allowed him to come because he insisted Daniel would be more comfortable with a friend in the house, but since his arrival, he'd been almost openly hostile towards Pat all day. Pat had the patience of a saint, and he didn't seem to notice, but Ellie did think he stuck a little closer to her side all day. Charlie had been outright flirting, trying to tickle her on the beach, grabbing her around the waist and throwing her into the waves; Ellie was furious at him. Part of her wished Pat was prone to jealousy so that he would demand Charlie quit flirting, but she didn't foresee that happening.

ELLIE WAS SITTING on the front steps, overlooking the dunes and the beach, when movement down the beach captured her attention. She sat up a little straighter, craning her neck. Blue Turtle Team shirt, red bucket—the woman kneeling in the dunes was definitely a Turtle Lady. Ellie jumped to her feet and hurried down the boardwalk.

"Do we have a new nest?" she called to the woman.

"It sure looks like it," the woman replied, smiling graciously. She pointed to the wide tracks in the sand. "I just called it in, so another Turtle Team member will be here shortly to probe for eggs."

Ellie clapped her hands together, childishly delighted. "Do you mind if I stay and watch?"

"No, of course not."

SHE WAITED EAGERLY until another Turtle Lady emerged from the nearest beach access, carrying the signature red bucket of the Island Turtle Team. The two women worked quickly to find the nest, using a long probe to gently poke the sand in the area the turtle had disturbed. When the woman's probe slipped easily into the sand, she nodded confidently.

"The nest is right here," she told the woman who'd found the tracks. "Time to dig it up."

Mesmerized, Ellie knelt beside them as they scooped handfuls of sand away until they finally unearthed the ping-pong shaped eggs buried in the sand.

"Look at all of them," Ellie exclaimed, her words barely more than a breath.

"The tide rarely comes up this high," the second Turtle Lady said. "We won't need to move this nest, but let's count it quickly and close it back up."

After the women hastily counted the eggs in the chamber, documenting the number for the Department of Natural Resources, they covered it with sand and erected the familiar wooden stakes and orange tape around the nest

"I'll keep an eye on it," Ellie told them. "I'm staying here for the summer, and I already check that nest over there every day."

The second member of the Turtle Team looked at Ellie and then at the beach house she'd pointed at. "Are you staying with Jim Wharton?"

"In his house," Ellie said. "He's my uncle, and I'm house-sitting for him this summer."

"You're the one he's always talking about," the woman surmised, finally smiling. "The one who loves the sea turtles."

Ellie nodded. "Yes ma'am, that's right."

"We appreciate what you do," the woman said. "I'm Betty, and this is Grace. We're members of the Island Turtle Team."

"I guessed as much."

"Here." Betty handed Ellie a business card out of her pocket. "If you notice anything with this nest or any others, don't hesitate to call me."

"I won't." Ellie took the card eagerly. It was the closest she might ever get to becoming an official member of the Island Turtle Team.

WHEN SHE TURNED to walk back to the house, she saw Olivia walking along the boardwalk towards the beach.

"What's wrong?" Ellie asked when they reached each other.

Olivia sank down onto the steps at the end of the boardwalk, shaking her head. "This weekend has just been a disaster."

Ellie sat down next to Olivia. "I can't disagree with you there. I swear, Charlie is pushing every single one of my buttons."

"I asked him to cool it, but he's in one of his moods," Olivia said. "Sorry."

"It's okay," Ellie shrugged. "They're leaving this afternoon."

"I know, and I'm glad. I feel suffocated with Daniel around."

"Have you heard from Ben?" Ellie was hesitant to ask the question, but she was also curious to know how he was taking the news.

"No," Olivia said in a very small voice. "I know I shouldn't care, but I do. I really like him. Not in the way you like Pat or anything, but I really enjoy spending time with him. I know it's not right, but I think I'm beyond caring at this point. Besides, I've made up my mind."

"You have?" Ellie's eyes widened.

"I want a divorce," Olivia said simply. "I cannot be married to Daniel anymore."

EVEN THOUGH CHARLIE and Daniel were planning to leave that afternoon, they spent the morning on the beach. Charlie was starting to grate on Pat's nerves, and Ellie could tell his patience was wearing thin. She couldn't wait for Charlie to leave; he hadn't been kidding when he said he wasn't going to give up, but Ellie wished that he would try to be a little more discreet. She kept telling herself he would leave soon, and life at the beach house would go back to the way it had been before Daniel and Charlie arrived, but the last few hours of their stay seemed to drag by.

They had been on the beach for nearly three hours when Ellie returned to the house to grab some chips and dips for them to snack on. When she emerged from the pantry, Charlie was standing in the kitchen, clearly waiting for her. She gasped loudly.

"Charlie! You scared me!"

"Sorry," he apologized. "I wanted to talk to you alone for a few minutes."

Ellie sighed loudly. "What now, Charlie? You've already made everything awkward this weekend, you've been rude to Pat, and now you want to talk to me alone? What's up?"

"Ellie, I'm sorry for the way I've acted all weekend," Charlie said, walking towards her and taking her hands in his. She pulled them away immediately, shaking her head at him.

"Charlie, what is this about?"

"I love you, Ellie Taylor," he told her. "I want to spend the rest of my life with you. I know you don't think I could make you happy, but I know I could, if you'd just let me."

Ellie took a step back, trying to put some distance between them, but Charlie stepped towards her again. "I've already told you I'm not interested, Charlie," she said firmly. "I should never have gotten your hopes up this spring—"

Charlie darted forward, trying to plant a kiss on Ellie's mouth. She pushed him away roughly, her eyes flashing angrily.

"Charlie Tanner, what the hell are you doing?"

"Pick me, Ellie. Don't pick that stupid fiddle player over me. It'll never last."

Ellie shrank back as if he'd struck her. "You don't know that!"

"Oh come on, El. It's so obvious he's only spending time with you so he can sleep with you and spend half his summer living at the beach."

For once, Ellie had had enough. She slapped Charlie across the face, hard. The sound of her palm striking his cheek echoed in the quiet house. His blue eyes darkened angrily, but he didn't flinch.

"Shut. Up," she told him angrily. "You have come to stay in *my uncle's* house twice this summer, but you're still so rude. You have no right to lecture me about Pat. You don't even know him!"

"I know his type," Charlie snapped.

"Listen to me, Charlie," Ellie said, enunciating every word so there was no misunderstanding. "You and I are not getting back together. Not ever. And don't you dare insult Pat again, understand? I have known you all my life, but I have never seen you act like such a jerk as you have this weekend. I had really hoped we could just stay friends and hang out like we used to, but you've made it clear to me that that will never work."

Charlie backed away. He ran his hands through his hair and glared at her. "I'm right, and I know it. That stupid Irish dude is just trying to get in your pants, and he succeeded, I guess. When he turns out to be everything I said he was, don't come running to me. I'm done with you."

He stormed out the back door, the screen door slamming shut behind him. Ellie slumped against the wall, emotionally drained. Yes, she had blatantly rejected his profession of love for her and his attempt to kiss her, but she never would have expected him to be so nasty. He knew she and Pat were dating, so why had he tried to kiss her? She felt the tiniest bit of remorse for slapping him, but not enough that she would ever apologize to him. Trying to mentally stabilize herself, she squared her shoulders and looked up.

Pat was standing in the doorway of the screened porch, watching her. His expression was unreadable.

"You okay?" he wanted to know.

"How long have you been there?"

He shrugged. "When Charlie followed you up to the house, I knew he was trying to undermine me."

Ellie laughed wryly. "You weren't wrong. He had a lot of things to say."

"He's lucky you slapped him. I was thinking about punching him," Pat muttered. "Good thing he went out the back door or I might've."

"So you heard everything?"

"Yep."

"I swear, I didn't say anything to lead him on. The last time he was here, I tried to tell him I didn't want to get back together." Ellie sank into one of the living room chairs. "But he just refuses to hear me."

"I'd be pretty upset if I thought I lost you," Pat said quietly.

Ellie looked up at him. "I feel like I'm surrounded by all this drama and that at some point, you'll have had enough of it and bail."

"Nope," Pat shook his head. "I told you before—I'm not going anywhere."

She smiled warmly, longing to tell him the depth of her feelings for him, but she wasn't sure the moment was right.

"Charlie just drove off in a hurry, so he probably won't be back for a while," Pat said, holding out his hand to her. "Let's go back to the beach, okay? Don't let him ruin your day."

Ellie took his hand. "You're right."

Pat pulled her to her feet and kissed her, long and slow, as if reminding her how she felt about him. "And for the record," he said when he pulled back, "I really don't like that guy."

CHAPTER TWENTY-FOUR

*W*hen Daniel left, Olivia finally felt as if she could take a deep breath again. His presence made her anxious and tense, and when he'd blurted out her secret to Ben, the happy little bubble she'd created for herself at the beach house had been popped. She had created a haven of sand, sunshine, and serenity for herself, but seeing him—arguing with him—had brought her crashing back into reality. Realizing he was the same Daniel who had no idea what it was about their relationship that disturbed her, that he literally could not understand—would never be able to understand, for that matter—forced her abruptly back into reality. Nothing had changed in their relationship. And nothing would ever change.

And to top it all off, she was certain her friendship with Ben was over; after all, how could he ever trust or respect her again? She was sure he felt deceived. And he had been. Olivia didn't know exactly what she and Ben meant to each other. She had met him for lunch a few times near his office, seen a movie with him, and spent countless hours in his company while they hung out with Ellie and Pat. Nothing they had said or done had been particularly romantic or even suggestive of deeper feelings, but

Olivia felt an unexpected connection with him. Daniel and Olivia had grown up knowing one another, but Ben knew her only as an adult. She felt as if that automatically made him take her a little more seriously, and she liked that.

Ben was, Olivia had decided soon after she met him, exactly the type of man she would want to date when she divorced Daniel. He was handsome, kind, and well-mannered. But as the weeks had worn on and they'd been thrown together more and more often, she realized she would like to date *him* when she divorced. She had no idea if it would turn into anything serious, but she wanted to find out. She wanted to know what it was like to hold his hand, to kiss him, and to snuggle up next to him on the couch and watch a movie. The few times that their hands or bodies had brushed, Olivia had felt an intense longing—so strong she fought to resist it.

Somewhere in the midst of all her daydreaming, Olivia had forgotten to factor in her baby. It was as if her pregnancy were separate from everything else, including Ben. She had planned to wait until she was further along in her pregnancy before announcing the news to anyone other than close family and friends, and Ben hadn't been included in that list. Pat only knew because Ellie had told him in confidence.

But Ben certainly knew now. Olivia hadn't had a chance to talk to him about it before his hasty exit. She hadn't heard from him since which made her think maybe he *did* care about her as more than just a friend. But now she was afraid anything that might have started developing between them was ruined. She should've told him from the start. She should have been upfront about everything—her tumultuous marriage and her unexpected pregnancy—but it was too late for that. She wouldn't blame him if he never wanted to see her again. Flirting with a married woman was one thing, but a *pregnant* married woman was something else entirely.

· · ·

A WEEK after Daniel and Charlie had returned to Georgia, and Olivia still had neither seen nor heard from Ben. She asked Pat about it once, but he politely refused to get involved. All he would tell her was that Ben had been surprised by the news and was busy at work. Olivia moped around the house, scolding herself for having ever allowed herself to get emotionally involved with another man. What had she been thinking? Ellie had warned her, but she hadn't wanted to listen.

Finally, when ten days had passed without a word from Ben, Olivia texted and asked if he wanted to meet for coffee. To her relief, he agreed. The next morning, she got up early and drove into Mt. Pleasant to meet him at a local coffee shop.

As soon as she saw him, she noticed the stark change in his demeanor; he wasn't his usual smiling self. He seemed subdued, almost as though he didn't want to look at her. Without ordering anything, they simply sat down across from each other at a small table.

"Hi Ben," she spoke softly.

"Hi."

Olivia bit her lower lip nervously. "I owe you an apology. I'm sorry I didn't tell you I was pregnant. I never intended for you to get blindsided by the news in front of everyone like that. You left so suddenly Saturday that I didn't have a chance to ...."

"You're married," Ben interrupted her, "and you're having a baby. It's none of my business why you didn't tell me."

"Oh." Olivia looked away, his words a disappointment. She wished he would at least admit that he was bothered by the news. At least then she would know that he actually cared about her, even just a little bit.

"Listen, I know you're unhappy in your marriage, and that's how I justified spending so much time with you, but this," Ben shook his head, "this is different."

"I know." Olivia bowed her head, ashamed of herself. "I should've told you. I should've been up front about my pregnancy. When we met, I wasn't telling *anyone* and then, I don't know, I kept putting it off. And after spending more time together, it seemed more difficult and awkward to tell you."

"Olivia, I think you're great," Ben said sincerely, looking directly at her. "And a part of me wondered what might happen if we'd met when you were single..."

"I know." A few tears pooled in Olivia's eyes, and she brushed them away quickly. "I thought about that, too."

Ben reached out and put a hand over hers. "You're beautiful, Olivia, and sweet. You deserve a man who is going to appreciate that and make you happy, but you have to decide what you want before that can happen. When you do, please let me know. I want to see you again, but you've got a lot going on right now."

"You're right," she said. "It's not fair to you."

"It's not about me," Ben said sadly. "You need to figure out what will make you happy."

Olivia smiled tearfully, dabbing her eyes with a tissue.

Ben pulled his hand back and stood up. "I need to go. I'm not saying I don't want to see you again while you're here, because I do, but I need some time to think right now."

"I understand," Olivia managed to say.

He turned to leave, then looked back at her one last time, smiling. "Are you going to divorce him?"

"I am."

Ben nodded. "Good. He doesn't deserve you."

OLIVIA KNEW she was moping around the house, but she couldn't seem to drag herself out of her slump. She spent a lot of time curled up on the couch watching sad movies. Ellie tried to coax her outside, but she wasn't in the mood. Finally, when Olivia was still in her pajamas at noon three days after meeting

Ben at the coffee shop, Ellie stood in front of the television, blocking her view.

"You have to get off the couch and out of this house," she told Olivia sternly.

"I don't want to go anywhere," Olivia mumbled, holding a pillow against her chest. "I'm down in the dumps."

"I don't care." Ellie folded her arms across her chest and tipped her head to the side. "We're going out today to do a little self-care."

"Self-care?" Olivia perked up a little. "What do you mean?"

"We're going to get manicures and shop for clothes and window shop, or something like that," Ellie said. "So go take a shower because we're leaving in an hour."

"Fine." Olivia tossed one of the couch pillows aside and stood up reluctantly. "It seems I have no choice."

An hour later, Ellie and Olivia left the island. Olivia had only made minimal effort getting dressed; she had showered and then pulled her hair into a loose, messy bun. She had applied the barest minimum of makeup and chosen an easy outfit of denim shorts and a white tee. Ellie drove them through Mt. Pleasant, across the Ravenel Bridge, and into downtown Charleston. She parked in a huge garage and then ushered Olivia to a nearby nail salon where they picked out fun summer nail polish colors for their manicures. The manicurists convinced them to get pedicures as well, and Olivia had to admit that it *was* relaxing to lie in a massaging chair with her feet soaking in a bath of warm water. When their nails were completely dry, Ellie led Olivia down the street to a restaurant Pat had recommended; it didn't disappoint.

Ellie hadn't asked Olivia what transpired between her and Ben when they met for coffee, and Olivia appreciated that. Ellie had never been the type of friend to pry for information, even when she was dying to know. All through their meal, Ellie kept up a steady stream of chatter, talking about her upcoming semester, what she needed to purchase before classes began, and what she and Pat were planning for the rest of the summer. After lunch, Ellie suggested they walk through the City Market, and Olivia agreed eagerly. She loved browsing all the local crafts and artwork in the market, and they walked several blocks before reaching it.

Olivia's eye was immediately drawn to the beautiful sweet-grass baskets, Lowcountry Gullah creations. The larger ones were far out of her price range, but she found a smaller one that wasn't too expensive. Ellie was fascinated by the jewelry creations of a local artist who fused colorful glass with sand from local beaches. Olivia could clearly see that her friend wanted one of the necklaces, but they cost more than she was willing to spend, so she finally walked away empty-handed.

Finally, when the afternoon heat was nearly unbearable, the girls bought gelato from a local shop and walked down to the Waterfront Park that overlooked the Charleston Harbor. They sat on one of the last remaining benches to savor their frozen treats.

"Thanks for pushing me to get out," Olivia told Ellie. "I really needed someone to do that."

Ellie smiled proudly. "You're welcome. I couldn't bear to see you sit inside feeling sorry for yourself."

They sat in silence together for a few minutes before Olivia spoke again, ready to talk about her conversation with Ben.

"He said he needs some time to process everything," she said quietly. "Ben did."

"That's understandable."

"I know it is. And I could tell that finding out about my pregnancy was a real shock for him. I don't blame him for not wanting to get involved with a married, pregnant woman." Olivia sighed, using her napkin to catch a drip of melting gelato before it fell.

"Me either."

"He did say he still wants to see me this summer, but right now he feels like we need a little space."

Ellie frowned, setting down her gelato cup. "What are your feelings for Ben? Did anything happen between you two?"

Olivia shook her head. "No, but I feel like if I'd been single this summer, something might have."

"There's no way to ever know, though."

"I know." She sighed again. "I keep wondering if Ben will still be single when I'm divorced and have a baby. And if he is, will he still be interested in me? Would he want to take on me *and* a baby?"

"You can't start thinking about that right now," Ellie said softly. "You need to focus on you and your baby right now. Take care of everything at home first, and then we'll check on Ben's relationship status."

"I should've asked him if he would be interested in dating me when I have a baby," Olivia muttered. "I can't believe that didn't come up."

"Well, I don't think that's something either one of you can decide right now."

"I can't believe I'm going to be a single mom," Olivia said, shaking her head. "How am I going to manage?"

"You've got lots of people who love and encourage you, Liv. You're going to have plenty of help," Ellie assured her. "And you're a strong, tough woman. If anyone can do this, it's you."

"Thanks, El." Olivia hugged her friend, never more grateful for Ellie's presence. "Nothing about this summer is turning out the way that I thought it would."

Ellie laughed. "That's for sure!"

CHAPTER TWENTY-FIVE

*E*llie stared at her closet, wondering why it was always so difficult to decide what she should wear. Only a few options were actually suitable for supper with Pat's parents, and she finally narrowed it down to two different dresses.

"Olivia, which one of these looks better?" Ellie turned to her friend. Olivia was busy reading on the window seat, oblivious to Ellie's struggle. She looked up and tapped her chin thoughtfully with the highlighter she was using to underline sections of her book.

"I like the white one," she said. "You'll be cooler in that, too."

Ellie agreed. "You're right. I want to be as cool as possible. It feels like it's a million degrees outside."

"Why do you think I'm inside reading?"

ONCE SHE WAS DRESSED, Ellie swept her hair up into a high, loose ponytail before selecting a pair of gold-and-pearl seashell earrings to wear. She was nervous about meeting Pat's parents, even though he had assured her she had nothing to worry about.

Instead of meeting them at a restaurant, his parents had invited Ellie to have dinner at their house. A restaurant would have been more neutral ground, but Pat really wanted her to see his home.

"You look great," Olivia told her when she finished dressing and was applying a hasty spritz of perfume to her wrists.

"Thanks. I'm a little nervous. Is it obvious?"

"A little bit," Olivia admitted.

"I just really want Pat's parents to like me, you know?"

"They will," Olivia said, setting her book down in her lap. "What's not to like?"

"I don't know," Ellie shrugged. "What if they don't think I'm good enough for their son?"

Olivia rolled her eyes. "Don't be silly. They will *love* you, I promise. Just be yourself. And relax!"

"If you say so."

"You really like him a lot, don't you?"

"Yes," Ellie confessed. "I'm in love with him."

"What?" Olivia eyes grew wide as her mouth fell open in surprise. "When did this happen? Why didn't you tell me?"

Ellie sat down on the edge of the bed to slip on her sandals. "I don't know. It was so gradual, and then suddenly I just knew."

"That's so romantic," Olivia said, pressing a hand to her heart. "I'm so happy for you. You deserve this."

"Did you feel that way about Daniel when you first started dating him? Did you have a specific moment where you realized you were in love with him?"

Olivia thought for a moment and then shook her head. "No, I didn't. Daniel and I started dating when I was so young, and I guess it just seemed natural that we would get engaged and get married. I know I loved him, but maybe not in the same way that you love Pat. Mine was more of natural progression of affection, I feel like." She grimaced. "That sounds awful when I say it aloud."

"No, it doesn't," Ellie said. "Not at all."

"I do love him, you know," Olivia said sadly. "Sometimes, I find myself wishing that love was enough of a reason for me to stay married to him, but it's not. I need him to step up, or at least try to meet me halfway. If he would make an effort—even the smallest one—I would actually consider staying with him."

"I know you would." Ellie smiled comfortingly at her friend. She did believe Olivia loved Daniel. She had known them both from the first date till their first dance as husband and wife, and no one could deny that they had been crazy about each other.

"But you and Pat are perfect for each other," Olivia said, clearly trying to change the subject from her problems back to Ellie's happiness. "I told you he really liked you."

"I know you did," Ellie sighed. "Doubt still creeps in from time to time, though. I worry that I'm going to wake up and it'll have all been some wonderful dream."

"It's not a dream!"

"I know, but I can't help it! I mean, Charlie's the only boy who ever really expressed serious interest in me. Since him, I've only had occasional dates here and there, so I just keep thinking something's going to happen, and I'll find out Pat has another girlfriend or that sex is the only reason he's interested in me, like Charlie said."

Olivia crossed the room and took Ellie by the shoulders. "Pay no attention to my stupid brother. He shouldn't have said what he did, and you need to let it go. Pat took you on so many dates and hung out with you so much before he even stayed over for a night. Why can't you get it through that thick skull of yours that Pat has strong feelings for you?"

Olivia's words stuck with Ellie as Pat drove her to his parents' house. Why was it so hard for her to accept that he genuinely cared for her? Why couldn't she believe that someone as handsome and attractive as Pat would want to date her? She knew that with every passing month she'd been single after her freshman year breakup with Charlie, her self-confidence had been knocked down a notch. She had classes with lots of different guys, several of whom she was friends with or studied with regularly, but they always saw her as a friend or study partner—not a datable girl. She was the one they relied on for class notes and test study guides, the one they talked to about problems they were having with their girlfriends, or the one they went to when they needed help buying a gift for their mothers or grandmothers. She hated being that girl, and she wasn't sure how she'd become that girl. She knew several of the guys she studied with were simply spending time with her because they knew she could help them get a better grade. Pat was nothing like them, though. He had flirted with her almost from the first moment he set eyes on her, and he often told her how beautiful he thought she was. Not once did she feel as if he took any part of her for granted, and his respect was refreshing.

WHEN PAT PULLED into the driveway of his parents' house, Ellie's eyes widened into saucers. The O'Sullivans lived in large, two-story house in an affluent Mt. Pleasant neighborhood. A shiny black Land Rover was parked in the driveway, and Ellie spotted a Mercedes-Benz coupe in the garage.

"Wow!"

"What?"

"Your parents drive really nice cars," Ellie said, not wanting to make a big deal out of it.

Pat laughed "Oh yeah. Dad has worked for Boeing for years, and he's done really well for himself. Mom's pretty high up in hospital administration down at MUSC."

Ellie swallowed tightly. "It's a little intimidating."

"Nah." Pat took her hand and squeezed it tightly. "You're gonna be fine. C'mon, I'll take you around back. Dad's probably grilling." She followed Pat through a gate into the back yard.

"I'm home!" he hollered.

When they rounded the corner of the house, Ellie felt her mouth fall open. She was met with a pristinely landscaped yard. Despite the scorching summer heat, bright flowers were blooming all around the fence-line and the grass was a healthy, vibrant green. A tall oak tree towered in the the back corner on the yard, and she spotted the remnants of a treehouse—probably from Pat's childhood.

Sure enough, Pat's dad was standing at the grill. When he heard his son's voice, he turned, and Ellie instantly recognized the resemblance. Mr. O'Sullivan was merely an older, white-haired version of his son, and he smiled at her instantly.

"You must be Ellie," he said, extending his hand to her. "We're so glad you could come and have dinner with us."

His Irish accent was much stronger than Pat's, and Ellie knew she could listen to him talk for hours. "Thank you for inviting me," she told him, shaking his hand.

"I'm grilling steaks for all of us. How do you like yours cooked?"

"Medium well, please."

Mr. O'Sullivan nodded. "Got it." He nodded towards the house. "Pat, your mother's in the kitchen. Take Ellie inside and introduce her. I'll be in shortly."

"Yes, sir."

PAT'S CHILDHOOD home was two stories with a deck that overlooked the back yard. He led Ellie up the back porch steps and through the back door, which led directly into the kitchen. His mother was pulling a pan of baked potatoes out of the oven, and her face lit up when she saw her son.

"You're here," she exclaimed, putting the pan down on top of the stove and coming around the counter. She greeted her son with a warm hug and then turned to Ellie.

"Ellie, we're so glad you could come. Pat has told us so much about you, and we're so happy that we have a chance to meet you before you go back to school." She hugged Ellie, too. "I'm Carol," Mrs. O'Sullivan greeted her warmly.

"It's nice to meet you. Thanks for having me. You have a beautiful home."

"Thank you. We've lived here for more than ten years now, so we have a lot of good memories here."

Pat's mother was nothing like Ellie had imagined. For some reason, Ellie had pictured a smaller woman with a soft voice and quieter demeanor. Instead, Carol O'Sullivan was an elegant woman, tall and slender with the confidence of a practiced hostess. Ellie admired the simple linen sheath and strappy sandals she was wearing and the way her hair was twisted up into a simple bun.

"I just took the potatoes out of the oven, and I've got a salad," Carol went on, removing the salad from the fridge. "I wanted to eat outside, but it's so warm."

"One of the hottest days we've had so far this summer," Pat commented, taking a seat on one of the kitchen bar stools.

"Can I help you with anything?" Ellie asked.

"No, thank you, I think I have everything ready to go. We're just waiting on the steaks. Can I get you something to drink before we eat? Wine? Water?"

"I'm fine right now, thanks." Ellie sat down on a stool beside Pat, her eyes sweeping around the kitchen. She loved the O'Sullivan's house; everything about it was homey and welcoming. The fridge door was covered in photos, invitations, and greeting cards. On the counter beside the stove, an apple pie-scented candle was burning, and the table was set with pineapple-print placemats.

"So, tell me about yourself, Ellie," Carol urged her, sipping a glass of red wine as she leaned against the kitchen counter. "Pat says you're a student at the University of Georgia?"

"Yes ma'am, that's right. I'm majoring in Public Relations, and I have only two semesters left before I graduate. Well, one semester of classes, and then a semester-long internship."

"That's wonderful. Do you know what you'd like to do with your degree?"

"I'd like to work as a spokesperson for a company or government organization, ideally, but we'll see."

"Do you like UGA?"

"Oh yes! I love Athens, and I'll be so sad when I have to leave. I love everything about, especially college football!"

Carol's eyes lit up. "We love college football, too. We're Clemson season ticket holders."

"I think Pat told me that." Slowly, Ellie felt herself relaxing. When she had first seen the exterior of the house, she had worried that Pat's parents were going to be the stereotypical affluent Mt. Pleasant couple, but they seemed the polar opposite.

The back door opened, and Mr. O'Sullivan walked in, carrying a platter of steaming steaks. Ellie's mouth began to water, and she was suddenly ravenous.

"Let's eat," Pat said, rubbing his hands together eagerly. "I'm starving."

THEY ATE at the kitchen table rather than the formal dining room that Ellie glimpsed through a large archway. Their meal was delicious, and she soon forgot about her earlier nervousness. She found herself talking about her family, her uncle's beach house, and her hometown of Warner Robins.

"Tell them about the Lights Out Club," Pat said when his

mom was clearing their empty plates and bringing out a home-made peach cobbler for dessert.

"What's the Lights Out Club?" Mr. O'Sullivan wanted to know, leaning back in his chair a little. Both he and Pat had the same mannerisms, and Ellie loved watching them sit side-by-side.

"Um, well," Ellie began, blushing a little. She always felt self-conscious when she told people about it, concerned they might think it was silly. "The Lights Out Club is something my friends and I started when we were kids. One of the island Turtle Ladies found a nest near our beach house, and she educated us extensively on the importance of keeping our beaches clean and making sure we turn out the lights at night on the beachfront. I got really excited about it, and that night, I saw this house with all its lights on, so I marched up to the front door and politely told the vacationer staying there that he needed to turn his lights out."

"How did he take it?" Mrs. O'Sullivan wanted to know.

"Not very well," Ellie laughed. "He said I was trespassing and told me to get off the property. So I told him I was going to stand in his front yard by the street until he turned them off."

"Tell them what happened next," Pat said, grinning. She had shared the story with him weeks ago.

"He said if I didn't leave—and I was standing on the right-of-way—he was going to call the cops. And he did. They came and told him that I was right, and then they gave me and my friends a ride back to our beach house in the patrol car. That night, we formed our own little club, and I walk the beach every night I'm here to pick up trash or check for lights shining on the beachfront."

"Every night," Pat repeated proudly. "That's dedication."

"You still do this?"

"Yes, ma'am," Ellie said. "I've been doing a long time now.

My friends aren't quite as dedicated as I am, but they still go with me sometimes when they're here."

"It's good that you do that," Mr. O'Sullivan said. "A lot of people who aren't from here don't know the rules about the sea turtles and the lights on the beach."

WHEN THEY HAD FINISHED their hearty portions of cobbler and vanilla ice cream, Mrs. O'Sullivan began to gather up the dishes. Ellie began scraping food off the plates, but Pat's mother shooed her away.

"Let Pat give you a tour of the house, Ellie," she suggested.

Ellie's eyes lit up and she nodded eagerly. "Yes, I'd love that, if you're sure you don't need any help with the dishes."

"I'm sure," Mrs. O'Sullivan reassured her. "Let Pat show you around."

"Okay then." Ellie turned to Pat and winked impishly. "Do you have any photo albums I can look at? With pictures of you as a kid?"

"No!" Pat exclaimed. "Absolutely not."

"C'mon!" Ellie pleaded playfully.

"Do you want to see the house or not?"

"Okay, okay."

THE HOUSE WAS BEAUTIFULLY DECORATED in coastal décor, and Pat showed Ellie the den, formal living and dining room, and office. His old bedroom was in the back of the house, overlooking the back yard.

"I haven't changed it much since high school," he warned her, hesitating before he opened the door. "So don't laugh."

"Why would I laugh?"

Pat narrowed his eyes. "I don't know, but you might." He opened the door and let Ellie walk past him into the room.

Ellie's attention was captured immediately by the large number of trophies that lined many shelves in the room. "What are all these for?" she asked.

"Mostly fishing tournament trophies," he said. "I did a lot of fishing when I was younger. I was actually pretty good."

"First place, first place, first place," Ellie read off the plaques. "I'd say you were more than pretty good! All of these are first place trophies!"

Pat sat down on the edge of the bed, shrugging. "What can I say? I knew how to catch the big fish."

"Clearly."

"So, what do you think about my parents?'

"They're great. You look exactly like your dad, too, except for the white hair," Ellie laughed.

"Yeah, I've got that to look forward to," Pat grumbled, patting his dark curls ruefully.

Ellie studied the photos on Pat's desk—one of him and his parents on a cruise ship somewhere, one of him in Ireland, and one of him and Ben at their high school graduation. "Y'all look so young here," she said, pointing at a picture. "Just babies."

"That was almost six years ago now, so we were pretty young back then," Pat agreed.

Ellie sat down on the edge of the bed beside him, noting the tide charts on the bulletin board over the desk. On one wall, a large poster listed the different types of fish often caught off the South Carolina and Georgia coast. Another map showed the water depth in the ocean, rivers, and coves all around the Charleston area. "Do you think your parents like me?"

"Definitely. You're the only girl I've ever brought home to meet them since high school?"

"Really?" Ellie couldn't hide the surprise in her voice. "Why?"

"I don't know." Pat picked at piece of lint on the bedspread, and studied it intently. "I guess I always thought that when I brought a woman home, she would be someone I seriously cared about. No need to let them get attached to someone that they might not ever see again."

"And you feel confident that they'll see me again?" Ellie asked softly, scooting a little closer to him.

"Oh yes," Pat whispered. "I fully intend for them to see you again. A lot. You know that."

"Yes, but I like for you to say it. It makes me feel better about long-distance." Ellie leaned in and pressed a chaste kiss to his lips.

"When do I get to meet your parents?" Pat wanted to know.

"Well," Ellie said, scooting closer to him, "we do spend Thanksgiving on Sullivan's Island every year."

Pat wrapped his arms around her waist tightly, pressing her body tightly against his. "Is that right?"

"That's right."

Suddenly, Pat pushed Ellie back onto the bed and knelt over her, his lips only inches from hers. "Good. I can't wait to meet them."

"Yeah?"

He nodded. "Yeah." With that, he kissed her, his body flush against hers.

"Pat, stop!" Ellie whispered, pushing him away. "Not here!"

"Why not?" he laughed quietly.

"Because!" She tried to push him away, but he was too heavy. Instead of budging, he began to tickle her. Ellie was very ticklish, but she tried to stifle her giggles.

"Please, stop," she begged him, laughing until tears ran down her face.

"I will, but you have to kiss me. All I want right is to kiss my girlfriend. Is that so much to ask?"

Ellie stilled beneath him, her eyes wide. "I'm your girlfriend?" He had never called her his girlfriend before, and it felt like a monumental moment between them. Her heart ached with love for him, and she felt the words on the tip of her tongue. She was still too scared to tell him, though.

"I sure hope so."

A wide smile spread across Ellie's face, and she looped her arms around his neck lazily. "Alright then, where were we?"

CHAPTER TWENTY-SIX

One morning, Olivia woke up and realized that August was only a few days away. Somehow, without her realizing it, the entire summer had flown by. Ellie had to return to college in a couple weeks, and Olivia would go back to Warner Robins, to an uncertain future. She lay in bed, wondering how she would go about finding a divorce lawyer. What would her first steps be? Would she and Daniel continue to live together? How would they split everything up? When they married, Daniel had made sure that everything they had—cars, bank accounts, insurance—were all in both their names. Olivia frowned; Daniel was the sole provider, and she was a full-time student and wife. Would lawyers decide that she didn't deserve half of everything. How would they work out custody of the baby? Daniel wouldn't be able to care for a newborn on his own, but Olivia didn't want to deny him time with their child. She wished there were a way they could just continue to live in the same house, but as roommates and not husband and wife. She would be free to date and find love somewhere else, but she wouldn't have to leave her home.

Olivia loved her little house. When Daniel proposed and

they started planning their wedding, Olivia had immediately started thinking about how she would decorate each room of the house he'd purchased only a few months earlier. She had transformed the ultimate bachelor pad into a warm, welcoming country-chic house, and she was proud of how well it had turned out. Most of the furniture she'd added had been purchased from thrift shops and refurbished. She had painted the walls and trim and planted an assortment of flowers and shrubs all around the front porch. If only she had spent more time with Daniel and less time thinking about the color of the bedspread, Olivia thought to herself. She glanced at her phone, checking to see what time it was. It was past seven, and she knew Ellie was probably awake already, having breakfast on the screened porch. Reluctantly, she rolled out of bed and headed down the hallway towards the stairs.

"Can you believe the summer is almost over?" Olivia asked, shaking her head. She was sitting at the small table on the porch, sipping a cup of hot tea, and Ellie was sitting next to her, eating a strawberry Pop-Tart.

"No," Ellie scowled darkly. "I've been trying not to think about it, actually."

"Have you and Pat talked about what will happen when you go back to school?"

Ellie leaned back in her chair. "Yes. We're going to do long distance until I graduate."

"And then?"

"And then I'll try to find a job in this area," Ellie said confidently. "I'm sure there will be some sort of opening for me somewhere. At least I hope there will be."

"I'm sure you'll find something," Olivia assured her. "I've seen your resume, and it's impressive. Once you complete your internship, you'll have more to add to it, too."

Ellie sighed, setting down her glass of milk. "What about you? Have you told Daniel about your decision yet?"

"No," Olivia shook her head sadly. "I know I need to, but I'm not sure how to go about it." She took a long drink of her tea. "Would writing a letter be too cowardly?"

"Yes!"

"I thought so." Olivia propped her chin in the palm of her hand and rested her elbow on the table, staring out at the ocean. "However I decide to tell Daniel, the second thing I'll need to do is find a lawyer," she told Ellie. "But I don't want it to be a nasty divorce. I wish we could just calmly go our separate ways."

Ellie ate the last bite of her breakfast pastry. "I hope y'all can avoid that, too. Hopefully you can both be amicable, if only for the sake of your baby."

"I feel like such a terrible mother already," Olivia admitted quietly, looking down at her hands. "I mean, I'm going to have a baby and be divorced when he or she is born. That's not fair to the baby."

"That's an unfair thing to say, Liv," Ellie said, placing a hand on Olivia's. "You're already a wonderful mother. I mean, look how much you've been reading and trying to learn about babies this summer. You've been eating cleanly and drinking plenty of water. You're a poster child for pregnancy. And this baby will come into the world having two loving parents. Sure, they may not still be married to each other, but your baby will still get to know his or her father. That's what you need to remember."

"Thanks. I'll try," Olivia said. "I'm also worried what people at home will say when the news gets out."

"Puh-lease!" Ellie waved Olivia's concern away. "They might talk about it for a week or two, tops, but then everyone's going to get caught up in throwing you showers and trying to make sure you have everything you need. Pretty soon some other piece of juicy gossip will come to light, turning your divorce and new baby into old news."

"I'm going to need you to come home from school more often," Olivia laughed. "You're so good at saying just the right thing."

"You can always call me, you know."

AFTER THEIR EARLY MORNING CONVERSATION, Olivia and Ellie decided it was too hot for the beach, so they drove into Mt. Pleasant to see a movie. It was a few minutes past noon when the movie ended, so they grabbed a quick bite at a nearby restaurant and then spent over an hour shopping at several different stores in town. Around two-thirty, they headed back to the beach house, reaching the causeway just as a large sailboat was slipping down the Atlantic Intracoastal Waterway, approaching the Ben Sawyer Bridge. The bridge swung to the side to allow the boat to pass through, and Ellie slowed the car and came to a stop behind a line of cars.

"We're gonna be here for a few minutes," she sighed. "There's another boat behind this one, and they're both moving at a snail's pace."

"I'm in no rush," Olivia said, looking down at her phone. "It's not as if we have anything we absolutely *have* to do. Ugh! It's going to be weird to go home and have all the usual obligations again."

"I know." Ellie wrinkled her nose. "I have to go back to classes and exams and studying in the—" Ellie's words were cut short by the sound of squealing tires behind them, and she jerked her head around to look over her shoulder.

The impact of the collision was violent, shoving Ellie's sedan forward into the truck idling in front of them. Olivia and Ellie were thrown forward, and Olivia's seatbelt dug into her chest as it locked tightly. The sound of crunching metal was almost deafening, and both airbags deployed with a loud popping noise.

When the dust settled, Olivia blinked slowly, dazed from the crash. She stared down at the airbag in front of her, expanded into her lap. *I've never actually seen one of these deployed,* she thought to herself. Steam poured from underneath the hood of Ellie's car. The front end seemed to be crumpled against the rear of the truck in front of them, and the windshield was a spider-web of cracks.

"Ellie?" she called. "Are you hurt?"

No response.

"Ellie?!" Again, no response. Panic crept in, and Olivia groped frantically for her seatbelt.

"I'm okay," Ellie finally mumbled, her voice weak. "Are you alright?"

Olivia looked down at her arms and legs. Nothing was visibly broken and she didn't see any blood, but her chest hurt from the restrictive seatbelt and when she turned to look at Ellie, her neck throbbed in protest. "I think so," she said. "But I hurt in some places."

"Me too."

Someone opened Olivia's door and knelt beside the car. "Are you okay, sweetie?" the woman asked anxiously. "Are either of you hurt?"

Olivia shook her head, still disoriented. One minute, she had been checking her Facebook account, and then suddenly they were sandwiched between two vehicles on the causeway.

"I'm calling 9-1-1," a man standing behind the woman said, holding a cell phone to his ear.

"I'm a nurse," came another voice. "Don't let them move! They need to be checked out by the EMTs."

"My neck hurts." Olivia's hand drifted down to her stomach, and she felt the faintest twinge in her pelvic area. "Tell them I'm pregnant," she said, closing her eyes and breathing a soft prayer for the safety of her baby.

. . .

WITHIN A FEW MINUTES, the police department, fire department, and EMS arrived. Immediately, the EMTs began evaluating Olivia and Ellie. Gradually, Olivia became more lucid, as though waking from a nap, hearing seemingly distant voices and other noises only to eventually realize they were close by. She became increasingly aware of her surroundings. Half a dozen people had offered their assistance, and they were standing nearby, talking to the police about the accident.

"Ma'am, someone said you're pregnant," one of the EMTs said. "Is that right?"

Olivia nodded weakly. "Yes." She sat still while he fastened a brace around her neck so she couldn't move it.

"How far along?"

"Sixteen weeks." Next to her, she could hear someone talking low and soothingly to Ellie, and she thought that she could hear her friend crying.

"Are you in any pain? Are you having any contractions?"

"No. A little at first, but not now."

"We're going to take you and get you checked out," the EMT said. "Just to make sure everything is okay with you and your baby."

"How is Ellie?" Olivia wanted to know.

"I'm okay, Olivia," Ellie said, her voice shaky. "Just a little banged up. Don't worry about me. I'll see you at the hospital."

ON THE SHORT, ten-minute drive to the nearest hospital, Olivia answered at least a dozen routine questions. One of the EMTs, the same man who had first checked on her, cleaned some cuts and minor burns on her hands—all a result of the airbag deployment.

"Is my baby going to be okay?" she asked anxiously. "Did the airbag hurt the baby?"

"We're going to check all of that out as soon as we get to the hospital, sweetheart. We've got an OBGYN waiting to see you."

"Was my friend okay?"

"I'm not sure what her injuries were, but she looked like she was going to be fine."

"Thank goodness." Olivia leaned her head back against the stretcher. She looked down at her hands and realized that they were trembling violently. Tears filled her eyes, but she couldn't explain why. "I don't know what's wrong with me," she sobbed.

"It's okay," the EMT assured her. "Take some deep breaths for me—you need to stay calm."

THE NEXT TWO hours passed in a blur for Olivia. In the hospital, several nurses and the ER doctor examined her. In no time at all, the on-call OBGYN came to check her out. He conducted an exam and ultrasound before assuring her that her baby was fine and healthy—not at all affected by the accident. He did, however, advise that she stay overnight in the hospital, purely for observation and peace-of-mind. While she waited for a room, one of the nurses poked her head around the curtain into the semi-private area.

"Your friend is here, honey—the one who was in the accident with you. Can I let her in?"

"Yes, of course."

Ellie ducked around the curtain, and Olivia eyes widened when she saw the gauze bandage taped over her friend's forehead. "Are you okay?"

"It's worse than it looks," Ellie said, smiling bravely. "I have a few stitches and a very sore collarbone, but otherwise, I'm fine. Just really stiff." She sat down on the edge of the hospital bed, and Olivia hugged her gently.

"What about you?" Ellie asked. "How are you and the baby?"

"We're fine." Olivia rested her head back against the pillows. "But the doctor who examined me thinks I should stay overnight for observation, just in case I start having any issues. So I'm stuck here for tonight."

"Wow." Ellie shook her head. "The police have already talked to me. I think the guy who hit us was texting and driving or something. Apparently he didn't see that we had stopped. The cop I talked to said he didn't even hit the brakes until the last second."

"That would explain why everything in my body hurts," Olivia grumbled. "I'd like to tell him exactly what I think of his driving skills."

"I called Daniel and your parents," Ellie said. "I thought they would want to know what had happened. Pat's on his way to the hospital, too. My car had to be towed, and several people said they thought it was a total loss."

"Oh, El, I'm sorry." Olivia knew how hard Ellie had worked to help pay for her car.

"It's okay," Ellie shrugged. "I just have to go deal with the insurance company and all that fun stuff. I'll call my dad, though. He'll help me figure it all out."

"What did Daniel say?" Olivia asked curiously. She had no idea what sort of reaction Daniel would have to the news of their accident. It would probably interfere with his daily routine and stress him out, she thought wryly.

"He said he was going home to grab some clothes and then he was coming," Ellie said, patting Olivia's arm comfortingly. "He was very, very worried about you. In fact, you should probably call him." Ellie handed Olivia her cell phone.

"I will," Olivia said, taking the phone gratefully. "He really shouldn't come, though. I'm going to be fine."

"Daniel's still your husband, and he's worried about you. We were in a serious car accident! It's normal that he'd come."

"Normal isn't always Daniel's strong suit, and hospitals make him uncomfortable." Olivia said doubtfully. "I wish my mom would come. She would take care of us."

"Well your mom isn't coming," Ellie said wearily. "Your husband is."

❀

DANIEL ARRIVED LATER that evening while Olivia was picking at the bland chicken-and-rice meal that a hospital attendant had delivered a few minute earlier. He knocked on the door hesitantly and popped his head in.

"Olivia?" he called uncertainly.

"Come in." She sat up a little straighter, adjusting the pillows behind her back.

He walked in slowly, anxiety written all over his handsome face. "How are you? Ellie called and said you were in a bad wreck, but then she called again to say that you and the baby were both ok."

"We're fine, but the doctor wanted us to stay overnight for observation," she explained. "I'm just sore."

Daniel's eyes landed on the gauze wrapped around her hands. "What happened to your hands?"

"The airbags."

Daniel glanced uneasily around the room. Olivia knew he must be anxious and miserable; he hated hospitals—the smells, the sounds, the closed doors, everything about them. She wasn't sure why, but it was evident that he was uncomfortable by the way he kept shifting back and forth. For several minutes, they sat in silence until, finally, Olivia felt compelled to speak.

"We didn't even see the other car coming," she said. "We were just sitting there, waiting for the bridge to close."

Daniel swallowed tightly. "I'm glad you're okay. And the baby, too."

Olivia put her hand to her stomach again, smiling softly. "Yes, the baby is fine. That was one of my first questions, too."

"I started cleaning out the office at home so we can turn it into a nursery," Daniel said quietly. "We can paint it, but we have to be careful because the fumes can be hazardous for you and the baby."

Olivia didn't know if it was because she was already emotional, but she melted a little when she realized that Daniel had been at home, preparing for their first child, while she was at the beach trying her best not to think about him. When he put forth the effort, Daniel really could be sweet and thoughtful. She hated to think about how much it would shake up his life when she filed for divorce.

"It's sweet of you to think about that," she told him. "Maybe we can talk about it later."

Daniel shifted nervously and looked down at the bed, his eyes darting back and forth. "I've also been calculating the cost of a baby—diapers, clothes, doctors' appointments—and we really need to start saving money. Especially for the future. You know, like college. I'm working on a pretty strict budget for us."

Olivia sighed wearily. One moment he was thoughtful and caring, and the next he said something that reminded her of all his obsessive-compulsive tendencies. Of course he'd been home crunching the numbers and analyzing every possible scenario. She closed her eyes, trying not to speak. The words were on the tip of her tongue, but she was exhausted and didn't want to tell Daniel of her decision until she'd had more time to prepare what she wanted to say. And yet, she wanted to get it over with.

"Daniel," she began slowly, "there's something I need to talk to you about."

"Yes."

"I've been thinking ever since you were here last, and I've made up my mind." She took a deep breath, "Daniel, I want a divorce."

Her words echoed in the quiet room, and she waited for a response. Daniel seemed to be processing her words, and she wondered if perhaps he hadn't heard her.

"I don't understand," he said. "We're having a baby together. How can you still want a divorce?"

"Because I'm unhappy and really have been since the day we got married, and I have begged you to try and work on our problems. But you won't."

Daniel frowned and shook his head adamantly. "We don't have any problems. You're just trying to change me."

Olivia's head was already pounding, and she didn't feel like arguing with him. "I don't want to talk about it now, but I *am* filing for divorce when I go home, and I thought I should tell you."

"But the baby," he stammered, standing up and pacing back and forth. "What will we do about the baby?"

"I'm not sure yet," Olivia admitted. "We have a lot to figure out, and I know it's going to be complicated, but this is what I want."

"Is there anything I can to do to change your mind?"

"I really don't think so," Olivia said. "You have had months to be a good husband to me, and you never were. You have had months to change your mind about therapy and counseling for your Asperger's, but you refuse to do anything. I begged you, but you refused to accept help."

Daniel looked down solemnly, digesting her words.

"I love you, Daniel—I really do—and I wish that was enough to make our marriage work. But it isn't." Once she started talking, the words tumbled out of her mouth faster and faster. She didn't want to say anything to hurt Daniel, but she couldn't stop herself. "You deceived me when we were dating and engaged," she went on. "You knew there was something different about you, and you intentionally hid it from me. I had so many plans for us—so many things I wanted us to do together—but you're just not the man I married!"

Bewildered, Daniel leaned against the wall. His lips moved; he was talking to himself softly, under his breath. "I think I'll go for a walk," he said slowly. "Can I bring you anything?"

Olivia shook her head sadly. "No, thank you."

WHEN THE DOOR closed behind him, Olivia let out a deep breath she didn't know she had been holding in. She was relieved she had finally told him. It was over; Daniel knew she wanted a divorce. His response wasn't exactly what she had imagined, but she never really knew what to expect from him anyway. His concern for her and the baby after the accident was admirable, but it wasn't enough. She had explained to him why she wanted a divorce, and he still hadn't agreed to seek counseling or work out their issues. He wasn't fighting for her.

She thought back to her wedding day—a day she had been blissfully, ignorantly happy. She had taken Daniel's last name proudly. She had been so eager to become his wife and have a family with him. Now, less than two years later, here she was—finally pregnant with Daniel's child and preparing to file for divorce.

How had her life turned out so differently from how she had expected? With that thought, Olivia buried her hands in her face and burst into tears.

CHAPTER TWENTY-SEVEN

hen Ellie awoke the next morning, every part of her body ached. Her joints had been slightly stiff when she climbed into bed the night before, but now her muscles were really tight and sore. As usual, Pat was still snoozing peacefully beside her. Ellie reached out and ran her fingertips softly along his arm. Watching him sleep like this, she realized just how much she cared for him and how grateful she was that he had come into her life. Ellie had called him from the ambulance to tell him about the accident, and he was at the hospital not long after she arrived.

In the bathroom, Ellie gingerly pulled her tank top over her head and stared at her reflection in the mirror over the sink. A distinct bluish bruise was already visible across her chest and abdomen where the seatbelt and shoulder harness had locked in the crash. On her forehead in the edge of her hairline, a small gash was pulled together by five stitches. Her left shoulder was sore and tender to the touch, and pain shot through it when she slipped her tank top back on. The emergency room doctor said the x-rays showed a possible hairline fracture in her collarbone, but nothing serious. He advised her to take it easy for the next few days.

Overall, Ellie knew she and Olivia had been lucky. They both could have been injured much worse, and Ellie cringed when she thought of anything happening to Olivia's baby. She had seen photos from the accident—someone posted them on Facebook, and Pat had shown them to her. Smashed in the front and the rear, her car was barely recognizable.

Booming thunder and cracks of lightning had disturbed Ellie during the night, but the storm had long since passed, and the sun was up now. She had skipped turtle patrol the night, but now that the storm had passed, she needed to check on the turtle nests in front of the house. She hoped that walking on the beach might ease some of the soreness in her muscles.

The night before, when Ellie and Pat returned to the hospital, Olivia had been visibly upset, prompting Ellie to worry that something had happened since she left Olivia in the emergency room a few hours earlier. Olivia assured Ellie that both she and the baby were fine physically, then tearfully recounted the conversation she'd had with Daniel about her plan to file for divorce. Ellie could tell that Olivia was exhausted, in pain, and also grieving for her failed marriage, so she'd stayed with her friend longer than she'd intended. Pat had waited patiently in the waiting room, but when she was ready to go home, he seemed to sense that Ellie was on the verge of collapse from the mental and physical toll of the day. He had driven her home, made her a quick omelet, and then tucked her into bed as if she were a child. She wasn't used to someone doting on her, and she was grateful for Pat's pampering.

ELLIE MADE her way stiffly and slowly down the boardwalk and breathed a sigh of relief when she saw that the small wooden stakes surrounding the nest were still standing. Though the tide had been unusually high, likely because of the storm, it hadn't reached the nest. Ellie trudged back to the boardwalk and gently eased herself down onto the steps at the end. She glanced back at the house, her neck muscles protesting, wondering if either Pat or Daniel was awake yet. When Olivia said Daniel had walked out of her hospital room and she hadn't seen him or heard from him since, Ellie texted him. She wanted him to know that he was welcome at the beach house. After all, Daniel *had* dropped everything and driven for several hours to check on his pregnant wife when he found out she'd been in a car accident. He had been waiting in the yard when Ellie and Pat returned from the hospital, and though he said very little before he headed to bed, Ellie sensed he was upset in his own subdued way.

Part of Ellie felt sorry for Daniel. He wasn't a bad person, and she didn't think he had ever intentionally tried to hurt Olivia. During his earlier visit to the island, Ellie had noticed him struggling to fit in, to act like the other guys, like Pat and Ben. He tried—he really did—but it wasn't enough for Olivia; she needed more than that. Ellie hated to see Daniel crushed over it, though. She had known him for years, and he had never been anything but kind to her. Ellie shook her head, rubbing her eyes sleepily. Divorce was never easy, she decided, no matter the circumstances.

BACK AT THE HOUSE, Pat was standing at the kitchen sink, gulping down a glass of ice water, when Ellie walked inside.

"You're up!"

"G'morning," he greeted her. "How're you feeling?"

Ellie grimaced. "Not great. I'm sore all over, and I've got an awful bruise on my chest and stomach." She held up her shirt for Pat to see, and he winced sharply.

"Damn. That looks painful."

"It is. I think it's time for more Advil now, actually," she said, reaching for the bottle. "The doctor said I should take it around the clock for a couple days."

"Olivia texted you," Pat said, handing Ellie her cell phone.

Ellie opened the text message and scanned it quickly. "She should be released somewhere around ten or ten-thirty, once the doctor checks on her and signs off on her release. She wants to know if I'll come pick her up."

Pat shook his head. "She can't avoid Daniel altogether. Besides, she should know you were pretty banged up, too. You shouldn't have to go pick her up!"

"It's fine, really," Ellie said. "I don't mind. If I were her, I probably wouldn't want Daniel to pick me up. They will have to see each other at some point today, though. They're going to be in the same house, for heaven's sake!"

Glancing at his watch, Pat cleared his throat and placed his glass in the dishwasher. "That reminds me, I've got to go call a buddy of mine. I was supposed to go fishing with him this morning, but I'm going to tell him I can't go."

"No, no," Ellie objected. "You should go! Really. I'm just going to be lying around all day, and I'd hate for you to miss out on anything because of me."

"Are you sure? Cause it's not a big deal if I don't go."

"I really want you to go. You can come back over as soon as y'all get back, but I have a feeling that Olivia and I will just be lying around for most of the day."

Pat's eyes lit up, and he grinned. "I've got an idea. I'll invite Daniel to come fishing with us. That way he won't be stuck here in the house with y'all."

Ellie pondered the idea for a moment. "Yeah," she said slowly, "that might work, if he'll agree to go with you. For all we know, he could be planning to go home first thing this morning."

As if on cue, Ellie heard muffled footsteps above the kitchen. Daniel was stirring around upstairs.

"You're sure you wouldn't mind having him along?" she asked Pat. "I mean, he's a little," she lowered her voice, "different."

Pat waved her words away. "Nah, it's all good. You know, he can talk college football stats better than anybody I've ever met. Besides, it's a boat full of men fishing—we don't talk that much anyway."

✿

"He's going to do WHAT?"

"I know! I'm as surprised as you!"

Ellie and Olivia were driving home from the hospital, and Olivia couldn't believe that Daniel had actually agreed to go fishing with Pat and his friends.

"How long will they be gone?" Olivia wanted to know.

"Pat said till mid-afternoon, assuming the fish are biting today."

"Wow." Olivia shook her head. "Well, good. Sounds like a good chance for us to rest."

"That's what I was thinking."

"Have you gone to check on your car?"

Ellie frowned. "Yes Pat thinks it's definitely totaled. We drove by the tow-yard today to clean it out, and I barely even recognized it."

"I'm sorry. What did your parents say?"

"That cars can be replaced. They're just glad we're both okay."

"My parents, too," Olivia agreed. "Your mom called my mom, and my mom called me... she was frantic!"

"Yeah, Mom mentioned it, too," Ellie said. "But I assured her that Pat and Daniel were here to take care of us."

Olivia leaned back against the head rest, closing her eyes and sighing. "This summer," she said, "has been one thing after another. I wish everything would settle down so we could enjoy our last two weeks here."

"Hopefully, this wreck is the last excitement we'll have," Ellie said wryly. "I just want to enjoy the time I have left with Pat before I go back to school."

"I understand." Olivia patted her friend comfortingly on the arm. "You've fallen in love, I've decided to get a divorce, and we were in a bad wreck. Honestly, what else could possibly happen?"

By four o'clock, Ellie was beginning to wonder when Pat and Daniel would be back. The last she'd heard from Pat was a text around eleven that morning when he'd told her they were about to leave the Isle of Palms Marina. Five hours of fishing? Surely they wouldn't be much longer.

"Do you want to order in tonight or should we go somewhere?" Ellie asked Olivia. The two of them were growing bored of sitting around the house all day.

Olivia thought for a moment. "We could get out and go somewhere. I'm tired of being cooped up in here all day."

"I agree," Ellie said. "We should go ahead and decide where we want to eat so we can tell Pat and Daniel where to meet us when they're done fishing."

"If Daniel even wants to come with us," Olivia muttered. "I mean, I haven't heard a word from him since he walked out of the hospital room last night."

"He was devastated," Ellie said sadly. "I saw him last night, and I know he can be hard to read sometimes, but he was clearly unsettled by your decision."

"I did warn him that this might be my decision, but I guess he didn't think I was serious."

Just as Ellie opened her mouth to speak, her phone rang, and she saw Pat's name and photo pop up on the screen. "Finally," she said, answering the call. "Hey, we were starting to worry about y'all! I take it the fish were biting pretty good, huh?"

For a moment, all Ellie heard on the other end was silence, but then she heard what sounded like a long, shuddering breath.

"Ellie," he said slowly. "Something's happened."

Immediately, Ellie froze. His tone was so grim. He didn't sound anything like himself. "What's wrong?"

"Am I on speakerphone? Is Olivia there?" he wanted to know, ignoring her question.

"She's here, but you're not on speakerphone."

"Okay." Another long pause. "Ellie, there was an accident..."

"What? What do you mean?" She didn't know what to expect from his next words, and he seemed to be struggling to find them.

"There was an accident, out on the water. Daniel..." he paused and exhaled a ragged breath. "Daniel fell overboard, and they haven't found him yet."

"Who is *they*?" Ellie wanted to know, standing up and walking to the window. Olivia's eyes bored into her, and Ellie didn't want her friend to see her facial expressions.

"Everyone's out here looking for him. The police, DNR— even the Coast Guard. We think he hit his head on the side of the boat before he went in the water, but we can't find him. We've been searching for almost an hour now."

"Oh, God." Ellie covered her mouth with her hand, her thoughts immediately racing to the worse-case scenario.

"It doesn't look good," Pat went on. "This is the first chance I've had to call you. You should let me talk to Olivia. I'll tell her."

Ellie nodded wordlessly, as if Pat could somehow see her.

She turned and held out her phone, swallowing tightly. "Olivia, there's been an accident. Pat needs to talk to you."

The color drained from Olivia's face, and her eyes widened. "It's Daniel, isn't it?

Tears blinded Ellie's eyes, and she nodded. "Yes. Something's happened."

CHAPTER TWENTY-EIGHT

*M*inutes crawled by, eventually turning into agonizing hours. Olivia sat speechless at the dining room table, staring out at the ocean, waiting for news of Daniel.

From the moment Pat had told her about the accident, everything around her seemed like a surreal nightmare. Nothing felt real. Ellie had already made half a dozen phone calls, and Olivia knew her parents, Daniel's parents, and Charlie were all on their way to Sullivan's Island. Two hours after he'd first called them, Pat arrived at the beach house, looking as if he'd aged ten years. He had tried to tell Olivia more about what had happened on the boat, but she barely heard his words. Daniel couldn't be dead. He simply couldn't. Olivia kept telling herself that he wasn't dead, repeating it over and over in her head. He was a strong swimmer, she reminded herself. Maybe he'd just gotten swept away in a current and they'd find him clinging to a buoy in the harbor soon. Perhaps he'd ended up on one of the small, uninhabited islands along the Atlantic Intracoastal Waterway, and he was trying to catch the attention of the search parties out looking for him.

Evening faded into nightfall, and Olivia's dread deepened. If all the people out searching for Daniel couldn't find him in the daylight, how could they ever find hope to find him in the darkness? Olivia bowed her head and clasped her hands together in prayer, silently begging for Daniel's safe return.

The guy driving the other boat was drunk, and he nearly hit us. Daniel had just gotten a bite on his line. He insisted he didn't need a lifejacket, but none of us were wearing them either. He hit his head on the side of the boat when he fell overboard. Pat's words kept echoing in Olivia's head, and she found herself picturing the entire scene. If he'd hit his head, had it been a hard enough blow to knock him unconscious before he fell into the water? Had he drowned? Was Daniel dead? Or was he alive somewhere, waiting for a rescue?

Wordlessly, Ellie sat down in the chair next to her and slid a cup of hot tea towards her. Olivia stared at it, but she didn't think she'd be able to swallow a single sip. All the waiting was choking her.

"Your parents will be here soon," Ellie said softly. "Daniel's parents, too."

Olivia nodded, moistening her dry lips and trying to swallow the lump in her throat.

"Can I get you anything? Do you need anything right now?"

"No," Olivia shook her head, finally finding her voice. "Not unless you can take back the last twenty-four hours." Tears filled her eyes and slipped down her cheeks. She turned to Ellie. "He was so hurt, and he didn't understand why I wanted a divorce. I told him he'd deceived me and that he wasn't the man I married. Please God, don't let that be the last thing I ever say to him!"

Ellie wrapped her arms around Olivia and pulled her close. "You can't think like that right now. We have to have faith. They're going to find him."

"It's been hours, and it's dark now," Olivia sobbed. "I told him I loved him, but that it wasn't enough. I think I broke his heart! Maybe this is God's cruel way of punishing me for not being a more faithful and devoted wife."

"That is not what this is!"

"Then what else? What if God is angry that I had feelings for Ben, and he's punishing me for this?" Olivia pulled back and wiped her eyes on her sleeve. "And why haven't they found him? If he's still alive and out there, treading water or something, why haven't they found him?"

Ellie seemed to search for an answer. "Well," she said uncertainly, "it's a lot of water to search. There are so many little spots he could've swum to for safety, you know..." Her voice trailed off, and Olivia knew she was grasping at straws. Even Ellie didn't think Daniel would be found alive.

"They're just out looking for his body, aren't they?" Olivia asked, her face crumpling again. "That's what they're doing, isn't it? They don't think he's alive, do they?"

Ellie glanced over at Pat, and Olivia saw him shake his head slightly.

"No," Ellie admitted, "they don't."

OLIVIA'S PARENTS arrived just before midnight, and she was grateful for their presence. She couldn't tell them about all the guilt she was feeling, though. She couldn't tell her mother that she'd found herself attracted to another man for many weeks, and that she'd considered what it would be like to have an affair with him. She couldn't tell anyone that she was scared Ben wouldn't find her desirable after she was divorced and had a baby. She certainly couldn't bear to tell them about the last conversation she'd had with Daniel.

An hour or so later, Daniel's parents arrived. Pat, Olivia's father, and Mr. Blakely, Daniel's father, all headed down to the Isle of Palms Marina where DNR, Charleston County Sheriff's Office, and other agencies were stationed while they searched for

Daniel. Olivia's mother ended up sitting with Mrs. Blakely in the living room, leaving Ellie and Olivia alone again.

"I need to get out of this house," Olivia told Ellie, twisting her hands anxiously. "I can't bear to sit in here any longer. Will you walk on the beach with me for a few minutes?"

"Of course." Ellie was on her feet in a moment.

At that moment, Charlie walked through the back door without knocking. He didn't say anything but immediately hugged Olivia, and she clung to her big brother.

"I'm so glad you're here," she told him.

"I left as soon as Ellie called," Charlie said, squeezing her tighter. "What can I do? What do you need?"

"We were just about to go walk on the beach for a few minutes," Olivia said. "Come with us?"

THE THREE OF them walked close together, shoulder-to-shoulder. Olivia felt as if she could draw strength from their touch, and she needed as much strength as possible.

"This is all my fault," she said quietly.

Both Ellie and Charlie came to an abrupt halt and turned to her.

"I told you it isn't," Ellie insisted.

"You can't blame yourself for this, Liv," Charlie added.

"Yes, I can! Don't you see? Last night I told Daniel I wanted a divorce, and this morning, Pat felt so bad for him that he invited him to go fishing! I know it was because y'all were worried it would be awkward between us because of what I told last night!"

"Liv, what happened was a freak accident," Charlie said.

"Charlie's right. Besides, if anyone's to blame, it's that drunken boater who nearly ran them over," Ellie said.

Olivia shook her head. "All summer long, I wanted to be as far away from Daniel as possible. I gave up on him. I gave up on our marriage. I had feelings for someone else, and look what happened!"

Confusion flashed across Charlie's face, and Olivia knew he was wondering who she was talking about. He didn't ask, though.

"None of this is your fault, and you need to stop thinking that way," he said.

"You already told me yourself—many times this summer—that you love Daniel," Ellie interjected. "And sure, maybe things weren't going to work out with you, but you still loved him, and he knew that."

"That's just it," Olivia said, looking up at Ellie. "I don't know that he did."

It was well past three in the morning when the three members of the Lights Out Club returned to the beach house, but Olivia doubted any of them would sleep. Instead, the night wore on slower than she could've imagined.

She was standing at the kitchen sink just after dawn when she saw two Charleston County Sheriff Deputy cruisers coming down the street. Her breath caught in her throat, and she gripped the sink for support. She watched them as they pulled into the yard and two deputies climbed out, both wearing grim, reluctant expressions. When they knocked on the back door, Ellie hurried to answer it. As soon she saw who was waiting on the porch, Olivia saw her face fall.

"Hello, we're looking for Mrs. Blakely. Is she here?"

Ellie nodded. "Come in," she told them, nodding towards Olivia. "This is Daniel's wife, Olivia."

Everyone—Olivia's parents, Daniel's parents, Charlie, and Pat, all gathered together, waiting to hear the news. Olivia held her breath, waiting to hear the words she knew were coming.

Both deputies removed their hats solemnly and turned to her. The one closest to her shifted his weight and cleared his throat.

"Mrs. Blakely, I'm so sorry to have to tell you this, but we found your husband's body this morning. He was found in the marsh near..."

Olivia didn't hear the rest of his words. The room spun around her, and she closed her eyes, finally letting out the breath she'd been holding in. Her legs crumpled as if she were a rag doll, and Charlie caught her before she collapsed completely. She clung to her brother, burying her face in his shirt.

I had so many plans for us—so many things I wanted us to do together—but you're just not the man I married.

Daniel was dead. That's what they had come to tell her. He was dead, and she would never be able to change the last words she'd said to him.

CHAPTER TWENTY-NINE

*F*or the first time since Ellie had arrived in May, the beach house was quiet. She sat on the screened porch, staring out at the ocean, searching for answers.

So far, she had found none.

Daniel was so young—only a couple years older than she was. Ellie had never lost anyone so close to her, and she wasn't sure how she was supposed to react. All she could think about was the moment that the deputies had delivered the news to Olivia. Ellie had never heard a cry filled with so much agony and anguish before, and she'd watched her friend collapse in shock. Daniel's parents were equally as devastated, understandably, and Ellie hadn't known what to do. Nothing she said or did would bring Daniel back.

If only they'd never been in that wreck on the causeway, if she and Olivia hadn't gone shopping, if that other driver had stopped in time, if Pat hadn't asked Daniel to go fishing—all the *what ifs* raced through her mind until her head throbbed. She had been sitting on the porch since everyone left hours earlier, and she hadn't bothered to shower or eat. In the past two days, she'd slept for only a few hours. Her mom had already called to check on her, but Ellie really didn't feel like talking. All she wanted was a few hours of solitude. Even Pat had gone back to his apartment to shower and rest.

She was all alone in the beach house for the first time since the beginning of the summer.

For nearly three months, she and Olivia had enjoyed day after day of sunbathing, bike riding, eating, and relaxing. Ellie had never anticipated that their summer would end so tragically. She wanted to close the blinds, crawl back into bed, and hide under the covers until she woke from this unspeakable nightmare. But instead, Ellie had promised to pack up all of Olivia's belongings and take them home to Warner Robins the next day. She needed to pack her own bags too, but her body felt like dead weight, and she couldn't summon the energy to move.

An hour or so later, Pat returned. Ellie could tell he hadn't slept at all; the dark circles beneath his eyes were more pronounced and he hadn't even bothered to shave. If he looked that rough, she could only imagine what she must look like.

"Can I get you anything?" Pat asked.

"No," Ellie shook her head and wiped her eyes hastily. "I'm alright. I just have to pack for home."

"Do you want me to come with you? I can if if you don't feel up to driving that far."

"I'm fine," Ellie snapped, her tone harsher than she intended. She expected Pat to flinch, but he didn't.

"Okay, well can I help you pack at least?"

"I can do it by myself."

"I know you can, but will you let me help? I need to do something."

Ellie stood up abruptly. She began pacing up and down the length of the porch. "I can't think about packing right now! I can't think about driving home! All I can think about it is how awful this is and how unreal it feels."

"I know what you mean," Pat said softly.

"No, you don't!" Ellie whirled around to face him. "You were always so nice to Daniel, but I was rooting against him the whole time. I wanted Olivia to divorce him. I was so proud of her for finally speaking up when Daniel came, and then you were all sweet and friendly, and you invited him to go fishing!"

"If I could take my invitation back, I would."

"But you can't. Just like I can't go back in time and prevent the car accident, which is the whole reason Daniel even came this week!"

"There's nothing we could've done," Pat told her, standing up and trying to pull her into a hug. "This isn't our fault."

Ellie tried to push away, but he held her tightly. "Olivia loved him—she told me she did—and now he's gone. And I don't know how to deal with that."

"Sometimes, we lose people we love."

"So why do we fall in love?" Ellie wanted to know. "Look at us—in the span of one summer I fell in love with you, and now I have to leave. I don't know when I'll see you again. Or if we can even make this long-distance work."

Pat suddenly pulled back and stared down at her. "You love me?" he asked softly.

"Yes. But it doesn't matter anymore." Ellie pushed away from him, freeing herself from his embrace. "Loving people just means that when you lose them, it's *that* much harder. And I fell in love with you, knowing that our time together had an expiration date!"

"No, it doesn't," Pat insisted. "Ellie, I'll come see you, and you'll come see me. And we'll make it work."

Ellie shook her head. "I've seen friends try to do long distance before, and it almost never works. We might as well go ahead and call the whole thing right here."

Pat's face darkened, and his brown eyes flashed. "No, I refuse to do that. I believe we can make our relationship work. You're understandably upset and emotional right now. I don't think you realize what you're saying."

"Yes, I do! I'm ending whatever we have before I get hurt." She shoved the screened door open and marched down the steps towards the beach.

"And what about me?" Pat called, following her. "What if I get hurt? I don't want us to break up. Don't I get some say?"

"Break up?" Ellie echoed. "We never even firmly established that we were a couple. Just think of me as one of those girls you seduced in high school. I was just a summer fling."

"Like hell you were!" Pat reached for her hand, but she snatched it away. "Ellie, I've spent almost every waking moment with you for the last two and half months because I *wanted* to. It wasn't about me seducing you or having a summer fling. You're the first woman I've ever met who made me want to fall in love."

"Yeah, right!"

"Ellie, you're acting crazy. I know you're upset now, but please let me be here for you."

"No," Ellie said, backing away from him. "I just need to be alone right now."

"Don't say that," Pat pleaded, reaching his hand out to her. "Ellie, I know you're going through a lot right now, but please don't push me away."

"Why? Why shouldn't I?"

"Because I love you, too, dammit!"

Ellie paused, his words sinking in. A week ago, she had wished he would tell her he loved her, but a lot had changed since then. Olivia had loved Daniel, and Ellie had seen how devastated her friend was at his loss. Sure, Pat might not die, but what were the odds that their relationship would survive the separation? And if their relationship ended, Ellie would be crushed. Maybe it was easier, she thought, to be alone and not love anyone.

"You should just go," she told Pat, tears filling her eyes. "I'm sorry if I led you on, but I can't do this right now."

Clearly agitated, Pat turned away from her, running his hands through his hair until it stood on end. After a few moments, he turned back to her. "You really want me to leave? That's it? After this entire summer we've spent together? You say you love me, and I tell you that I love you too, and now you're telling me to leave?"

"Yes," Ellie nodded wearily. "I am."

"Fine." Pat inhaled deeply and exhaled with a shudder of raw emotion. "But I just want you to know this. I love you. Not in some summer fling kind of way, but real love. The kind I've never felt before. You asked why I don't take many girls to meet my parents. I took you home because I already knew I loved you, and I wanted you to meet them. And one day, when all of this craziness from Daniel's death has passed, I think you'll realize you do want to take a chance on me. And I'll be waiting when you do."

With that, Pat turned and walked away. Ellie stayed behind, standing on the boardwalk until he disappeared around the corner of the house, and then she sank to her knees, sobbing.

"What have I done?" she asked herself. She pulled her knees to her chest and cried quietly, grateful for the privacy. Had she just saved herself from future heartbreak?

Or had she just made the biggest mistake of her life?

CHAPTER THIRTY

Olivia felt as if she was watching herself plan Daniel's funeral from outside her own body. Without the help of her mother, mother-in-law, and Ellie, she never would have been able to handle all the details. Every time Olivia saw Daniel's parents, guilt overwhelmed her. They had no idea that in their son's last hours alive, Olivia had told him she wanted a divorce. In their eyes, she was the woman who had loved their son and was carrying his baby—their first grandchild.

Condolences poured in. Olivia's doorbell hardly stopped ringing with people dropping by with food and words of sympathy. Ellie answered the door, graciously accepting containers of fried chicken, bowls of potato salad, and plastic-wrapped pound cakes and then rearranging to make room for them on the kitchen countertops and in the full-to-the-brim refrigerator. Together, Ellie and Charlie manned the phone, tactfully explaining that Olivia just wasn't up to talking with anyone. Both of them accompanied Olivia to the funeral home to finalize arrangements. When Olivia was confronted with the incredibly heart-wrenching task of choosing what clothing Daniel would be buried in, it was Ellie and Charlie who were right there with her discussing which suit, which tie, and what color shirt. And it was Ellie who reminded Olivia to eat and to take her prenatal vitamins. Olivia had never been more thankful to have Ellie as her best friend or Charlie as her big brother. Even in her grief, she appreciated that they were willing to put away their differences to help her.

Four days after Daniel's death, a visitation service was held at the funeral home Daniel's parents had chosen. The funeral director invited Olivia and the rest of the family to come early for a private viewing of the body. With her mother on one side of her and Ellie on the other, Olivia walked reluctantly up to the casket, purposely keeping her eyes down until she was standing right beside it. When she raised her eyes, there lay Daniel—quiet and peaceful as though he were merely sleeping. Suddenly her throat felt like it was constricting; she couldn't swallow. Panicky, Olivia turned away.

"I can't," she managed, a sob welling up in her throat. "I can't do this."

"It's okay," Olivia's mom told her. "I know it isn't easy, but you need to do this."

"We're right here for you, Liv," Ellie said softly.

Slowly, Olivia turned and moved back towards the casket. Her hands were trembling, and she held her breath. "He's really gone, isn't he?"

"Yes, he is," Ellie said quietly.

"This doesn't feel real," Olivia said to herself, closing her eyes. She wished she could rewind time and change what she'd said to Daniel in the hospital and at the beginning of the summer, when she left for the beach. "This can't be real."

That evening during the visitation, a line of family

members, friends, and various acquaintances—a line so long it wound through the funeral home, out the front door, and onto the lawn—filed by to offer their condolences to the immediate family. To Olivia, their words all sounded far away, but she nodded with gratitude at each person in front of her, hoping no one could see how close to the surface her pent-up sobs were. She heard herself talking, but she couldn't remember what she said. Everyone who hugged her or shook her hand blurred together. Ellie stayed close by, sensing Olivia's every need, whether it was a fresh tissue, a cup of water, or being tactfully rescued from a well-meaning visitor whose words seemed to be upsetting her. The evening wore on for what felt like forever.

When visitation was finally over, Olivia's mother drove her home. Her parents had been staying with her, and though she was grateful for their presence, she desperately wanted time alone. She lay in bed in the dark until her parents turned out their lights and the house fell silent. Once she was sure they were asleep, Olivia tiptoed through the house, turning on a few lamps. When she had initially decorated their home, she had framed numerous photos of her and Daniel together, especially her favorites from their wedding. Olivia trailed her fingertips over the furniture, thinking of all the memories the two of them had shared. She sank down onto the gray slip-covered living room couch, recalling the day they shopped together to buy their first couch and about all the nights they had curled up together to watch TV on it. Olivia pulled her knees up, tucked both feed under her, and clutched a throw pillow to her chest. Every inch of this house held memories of Daniel—some of them warm and happy, others more complicated and troubling.

Surely, if Daniel had been willing to work with some Asperger's specialists, they could've resolved their marital issues. Olivia had read about couples with successful marriages where one partner had Asperger's and the other did not, so she knew it was possible. She asked herself why she hadn't been more patient with Daniel. She *did* love him, even if it was a love now tainted by the knowledge and reality that Daniel had Asperger's, that he was very different, and that nothing she could do would change that. He was her husband—the one she shared a bed with, picked out a Christmas tree with, and baked chocolate-chip cookies for on Saturday nights. Olivia wiped tears off her cheeks and hugged the pillow tighter. She had never actually fallen out of love with Daniel, but she had been deeply hurt by the complete change in his behavior. Of course, he hadn't really changed at all; he was merely being the person he had been all along—the person he had cleverly managed to hide from Olivia. Love simply hadn't been enough to make their marriage work.

Olivia sobbed quietly to herself, curled up in a tight ball. She pressed her hands against her stomach, crying for her baby who would never know its father. No matter how many stories she told her baby or how many pictures she showed her baby—her child would never truly know what Daniel had been like.

WHEN OLIVIA WOKE up the next morning, she was lying on the couch. Her head ached dully, and she sat up slowly, groaning.

"Good morning," a familiar voice greeted her quietly, startling her.

"Ellie! You scared me!"

"Sorry," Ellie apologized, sitting down in the chair opposite her.

"What time is it?" Olivia wanted to know, rubbing her eyes wearily.

"Seven-thirty."

"I slept all night!" Amazed, Olivia took a deep breath. "That's an improvement."

Ellie handed her a glass of ice water. "That *is* good. I'm glad you finally got some rest."

Olivia leaned back against the back of the sofa, sipping the water. "Why are you here so early? You have to be completely exhausted."

"I'm fine," Ellie said, shrugging nonchalantly.

Olivia squeezed Ellie's hand, trying to muster a smile. "Thank you for everything you've been doing."

"I'm here for you—anything you need."

Finally, Olivia stood up and inhaled deeply. "I guess I need to shower."

"You shower, and I'll make breakfast," Ellie told her. "Scrambled eggs okay?"

"Yes, that's fine."

When she had almost reached the hallway, Olivia turned and looked back. "I just can't believe he's actually gone, you know?"

Ellie nodded sadly. "I know. I can't believe it either."

IN THE MOVIES, widows always wore black to funerals, but when Olivia stood in front of her closet, she couldn't bring herself to pick out anything dismal. Instead, she chose a royal blue dress that Daniel had loved. He had been so proud to take her out to dinner in that dress, and he had told her how beautiful she looked when she wore it. Daniel always appreciated when Olivia dressed elegantly, and she had always cherished the admiring gazes he gave her when they were out together.

Olivia dressed quickly, grateful that the dress was a simple sheath cut because it hid her growing baby bump. Her pregnancy wasn't a secret anymore, but she didn't want people to dwell on it at the funeral. Her long hair went up into a high, tight bun—off her shoulders and neck for the hot August day. She kept her jewelry to a minimum—her wedding rings, of course, and the diamond solitaire earrings Daniel had given her on her twenty-first birthday.

. . .

SHE MANAGED to hold herself together until they reached the church and she saw the number of people who were piling into the sanctuary. She stepped out of the car slowly, swallowing tightly.

"Olivia?" Ellie asked, "What is it?"

"I don't think I can do this," Olivia said, shaking her head. "I can't face all these people. I know they mean well, but I don't think I can do it."

"You *can*," Ellie told her, "and you *have* to do this. For Daniel. We'll be right there with you."

"Okay." Olivia took a step forward and let the door shut behind her. "For Daniel." She took her Dad's arm, and they walked towards the church. She focused on putting one foot in front of the other, trying not to think about all the people who were watching her approach. She stopped short when she saw Ben and Pat trailing behind a group of several people. Olivia hadn't really expected to see Ben again, and she certainly hadn't expected him to attend Daniel's funeral. She hadn't even thought of him since the boating accident.

"I didn't know they were coming," she said, her eyes welling with tears.

"Me either," Ellie said.

Olivia frowned. "Pat didn't tell you?"

"No," Ellie shook her head. "We didn't end things well."

"I'm sorry." She squeezed Ellie's hand. "I want to talk to them. I should thank them for coming." She looked at her Dad. "Go ahead without me. I'll be there soon."

BEN GREETED her with a warm hug. "Olivia, I am so, so sorry," he told her. "I hope you don't mind my coming."

"Of course not. It means a lot to me that you're here," Olivia said, wiping her eyes. She turned to Pat and hugged him, too. "Both of you."

Pat nodded solemnly. "If you need anything, don't hesitate to ask," he said. Then, he turned to Ellie. "Can we talk?"

"Sure."

Pat and Ellie walked away, and Olivia found herself standing alone with Ben for the first time since their unpleasant conversation weeks prior.

"How are you holding up?" he asked, shoving his hands into his pockets

Olivia shrugged. "I don't know really. Without Ellie, I'd probably still be curled up in a dark corner somewhere. She has been so sweet and devoted."

"She's a good friend."

"Yes, she is."

"I wanted to reach out to you sooner, but I wasn't sure if I should," Ben said quietly. "I wasn't sure you would want to talk to me."

"I'm not sure if I would've wanted to, either." Olivia twisted her wedding rings around on her finger. "A lot of things have changed."

"I understand."

They stood together awkwardly for a few more seconds before someone else approached Olivia, waiting to speak.

"I'll let you go now," Ben said finally. "I know other people want a moment with you."

"They all do," Olivia sighed wearily.

He turned to walk away but stopped abruptly and looked back at her. "Whenever you need anything—if you ever do—I hope you still think of me as a friend."

"I do. Really."

As HE WALKED AWAY, though, Olivia knew she would never call

him. She had been attracted to Ben. She had flirted shamelessly with him. No matter what Ellie said, Olivia still felt ashamed about her feelings for Ben. He was a reminder that, while she hadn't engaged in a physical affair, she had had an emotional affair with him. She had confided in him, trusted him, and longed for his touch. Now Daniel was dead, and Ben only reminded her of the oppressive guilt she felt. Olivia had spent so much time wondering what life would be like if she weren't married to Daniel, and now she was going to find out. She was Daniel's widow, and her baby would be born without a father.

No matter what Ellie said, Olivia would forever blame herself for what had happened.

CHAPTER THIRTY-ONE

*E*llie could hardly believe Pat would still want to talk to her—not after the awful words she'd spoken before she left Sullivan's Island. She had been kicking herself ever since Pat had walked out, but she was too embarrassed to call him.

While Olivia and Ben talked, Pat took Ellie's hand and led her around the side of the church where they would have a little more privacy. She was about to speak when he pulled her into a tight hug, wrapping his arms around her waist and pressing his hands against the small of her back.

"I've missed you so much," he told her. "I've been so worried about you."

"I'm so sorry, Pat," Ellie cried softly, burying her face in his shirt. "I don't know why I said all those awful things to you. I didn't mean them, I swear."

"I know you didn't. I know."

"I was so upset and confused, and I'm so sorry, Pat," she went on. "I love you—I do, really. And I don't want to lose you."

"You're not going to lose me, Ellie. I'm right here for you, now and always."

Ellie pulled back, wiping her cheeks with one of the tissues she'd brought for Olivia. "I wanted to call you, but I was too ashamed."

"I wanted to give you space. A lot has happened in the last week."

"Yes, it has."

Pat cupped Ellie's chin in his hand. "I know you have to go back to school soon, but will you be able to come back to Sullivan's at all before classes start?"

"I might," Ellie said slowly.

"I wish you would. I want us to spend some time together— just you and me."

Ellie nodded hopefully. "I'll find a way to come back, I promise."

"Good." He nodded towards the church. "Let's go. Olivia needs you."

❦

"Are you sure you don't mind if I leave?"

"I'm sure. You need to go and make everything right with Pat."

Ellie was sitting on the couch, shoulder-to-shoulder with Olivia. It was well past midnight, but neither one of them could sleep. Olivia's parents were asleep down the hall, but the two girls had stayed up to watch late-night episodes of their favorite TV show.

"If you need me to stay, I will," Ellie insisted. "I feel like I'm abandoning you."

"El, you have done so much for me in the last few days, and I hope you know how much I appreciate it." Olivia leaned her head against Ellie's shoulder. "You've been such a good friend, and you were here when I needed you most."

"What will you do next?"

"I'm not sure," Olivia admitted. "Pick up the pieces one by one. Figure out what my next steps are."

"Are you scared?" Ellie's voice was very small, and she almost wished she hadn't asked the question.

"I'm terrified." Olivia gulped. "Daniel took care of so many things for us, and now I have to figure out how to do it all my own."

"You know you can call me anytime, right?" Ellie said. "Anything you need, just call."

"I will." Olivia covered her eyes with her hand. "The first thing I have to figure out is how to sleep."

Ellie yawned widely in response, her eyelids drooping. "Maybe we should watch one more episode. Maybe that'll do the trick."

"What happened between you and Pat?"

"I made a fool of myself—that's what."

"What is that supposed to mean?"

"It means I freaked out. Pat told me he loved me, and I couldn't handle it right then. I don't know why exactly. I know I love him, but I had just watched you lose Daniel, and I guess I was scared of getting hurt..." Ellie's voice trailed off and she shook her head. "See, it's stupid."

"I don't think that's stupid. It's true, loving someone can mean you might get hurt, but loving someone is indescribably wonderful. As hard as it is for me to say this, loving someone is worth it, even if you do get hurt."

"You think so?"

"I know so." Olivia nudged Ellie's shoulder. "Now please go back to Sullivan's and make things right with Pat. You two are meant for each other. You belong together."

Ellie nodded. "Okay, you talked me into it."

WHEN SHE WALKED through the back door of the beach house, Ellie was immediately struck by the deafening silence. She set her purse and keys down and hugged her arms close to her body.

Ellie's mother had been surprised when she announced she was heading back to the island for a final week before school started again, but Ellie needed an escape. She needed a chance to breathe and process before she settled back down to the daily grind of classes and exams. But, most importantly, she needed a few more days alone with Pat. He was using four of his vacation days so he and Ellie could spend every possible moment together before she left for school.

While she waited for Pat, Ellie eased herself into the hammock and closed her eyes wearily; she hadn't been able to sleep well for the last few nights, and she was exhausted. A light breeze was blowing across the dunes, and Ellie could clearly hear the people down on the beach. Talking. Laughing. Enjoying themselves. She swallowed tightly, resenting their happiness the tiniest bit.

"ELLIE?" a welcome voice called from inside just as she was falling asleep.

Easing herself out of the hammock, Ellie smoothed her messy hair. "I'm out here!"

Pat walked out onto the porch and engulfed her in a warm, tight hug. "I'm so glad you came back," he whispered softly, kissing her forehead.

"Me too."

"How're you holding up?" Pat asked, holding her face gently between his strong hands.

"It's all still really fresh. I'm mentally and physically exhausted. It's been a long week."

"What can I do?" Pat asked. "What will help take your mind off everything?"

"I think I need to be doing something—anything," Ellie told him. "Is there any way we could go kayaking or something this afternoon? That sounds so good to me."

"Of course. If you're sure you're not too tired." Pat smiled softly down at Ellie. "I'll make it happen."

AFTER A QUICK BITE OF LUNCH, Pat drove them to his parents' house where he stored his kayaks. Ellie sat beside, him staring out the open window as they drove. She sensed him glancing over at her every now and then, so she reached across the center console and took his hand in hers, squeezing it tightly.

"I'm not used to you being so quiet," he finally admitted, turning the radio down so she could hear him.

Ellie nodded. "I know." She bit her lip nervously. "I just keep thinking that it's not fair."

"What's not fair?"

"It's not fair that Daniel won't see his child born. He won't ever see his child grow up." Ellie pinched the bridge of her nose, closing her eyes tightly.

"I know. I keep thinking about that, too. He was my age," Daniel pointed out, tightening his grip on the steering wheel. "I should've insisted he wear his life jacket. If only I'd seen that other boat coming sooner..."

"I know what you're trying to say. You and I both feel like we could have prevented it somehow, and Olivia feels like she's being punished for the feelings she had for Ben."

Pat nodded. "Yeah, I know he feels pretty bad about it. He wasn't sure if he should even attend the funeral."

"It meant a lot to Olivia that he did."

"How was she doing when you left?"

Ellie hesitated before she answered. Olivia was going through a terrible time, but she was strong, and she would recover. "She'll be fine, but it's safe to say that her life—and mine, too, for that matter—will never be the same again after this summer."

CHAPTER THIRTY-TWO

*O*ver the next three days, Ellie and Pat spent every possible moment together. They rode bikes, rode the waves, and napped in the hammock. In the evenings, Pat took Ellie out for romantic date nights in downtown Charleston. She loved walking hand-in-hand with him along the Battery in the moonlight. They made love frequently, often lying tangled in the sheets for hours.

"I wish I didn't have to leave you," she whispered one night as they lay side by side. Her fingertips were dancing across his skin, occasionally finding a ticklish spot.

"We'll see each other soon, though," Pat promised her, kissing her forehead. "I'll come visit, and you can show me all around the campus and introduce me to all your friends."

Ellie nestled her head against his chest. "I know, but that doesn't make me dread leaving any less. Do you ever wonder if we still would've met somehow if Olivia hadn't needed to buy pregnancy tests?"

Pat laughed, and Ellie smiled to herself when she felt the vibrations through his chest. She found his laugh sexy, and she propped up on one elbow to look down at his face.

"I think we still would've met," Pat said. "But it certainly wouldn't have made for such an interesting story. You and I have a great story to tell people when they ask how we met."

"That's true." Ellie traced lazy circles on Pat's chest. "Our story is a good one."

"What did you think about me when you first saw me in Dunleavy's?"

"Lots of things," Ellie giggled girlishly.

"Like what? Be specific," Pat told her finally sitting up in the bed and tucking some pillows behind his back.

Ellie yawned, sitting up, too. It was past midnight and she was sleepy, but if Pat was wide awake, she would make the effort to take advantage of every minute they had left. They only had one more full day together before she went back to UGA, and she wanted to spend as many waking hours with him as she could.

"Well," she began, "the first thing I remember noticing was that you were really tall. So tall that your head almost touched the rafters in Dunleavy's."

Pat rubbed the top of his head, wincing. "I've definitely hit those beams before."

"And of course, there was your accent. It was so deep and Irish, and I found it very attractive."

"It does tend to come out a little stronger when I'm singing Irish music."

"There. Does that answer your question?" Ellie snuggled up closer to him, closing her eyes drowsily.

"I think so." Pat said, wrapping his arm around her waist. "By the way, I have something for you."

"Huh?" Ellie, in that deeply relaxed state just before sleep takes over, willed herself to stay awake.

Pat climbed out of bed and walked across the room to the small overnight bag he'd packed. "I found something that made me think of you, and I bought it for you."

Ellie pulled the sheet up around her body, admiring the sight of Pat walking naked across the room. He really didn't know how sexy he was, she thought. "What is it?"

Returning to the bed, Pat held out a small box to her. Ellie took it hesitantly, curious about what was inside. She removed the lid carefully and gasped when she saw the beautiful glass pendant in the shape of a sea turtle. Ellie picked it up carefully and watched with fascination as the colors of the glass danced in the lamplight.

"Pat, it's beautiful," she breathed. "I love it!"

He grinned. "I thought you might. I knew I had to get it for you. And you know what the coolest part is?" Pat picked up the small card that was still lying in the box and handed it to her.

Ellie's eyes skimmed the words quickly. "This glass is fused with sand from Sullivan's Island," she read aloud. "That is so cool."

"A local artist makes the jewelry, but this one really stood out to me."

"It's amazing." Ellie traced the glass turtle with her finger-tips, admiring the necklace from every angle. "Thank you so much." She turned her face up towards him, and he leaned down to kiss her.

"And I was thinking that if you ever end up living here—in Charleston—you need to volunteer to be a Turtle Lady," Pat said.

"Oh yes," Ellie agreed enthusiastically. "I plan on it."

Pat's eyes lit up. "Do you think you might want to do that one day? Move to Charleston? Maybe after college?"

"I've already been looking for places I might get a job," Ellie admitted.

Instead of responding, Pat scooped Ellie into his arms and pulled her down beside him on the bed, covering her body with his. The way he kissed her told her everything she needed to know.

❀

ELLIE AND PAT spent their final day together lying on the beach. At low tide, they walked out to the sandbar and stayed until the ocean began to swallow it up again. Pat suggested that they go into Mt. Pleasant and eat at one of the nicer restaurant he knew of, but Ellie declined. Instead, she wanted to eat one final supper at Home Team, and they decided to ride their bikes to the restaurant. Afterwards, they pedaled leisurely back to the house, giving Ellie time to say silent goodbyes to some of her favorite spots on the island. Pat didn't say much, and she appreciated his silence. He seemed to sense that she needed a few minutes to reflect.

"Let's go sit on the beach and watch the sunset when we get back," Ellie suggested. "We should be right on time to see it."

"Sounds good to me."

ELLIE TOOK a large blanket down to the beach with them and spread it out over the sand. They sat down, facing the Harbor. The sky was already beginning to change colors, melting first into orange and then pink. Ellie sat between Pat's legs, leaning her back against his chest and resting her arms on his legs.

"I wonder if Olivia will ever be able to come back to Sullivan's Island after what happened," Ellie said quietly. "Will she remember any of the goods parts of this summer? She and I spent so much enjoyable time together before the accident."

"It might be tough for her to ever forget about what happened here, but I hope she can."

"I hope so too." She looked up at Pat and smiled. "I'm so glad you were able to take these last couple of days off from work. This time we've had together has meant so much to—"

Ellie stopped mid-sentence when she saw something out of the corner of her eye. She turned slowly, her eyes wide as she watched a very small creature crawl past the blanket, headed towards the ocean.

"Is that a..."

"Uh-huh," Ellie breathed. Slowly, she turned her head and looked towards the dunes. "Pat, look! Look at all of them!" She jumped to her feet and squealed with delight.

Dozens of tiny loggerhead sea turtles were spilling out of the nest Ellie had been watching all summer. They scrambled towards the ocean, crawling all over one another in their rush.

"Look at those little guys go," Pat laughed, putting his arm around Ellie's shoulders.

"They're incredible," she said, dropping to her knees in the sand so she could be closer to them. Tears filled her eyes and began to stream down her cheeks, but she didn't bother to wipe them away. "I've never seen one in the wild before. I can't believe this is happening! It's amazing!"

THE BABY TURTLES were half the size of her hand, and although Ellie knew that only a small percentage of them would reach adulthood, she hoped that at least one or two of them would survive.

"Goodbye, little buddies," Ellie told the sea turtles, smiling tearfully down at them. "Swim fast and swim safe."

And as she watched the first of the turtles reach the ocean, Ellie stood up and leaned back against Pat. "Everything's going to be okay," she said quietly. "It's going to take some time, but I know it will. We're all going to be okay—Olivia, too."

Pat hugged Ellie close, then pulled back and looked down at Ellie. "I love you, Ellie."

"I love you, too, Pat." She grinned brightly, laughing and crying a little. "I don't know why I'm emotional over this. It doesn't make any sense."

"It makes sense to me. Look at those little guys." Pat shook his head. "So brave and courageous, just like you—the woman who has spent years making sure the beach was a safe environment for them."

"I can't believe I finally saw a turtle nest hatch. I've dreamed of seeing this for years, and now it's happening. And having you here to share it with makes it even more special. What a perfect way to end the summer!"

ELLIE WATCHED until every single one of the hatchlings emerged from the nest and scampered down the beach. She walked the last hatchling down to the water, offering him words of encouragement. When he finally disappeared beneath the water, she stood alone in the surf for a few minutes. When she finally looked back to see where Pat was, he was only a few feet away, waiting behind her. She reached out a hand to him, and he waded into the knee-deep water with her.

"I wish I knew that they would all live and grow up," Ellie said sorrowfully. "But the odds are stacked against them."

"Don't think like that," Pat told her. "Maybe one of those little turtles will come back to this very beach and lay her nest here."

"Maybe."

"Go ahead—tell them bye. You know you want to," Pat teased her.

Ellie laughed a little, but she did raise her hand and wave. "Goodbye, tiny sea turtles. Safe travels." She choked on the words, still emotional.

Even as she spoke, Ellie knew she was saying goodbye to more than just the sea turtles. She was saying goodbye to the summer, goodbye to Daniel, and goodbye to life as she had known it before her summer on Sullivan's.

CHAPTER THIRTY-THREE

*W*hen Ellie woke up on her last morning on the island, she realized the summer had officially ended. In another week or two, most of the tourists would vacate the island, and the locals would no longer have to fight for a seat at the island restaurants or a place to park along the streets. Gradually, life on the island would return to a quieter, less-hectic pace for the short fall and winter months.

Pat helped Ellie take out the trash and make sure all the windows and doors were locked. Her uncle wouldn't be home for another week, and she wanted to leave the house locked up securely. Pat had to leave for work by nine, though, and Ellie fought hard to keep her tears at bay, but she started crying when he kissed her goodbye.

"I love you so much, Ellie," he told her. "But I'll see you in two weeks, I promise."

Ellie nodded through her tears. She and Pat had already planned for him to come visit her in Athens so she could show him around the University of Georgia campus. "I love you, too. And I'll miss you so much."

Pat hugged her tightly, burying his face in her hair. "Will you let me know when you get back to school safely?"

"I will."

He held her face in his hands and looked deep into her eyes. "I'm so happy that you walked into Dunleavy's three months ago," he said quietly.

"And I'm so glad I came to hear some local Irish band play."

"I'll talk to you soon." He kissed her one last time, and Ellie's chin trembled when she pulled away.

"Goodbye, Pat."

"Bye. Ellie."

Ellie stood outside at the bottom of the stairs, watching as Pat away. She didn't want to cry, but she couldn't help it. She couldn't help but think back to a week ago, when she'd pushed Pat walked away because she was so upset after Daniel's death. She had cried when he left then, but these tears were different. She knew she would see Pat again, but it didn't make parting any easier. Reluctantly, she turned and climbed the stairs, glancing back over her shoulder one last time to see Pat's truck disappearing up the street.

THE WARPED WOOD of the boardwalk was warm beneath Ellie's bare feet, and the coastal breeze tugged at loose strands of hair around her face. It was still early, but quite a few beachgoers were already out—mostly people taking their dogs for early morning runs. Ellie walked all the way down to the water and let the gentle waves lap at her feet. She stared out across the ocean, watching a shrimp trawler ease its way back into the harbor.

It had been a bittersweet summer—one filled with love *and* loss. For the rest of her life, Ellie would remember the three months she had lived on Sullivan's Island. She had learned what it meant to fall in love with someone—the deep, passionate love she had never experienced before. She had created lasting memories and strengthened her friendship with Olivia. And finally had come Daniel's traumatic and untimely death. Although she and Daniel had never been particularly good friends, Ellie knew that day would haunt her for years to come. To Ellie, Daniel would always be the man who loved her best friend and who simply wanted to fit in with everyone else.

Finally, Ellie returned to the house and gathered her purse and keys. She locked the back door lovingly and walked down the back steps slowly, then she turned and stared up at the weather-beaten boards that made up the exterior of her uncle's beach house. Once more, the house had documented another year of Ellie's life.

"Goodbye," she said softly, smiling up at the house and blowing a soft kiss in its direction. "See you next time."

THE END

ACKNOWLEDGMENTS

I did it! I finally published a book! It certainly took me long enough, but I finally did it.

When I first started writing *The Lights Out Club*, I wasn't sure I'd ever reach this point. And yet here we are, almost two years later, and I've finally done it! Please excuse me while I shout it from the rooftops! *I'm an author! I'm an author!* In all seriousness, though, I need to thank so many people. Without the family and friends who comprise my support system, I don't think I ever would've reached this point.

I want to thank the wonderful friends in my Instagram Writing Community. You have inspired and motivated me, encouraged me when I was burnt out, and helped me feel a strong sense of pride in being a writer. I also want to thank Peggy Spencer, my wonderful critique partner, who helped me talk through difficult scenes, offered constructive feedback, and listened when I whined about my struggles. To my friends Cait, Bethany, Bruna, Brittany, Rylee, Marla, and so many more—you helped me more than you know. I wouldn't be where I am without your support and encouragement. Each one of you is chasing your dreams and writing your books, and I can't wait to see what the literary world holds for all of us.

I also want to thank my beta readers who helped mold my story into what it is now. Without your feedback, I'm certain my book would be a hot mess, and I'm grateful for all the time you dedicated to it. You helped me see flaws and plot holes that I was blind to, and you suggested changes that greatly improved the story.

To all the friends and family who never doubted I would be an author, thank you for your unfailing support. Each time you asked how my writing was going, you gave me an extra boost of confidence. When you asked when I was going to publish my book, you encouraged me to keep going.

I especially want to thank my coworkers, Leah and Blaine, who teased me about "building my empire". Despite all your jokes, you both believe in me and encourage me daily. We've been through a lot together, but I always know that you two have my back, both on and off the clock. So many of my sweet clients also deserve thanks; when they found out I was writing a book, they were so excited and enthusiastic. Russell Robinson, you're my #1 fan, and whenever we decide to buy a house, you're going to be my realtor!

Many of my best beach memories involve two of my closest childhood friends, Catie and Joseph. While *The Lights Out Club* is purely fiction, Catie and Joseph were the inspiration behind the brother-sister dynamic of Olivia and Charlie. When we were kids, the three of us explored every inch of Edisto Island. We knew every bike trail, every seashell, and every sand dune. We snuck into the Wyndham Resort hot tub at night and drank our first beers. We even have a time capsule buried behind a certain beach house on the island, and we'll go back in six or seven years to dig it up...

Two people who also deserve a lot of credit are my parents, Emmye & Larry Collins. They raised me to work hard for what I wanted in life, and I honestly think that mentality got me where I am today. Mama, you also deserve special credit because you taught me everything I know about writing and grammar. In addition, you were my editor for *The Lights Out Club,* and you devoted hours of your time to this book. I truly believe you're responsible for fostering a love of reading and writing in all of your children, grandchildren, and great-grandchildren, and I am so grateful for that. The older I get, the more I think that I'm turning into you! Just ask Ryan!

Lastly, I want to thank Ryan, my ever-supportive husband, who has put up with all the crazy moods and whims of his wife the writer. After seeing me start several stories and then lose interest over and over, Ryan finally asked me, "when are you actually going to finish something?" He was absolutely right, and his question motivated me to finally complete a full draft. I am so grateful to Ryan—not just for giving me that nudge I needed back then, but for also persevering with me through this entire process. I know I've been difficult to live with at times, that we ate way too much take-out some months, and that we missed a lot of Netflix shows because I was writing. I promise that we will finally watch Game of Thrones now!

Ryan, you're the most patient, easygoing man in the world, and I'm lucky to be your wife. Together, we are an unstoppable team. We both have big dreams, and I can't wait to see what the future holds for us. I love you!

Love, E.C.

ABOUT THE AUTHOR

E.C. Woodham is a Charleston, SC-based author of new adult fiction. She has been writing stories almost since before she learned to spell. Woodham has been enchanted with the South Carolina Lowcountry since she was a child and vacationed on Edisto Island, SC annually, but she never imagined she would end up moving to the Charleston area in 2016. Her time living in the Holy City has given her a deeper appreciation for the natural beauty of the Lowcountry, and she is currently in her second season as a Turtle Lady on Sullivan's Island. She still hasn't seen a sea turtle in the wild.

When she isn't plotting, writing, or editing, Woodham is working on her Charleston lifestyle blog, Peaches & Palmettos, and exploring Charleston with her husband, Ryan, and their two dogs: Goose & Poppy.

www.authorecwoodham.com
Instagram: @ecwoodham
www.peachesandpalmettos.com
Instagram: @peachesandpalmettos

Made in the USA
Columbia, SC
28 July 2019